# PRAISE FOR GAIA GIRLS ENTER THE EARTH

"[A] well-written supernatural adventure...Welles deftly handles the increasing tension...presenting an interesting, exciting story. We eagerly await the next installment." -Kirkus Reviews

"Gaia Girls is an engaging parable of taking responsibility for one's place on the Earth... for all ages." -Midwest Book Review

"Gaia Girls is a page-turner with a message that neither kids nor parents can afford to miss." -Writer's Voice

"This is the first book in a very engaging and thought provoking new series which explores the idea that the earth is a living breathing organism. The author's descriptions of Elizabeth's magical experiences with nature are so special that many readers may find themselves envying her her abilities and her connections with the natural world around her." -TTLG Children's Book Review

"...the environmental focus of the book is worked in so well that a reader might not even realize that they are learning something along the way." -YA Books Central

"Gaia Girls is a delightful book with a powerful message. An exciting story that will get kids thinking about the world around them and how they can make a difference too!" -Kids Bookshelf Review

"Following in the vein of Nancy Drew, the Babysitters Club, and, dare I say it, Harry Potter, the Gaia Girls series is the next group to offer heroes battling modern day villains for the kid with an eco-conscience. Enter the Earth is a great read." -Treehugger.com

"Despite this book (and the music, secret codes and website) being aimed at a younger audience it does capture adults with all the ease of Harry Potter. I for one will be lining up for copies of the next books." -CityHippy.com

"Harry Potter meets Sierra Club...While the book is intended for younger readers and is full of whimsical elements, like talking otters, Welles manages to balance the cuteness with frank depictions of fa[...] animal operations. Enter the Earth is an engrossing story for all ages." -Co[...]

# THE GAIA GIRLS SERIES

What would you do if you could hear the Earth asking for help? Would accept the challenge? Would you accept the powers? In the Gaia Girls Book Series, that is what happens to four girls, each from a different region of the world. Gaia, the living organism of the earth, approaches each because they have a love of place and willingness to listen to the world around them.

In the first four books of the series you will meet the girls, each endowed with powers of one of the four elements: earth, air, fire and water. Using their powers, they help Gaia survive modern humanity and grow to better understand the connectedness of all things.

In books 5, 6 and 7 the girls come together as a team. Of course, powers can clash—as can personalities. The girls come to learn what we all must learn—we share this earth. To keep it a wonderful place to live, we sometimes have to put aside what we want, listen to each other and act for the greater good.

# Gaia Girls
## Way of Water

# Gaia Girls

## Way of Water

# LEE WELLES

### ILLUSTRATED BY CAROL COOGAN

Chelsea Green Publishing Company
White River Junction, Vermont

Gaia Girls and associated logos are registered trademarks of
Gaia Girls LLC. www.gaiagirls.com
This is a work of fiction. Names, characters, places, and incidents are either the
product of the author's imagination or, if real, are used fictitiously.

The lines from "Childe Harold's Pilgrimage" by Lord Byron at page 14, "The Sea" by Bryan W.
Procter at page 53," The Tao Te Ching" by Lao Tzu at page 264, "Auguries of Innocence" by
William Blake at page 295, and "The Forsaken Merman" by Matthew Arnold at page 298 are from
The Book of Waves, text copyright © Drew Kampion, published by Roberts Rinehart Publishers,
Niwot, Colorado. The lines from "Young Sea" by Carl Sandburg at page 163 are from Chicago
Poems unabridged by Carl Sandburg, copyright © Dover Publications, Inc., Toronto, Ontario.

**Our Commitment to Green Publishing**
Chelsea Green sees publishing as a tool for cultural change and ecological stewardship.
We strive to align our book manufacturing practices with our editorial mission, and to
reduce the impact of our business enterprise on the environment. We print our books
and catalogs on chlorine-free recycled paper, using soy-based inks, whenever possible.
This book may cost slightly more because we use recycled paper, and we hope you'll
agree that it's worth it. Chelsea Green is a member of the Green Press Initiative (www.
greenpressinitiative.org), a nonprofit coalition of publishers, manufacturers, and authors
working to protect the world's endangered forests and conserve natural resources.
Gaia Girls: Way of Water was printed on 55# Rolland Enviro Natural 100, a
100-percent postconsumer-waste recycled, old-growth-forest–free paper supplied by
Thomson-Shore, Inc.

Previously published by Daisyworld Press.
First Chelsea Green Publishing printing May, 2007.
Printed in the United States of America.

10 9 8 7 6 5 4 3 2   08 09 10 11

ISBN: 978-1-933609-02-7
ISBN: 978-1-933609-03-4 (pbk.)
Library of Congress Cataloging-in-Publication Data on file.

Chelsea Green Publishing Company
P.O. Box 428
White River Junction, VT 05001
(802) 295-6300
www.chelseagreen.com

-For My Mother-

You did what all great mothers do: told me I could do it...over and over.

You also did what a lot of mothers *wouldn't* do: slash and hack at early drafts with a red pen!

It is because of you I love books. It is because of you I love Gaia. Therefore, it is because of you this book exists—I love you!

# ACKNOWLEDGEMENTS

In this story, the main character often finds herself with no choice but to move forward through her own fear. I think this reflects how I felt as I began writing the second book in the Gaia Girls Book Series. I had no choice but to write it. After all, it wouldn't be a series if it were just one book! I have had so much positive feedback for Gaia Girls Enter the Earth; I worried intensely that I couldn't match it.

Therefore, I want to begin my acknowledgements with the people who eased the fear and kept kicking me in the butt to, "write it already!" First and foremost—my champion, partner, cheerleader and harshest critic...my hubby; he knows what kids like and won't let me get away with going under the bar!

I want to thank some people who kept me connected to the water: Gil and Harriet Sweet, who generously opened their lake house to me. There is a lot of Keuka Lake winking out of these pages. Melissa Williamson, a great friend and fellow lover of water—thank you for time on Seneca Lake, laughing with the whale song, and your unbridled enthusiasm for the work!

Thank you to Carol Coogan, an intrepid and talented

illustrator. The re-writing I did after talking with you was like tucking in my shirttails and losing the extra jewelry; the story became much neater and more pulled together.

Many thanks to Sharon Nakazato of the Yasuragi Center—our conversations inspired some interesting additions to the story, and she was tireless in answering my questions about Japan, the language, and Shodo. I discovered that Japanese culture is much like the ocean itself; when you look at it from the outside, you are only seeing a tiny bit.

To Ann Hameister, your attention to detail for the cover and long view of the series is deeply appreciated!!!

Thank you to Ted Hayden, English Teacher at Prattsburgh Central School. While your feedback was valued, your eye for errors and typos was invaluable!

I would like to thank my nephew Nicholas who prodded the first sentence out of me—because the first sentence is the one that starts the ball rolling! To my niece Ava, a real Gaia Girl, you never cease to amaze and inspire me with your imagination. The "original" Gaia Girls Way of Water cover is still on my refrigerator and will be cherished forever.

# CONTENTS

# 1
# Winging West

Miho sat on the plane and thought of the shark. She leaned her head against the thick, double-paned glass and let her gaze travel 30,000 feet down to the ocean below.

*He could be down there now,* she thought.

Then she chided herself. The big, jumbo jet that was winging her across the Pacific Ocean was, most likely, already five thousand miles away from the Mexican bay where the beefy bull shark had tried to take a taste of her.

She rubbed the knuckles of her right hand with her left thumb. On the back of her right hand, a whisper of scar swept out from the knuckles. If she turned her right hand sideways, as if she were trying to look at a watch, the streaks of scar were in the shape of a cresting wave.

Miho closed her eyes and continued to rub her

thumb over the skin that was ever so slightly raised. She remembered the day she got the scar. She had been snorkeling while her parents ate their lunch on the boat. She was about 15 feet down and following a small rainbow wrasse around a ledge of coral. The sunlight above dappled the reef and made the colors shine. Healthy coral reefs are magical places.

A reef is a riot of color and life. The coral itself is a wild thing; it is both plant and animal and, in some ways, mineral. The living coral builds itself on the bones of old coral. The resulting kingdoms have many rooms. Fan coral lends a fragile beauty while the brain coral is round with winding curls that actually look a lot like a human brain!

· The peaks and valleys of a reef are home to a crazy array of life. Parrotfish, damselfish and angelfish bring such color and flash it reminds one of a summer festival. Small fish dart in and out of the shadows and larger fish linger along the edges, waiting for an inattentive small fish to become its next meal. Spiny urchins look like walking shadows and if one were lucky enough, a lion fish, sea turtle or ray could swoop in to dazzle the eyes.

Some kids might be bored to have to go to work with their parents, but Miho was very fortunate. The sea was her parents' office and understanding it, their work. More specifically, as her mother put it, "the minds in the water." Miho was always happy to don a mask and snorkel and go explore. She was never bored.

It was while she was exploring that she had rounded a spire of coral and found herself nose to nose with a shark! The bull shark had been cruising the ledge where the coral dropped away into a dark and cold trench. They both had been surprised. Miho had been so surprised she had yelled and lost the air she had been holding.

She began to kick to the surface, hoping her air would hold out. She surfaced with a gasp and then began yelling toward the boat, "Shark! There's a shark!" She started to swim hard toward the boat. The fear in her body filled her with a cold that balled up in her neck and back.

Her father was at the rail, already unhooking the lifesaver, preparing to throw it out to her. "Swim, Miho!" he had yelled. "Swim hard!"

The cold ball of fear in her neck seeped into her arms, making them move slower than she wanted. But she continued to kick her feet, pull with her arms, and keep her eyes riveted to the floating ring. She finally grabbed on.

Her father pulled the rope of the lifesaver ring.

He pulled, hand-over-hand, his face bunched up in concentration. Miho's cold fear had just begun to warm when she saw her father's face go white and his eyes go wide.

"Miho! Face him! Turn and face him!"

Miho turned and looked into the bright blue water below. The bull shark was coming at her like a speeding car! Miho yanked her legs up tight beneath her, curled her hand into a fist and directed the remaining cold fear down her arm. She pulled her fist back and punched that shark right in the nose! Her hand skidded across the shark's rough skin and starbursts of pain flashed. The shark turned sharply and dove.

Her father was still pulling her toward the boat. She stayed curled up tight, practically on top of the lifesaver ring, not daring to let her feet dangle back into the water. Once onboard, she saw her hand. The back of it was scraped raw and bleeding from a scattering of cuts.

Miho's bones shook. She couldn't stop her jaw from chattering as her mother dressed her wound and her father rushed the boat to shore.

"You were very brave, Miho," her mother had said, as she swabbed Miho's hand. Her mother's voice had been steady, but her hand shook almost as much as

Miho's bones.

Miho nodded and gritted her teeth against the hot burn of rubbing alcohol. She didn't feel brave. She felt small. She was shivering, in part, because she now knew she was a tiny little drop of person in the great vastness of the ocean.

The wrasse was still going about its own little rainbow wrasse life, unaware that Miho had ever cared for it. The bull shark was going about his own bull shark business, unaware that he had given Miho a moment she would never forget.

"You know, that shark didn't know you were a little girl," her mother continued. "They don't see very well. You ran away and he was sure you were a tasty harbor seal." She had given a little laugh and winked at Miho. "But…seals don't punch like little girls! You were very brave."

Her mother stepped back and looked Miho in the eye. "Remember Miho, nothing in the sea wants to hurt you. The sea follows its own rules. You acted like prey, so the shark acted like a predator. Learn to be part of those rules; be one with the sea."

Now, two years later and a thousand miles away, Miho sat on the plane and, as she rubbed her hand, felt almost thankful that the shark had left her with this memory. Miho dove back into that memory, into that place where she could still hear her mother's voice the day they had unwound the bandage from her hand.

"Ah, Miho!" her mother had said, her voice filled with delight. "Miho. Miho. This is you! In Japanese, 'Miho' means 'beauty in the crest of a wave.'" Her mother's finger had traced the line of the abrasion and showed her the wave shape, a great arch that spread into little curling fingers which seemed to be reaching or grasping at something.

The next day, Miho's mother had brought home a present wrapped in a long tube shape. When Miho had opened it and unrolled the print, she gasped. It was the most beautiful image of a great cresting wave.

Like the developing scar on her hand, the blue wave arched into many white, curling, grasping fingers. In the background, seen through the trough of the wave, was a snow-capped peak. The image was so striking, Miho could almost smell the salty air.

"This is Hokusai," her mother's soft voice had said. Miho loved the way her mother's voice seemed to speed up a little when she used Japanese words. "Hokusai made hundreds of pictures with Mt. Fuji," she pointed to the snow-capped peak. "Hokusai is a very famous Japanese artist. Although, when he made this 'Great Wave,' it was looked on as more European than Japanese."

"Why?" asked a young Miho.

"At the time he made this woodprint, no Japanese artist would show a fisherman or a distant mountain." Her cheeks dimpled with a little smirk, "But now, this print is seen by the world as very Japanese!"

Miho had tacked up the print on the corkboard wall at the foot of her bed and then watched as the red, angry abrasion the shark had given her, slowly became her own personal Hokusai wave.

Now, so much time later, Miho sat on the plane, thought of the shark and dwelled on that day. The plane was heading west—they were chasing the setting sun. She gazed down at the sparks of sunlight bouncing off the peaks of deep ocean waves. The light of the reflected sun winked up at her, like stars.

Miho had been told, and always believed, there was magic in the tips of waves. This place, which only existed for a moment, was where air and sun and water came together to present something of such golden magnificence, that any one person only had a half-second to behold it.

A game that she and her mother often played while sitting dockside was to make "wave wishes." The trick was to perfectly form your thought, your wish, at the very moment a wave winked at you. However, Miho didn't believe in wave wishes anymore.

If wave wishes were real, she wouldn't be traveling all alone, at the age of ten, to a place she had never been and to live with an uncle she had never met. If wave wishes were real, she would've been on the dory, the small boat, with her mother and father. If wave wishes were real, there would not be two pieces of paper in a sealed folder that had the awful words, *"Lost at sea; presumed dead"* on them.

Miho didn't believe in wave wishes anymore.

# 2
# In the Dream

Miho fell asleep with her head against the cool, thick window, still holding her wave-imprinted right hand. Perhaps it was the reminder of wave wishes that sent her sleeping mind back to the otter.

In her dream, the tide was rising and likely the whales would be returning. Her parents were loading their gear: hydrophone, recorder, cameras, notebooks and reference books full of pictures of whale fins and snouts and tails. Each picture showed the scrapes and bumps and shades of gray that patterned each whale with its own, individual marks.

Miho knew these marks, these humpbacked whales, almost as well as her parents. Each winter they followed the whales to Hawaii to listen and record their song. Each summer the family went to Alaska to watch them feed and try to figure out why the whales only sang while in Hawaii. Miho often went out on the water with her parents while they worked and stood with her feet braced on the pitching deck, binoculars in hand, waiting to hear the distinctive sound of whales surfacing to breathe.

In the dream, Miho stopped her play in the shaded stream, stopped looking for another one of the odd animal tracks in the mud. In the dream, Miho didn't see the otter that stood tall on its back legs and waved its right front paw. She never begged to stay and follow the creature. In the dream, she climbed onboard with her parents and therefore, her mother never called back over the clattering outboard motor, "Miho, take one of the tape recorders; when you find your otter, ask her why she's here!"

In the dream, Miho went with her parents and motored out, as always, past the great rocks that marked the inlet of Kaumet Sound. In the dream, they were laughing about some silliness, probably another of her father's poems, when a great wave rose up! The dream wave's white fingers curled and raged and grasped the very air from the space around them before all ended in an enormous roar and crash.

Miho sat up fast and hard. Sweat rolled down her temples and her heart thumped against her breastbone hard enough to make it ache. The only white she saw was the plastic of the plane's overhead compartment.

"Mizu?" a woman's voice asked.

Miho rubbed her eyes with the heels of her hands and shook her head. She clambered through her mind for the meaning of 'mizu.' She knew that she knew it, but the dream had made her mind all fuzzy. Miho gave up and said, "Watashi wa wakarimasen." This meant, "I do not understand." It was a phrase that she had decided she had better know well.

The smiling flight attendant held up a bottle of water. "Mizu?"

"Hai, domo." Miho had often said this to her mother. In Japanese, it meant, "Yes, please."

The flight attendant's eyes scanned the laminated card that hung around Miho's neck. Miho couldn't read much of it herself. It was written in hiragana. In Japan, they used three different kinds of writing. Miho knew some kanji. In kanji, a whole word, sometimes a whole idea, was represented by a single symbol. Kanji was fun to draw in the sand, like pictures. But she had only just started to learn hiragana and katakana. They were a sort of alphabet, not made of letters, but of shapes indicating the sounds that made up a Japanese word.

Miho knew the flight attendant was learning her sad

tale by reading the card around her neck. She knew the card said she was traveling alone, what flight she should be on and who was meeting her at the airport in Nagoya, Japan. She suspected it said the sea had taken her mother and father because she saw the flight attendant's lips purse together and a sad cloud cross her eyes. But then she brightened, like all flight attendants are trained to do.

"If you need anything…special, ask for me, Keiko." She gave Miho a wink and moved on to the row behind her.

*I need to get off this plane!* thought Miho. The problem with spending 20 hours in the air is it gives you much too much time to think. Miho thought about all the places she would rather be than on this plane.

Miho had lived with her parents in many interesting places, always by the sea, always near the whales.

Her mother, who was born and raised in Japan, recorded whales. When she worked, she often called Miho into her office, unplugged her headphones and whispered, "Listen!" The sounds that came from the speakers could sound like squealing, rattling, doors creaking, or low booms. Many sounds could not be heard at all unless her mother sped up or slowed down the tape.

Her mother said whales sang, looked around, and said things as simple as, "Where are you?" She often told Miho that whales and dolphins were great minds in the water and she wanted to be able to talk to them. This was so important to her that she had left her family in Japan to study in America and follow the whales around the globe.

Miho's father, an American, helped her mother with this work and took amazing photographs of the whales and dolphins they saw. He took pictures of the oceans and seas that they traveled. His photos captured the many moods of waves and his pictures had been in magazines and books; some had been used in advertisements. Like her mother, he loved the humpback whale songs best. He would listen for hours and hum along. Her father said that humpback whale song was the first poetry of the world. And her father knew a lot of poems. He often quoted great poets and Miho dearly missed his habit of marking a moment with an appropriate verse.

Sometimes he would say the whole poem, sometimes just a piece. He was funny with his poems. Practically every time their boat set out her father would call, "Once more upon the waters! Yet once more!" If Miho was nearby, he would turn to her and say, "Lord Byron."

Miho had not been born in America or Japan, but

on a boat in the searing blue waters far off the coastline of Kauai, a Hawaiian island. Her father loved to tell the story of the great humpback whale songs that had been booming through the hull as her mother groaned and yelled with Miho's coming.

"Here she was, my darling Yoko, covered in sweat, obviously in pain, but yelling at me to 'get the hydrophone in the water!' I asked her why she had waited so long to tell me about her labor. She said that she was waiting for the song she was recording to end before she said anything. That's why I love her; she appreciates fine poetry!"

So Miho had come into the world on a wave of whale song. She had been listening to the whales ever since. Her family had lived in California, Hawaii, Mexico, British Columbia and Alaska. Alaska was where they were, working in the summer feeding-grounds of the humpback whales, when the ocean turned against them.

Of all the places Miho had lived, she liked Mexico best. She understood why the gray whales came there to have their babies. In Baja, there were endless calm, sunny days. The whales rolled and sported and lounged and the people did too.

Her family made friends with other people who studied whales and dolphins. Some evenings they grilled dinner over an open pit with Mr. Hernandez, a big man with a wide face and a booming laugh. Mr. Hernandez liked to tease Miho about her name.

In Spanish, "Miho" was an affectionate thing to call a boy, like saying "buddy." "Miha" was sort of like an American saying "sweetie" to a girl. Mr. Hernandez started calling her, "Miho-Miha." He said it was her name in a crazy mix of Japanese and Mexican. He dubbed it "Japican."

There were a lot of kids in Mexico; they called her Miho-Miha too. She loved Baja and spent many afternoons exploring, fishing and body surfing waves. Each place they went, Miho tried to make friends with other kids. But sometimes, she didn't meet any until it was almost time to leave. When she did find some kids to play with, she asked to learn their songs, jokes and jump rope rhymes. She discovered that everyone liked to teach the songs they liked to sing.

But Miho and her family moved with the whales. She sometimes wished they could just stay in Baja, where it was warm and fun and she knew people. After it was certain her parents wouldn't be found, she had begged the lady at the Japanese Consulate to contact Mr. Hernandez. "I could live with him!" she had argued. Why did she have to go and live in a country she had never been to, with an uncle she had never met? The answer was, "Because Kazuki Kiromoto is your family."

Miho sat on the plane and thought of the shark. She knew that shark better than she knew Kazuki Kiromoto. The plane continued westward. When it crossed the International Dateline, somewhere over the vast blue Pacific, it would instantly be tomorrow. Miho leaned against the window, looked at the winking waves, and wished that the plane could go so far, so fast that she could go all the way back in time to the day the otter waved.

# 3
# Stolen Property

Miho was scared to get off the plane. Her fellow passengers were moving out slowly, chattering away in Japanese. She realized how little Japanese she really knew, because the sounds surrounding her were more like the twitter of birds than language she could understand. How would she recognize her uncle? How would she find him in the Nagoya Komaki International Airport? How would she ask for help?

She clutched her backpack tighter to her chest. In it was everything most important to her: a Japanese phrasebook, a small stuffed dolphin her mother had named Shinju, which meant 'pearl,' a small photo book with pictures of her small family, and a larger photo book with pictures of the whales she had known. She also had her portable CD player, extra batteries, and stolen property.

The stolen property was a small zippered case with ten CDs in it. The CDs had labels such as, "Beakman's Point, Fins 6/24/05," "Lat64 Long12 Sei 3/4/05," and "Maui Humpback 1/11/06." They were her mother's recordings. Actually, they belonged to The Foundation that paid her mother to record and study whale sounds. When the man from The Foundation had come to their little house in Alaska and started packing up equipment, Miho had acted fast. She had called their house phone from her mother's cell phone, which was still plugged into the kitchen outlet.

She then answered the house phone and called out to the man, "It's for you!" When he had found no one on the other end of the line, Miho told him that The Foundation had called right before he arrived, looking for him—perhaps they were calling again.

While he dialed and talked to an understandably confused person on the other end, Miho raced around the office grabbing the CDs she knew and loved the most. Not only did she sweep up CDs of the grand, hours-long, humpback poetry, she had grabbed CDs of the other rorquals, the whales that had baleen instead of teeth and long grooves that allowed their throats to expand. While the humpbacks sang songs that took hours to complete, the other rorquals sent low, booming pulses that sounded like the very heart of the earth.

Miho found the sounds settling and calming and she had listened to them every day since the sea had stolen her mother and father. She liked to close her eyes and imagine that the deep pulses were slicing through the dark waters of all the oceans of the world and seeking out the lost boat. She dreamed more than once that her parents returned, riding into the bay on the backs of two fin whales.

Miho told herself the CDs really belonged to her family because they had spent all the long hours in the sun, on the waves, searching the depths for those lonely calls. She was sure The Foundation had already found some other scientists to take their money and go out on their boats.

Miho hugged the backpack and waited to get off the plane. She squeezed the backpack tight to her chest and wished she wasn't too old to pull out Shinju, the tatty little dolphin that she slept with and talked to, even though she knew that a stuffed dolphin couldn't really hear her. She loved Shinju so much over the years that the poor thing now only had one eye. But it was okay if she didn't see so well. She could listen. Shinju was the only one that really knew how Miho felt when her parents left and never came back.

"Miho, you can come with me." The flight attendant's smiling face was looking down at Miho and her hand was extended. "Your uncle will be waiting for you after you go through Immigration and Customs. I will take you there."

At the front of the plane, the other three attendants stood saying goodbye to people. Miho remembered her manners and stopped, bowed slightly and said, "Domo arigato. Sayonara." (Thank you. Goodbye.)

The oldest of the attendants, a woman whose lipstick was creeping into the wrinkles around her mouth, turned just the corners of her mouth up in a put-on smile, patted Miho on top of the head and said, "Good luck, Gaijin-ko." The other attendants smirked.

Miho felt strange. She didn't know what to say or do, so she bowed again and said, "Domo arigato," which made the attendants smirk even more. Miho looked up at the nice flight attendant; she was shaking her head and rolling her eyes.

"Come, Miho." She took her hand and they left the plane.

# 4
# Gaijin-ko

M iho almost had to jog to keep up with the flight attendant's long, purposeful stride. The pretty young woman kept glancing at her watch as they walked. Miho hardly had time to look around as she was pulled forward.

The noise of the airport was terrific. Outside, jets pulled into and out of their gates, engines revving. Inside, it seemed like a thousand people were rushing to or from the gates. All around her, men in dark business suits, pulling small suitcases and carrying briefcases, were coming and going with looks of great concentration. Many were talking rapidly into cell phones. Overhead, a voice streamed from an intercom; it sent out a stream of directions, warnings, and flight information in Japanese, English and what might have been Chinese or Korean.

They passed restaurants and bars and stores full of shiny new things. Miho had no idea that an airport could look so much like a shopping mall. Music poured out of each establishment and often a store clerk stood in the doorway and called to passers-by. Miho's ears felt full.

Finally the rush of people thinned out and the remainder formed into lines. The signs overhead were in many languages. Miho's eyes went automatically to the English, "Immigration." The flight attendant looked ahead at the long lines and sighed. She checked her watch. "Miho, do you have your passport?"

Miho swung her red backpack around and unzipped a pocket. There it was—the little blue book that had followed her so many places. Miho loved to look through the pages at all the round and square stamps with their dates and place names. It was almost better than a photo album to remember the places she had been.

She liked to show her passport to people. Not only was it proof of all the places she had been, it showed that she was a citizen of two countries. Miho knew that was special. Most people were only the citizen of one country at a time, but Miho got to be both Japanese and American.

"Good. Keep your passport in the pocket until you get to the counter. After you are done, just keep walking and you will get to Customs." The flight attendant straightened up and looked at her watch yet again.

"Are you leaving?" Miho asked, happy she didn't have to try to say it in Japanese.

The flight attendant looked a little embarrassed. "I have to go. I am late to meet a friend." She looked Miho square in the eye. "You will be fine. Just stay in the line."

"Can I ask you a question first?"

"Only a question with a short answer."

"What is Gaijin-ko?"

The flight attendant sighed again and rolled her eyes a little, as she had when they left the airplane.

"Gaijin is…Gaijin is stranger, someone who is not Japanese. Ko means child. So…stranger child." She smiled brightly, as flight attendants are trained to do.

"But, I *am* Japanese." Miho pulled out the passport and opened it.

The flight attendant leaned down and squinted a moment at the text. Then she stood and put her flight-attendant smile back on her face.

"In that book, you are Japanese. But in Japan, you are Gaijin. You will always be Gaijin because you are half." She waved her hand as if to send any other questions Miho might have sailing away. "Good luck, Miho." She pivoted on her high heel and strode off before Miho's next question could come out.

*Half?* Miho looked at her passport. American and Japanese. *That's what she must've meant by half.* But in America, Miho was American. Why couldn't she be Japanese in Japan? She turned this question over and around in her mind as the line inched forward. She decided she would have to ask her uncle.

Miho finally reached the counter. She slid her passport across it to a man with tiny eyes behind thick glasses. He picked it up and began to flip through it.

"You came from Canada?"

"Yes," Miho said and then added, "Hai," for good measure. She would do her best to be Japanese.

"Hmmm." He flipped through the passport again. He stopped to peer over his glasses at Miho.

Finally, he began writing on a piece of paper. He pushed it across the counter and said, "Sign here." Miho carefully used her best cursive to write out her full name, "Miho Mary Rivolo." She pushed the paper back across the counter.

BAM! BAM! The agent hit the passport twice with his stamps and then thrust it back across the counter. Miho waited to be told what to do next. The agent leaned around her and started speaking to the person behind her.

*I guess that means I'm done.* This was scary. In the past,

her parents were always there to steer things. Now she had to steer herself. She resisted the urge to stop and get little gray Shinju, her stuffed dolphin, out of her backpack.

At Customs, the stern-faced agent asked her if she had anything to declare. She wanted to say, "I declare this to be the worst year of my life!" But she simply said, "No." The man gave her backpack a quick glance and then waved her on.

*Now what?* Miho felt her heart beat faster and her legs began to feel like lead. She stood rooted, looking at the massive baggage claim area beyond. *There are hundreds of people! How will I know my uncle?*

Somebody bumped her from behind and that made her legs start moving forward. She walked as slowly as she could, afraid to get too deep into the sea of dark haired, mostly Japanese people. She felt she would get lost. *But how can I get lost if I don't know where I am supposed to be?*

Then she saw the man with the small white sign. It had her name on it! "Oji!" (She had been sure to know the word for uncle.) Her voice was high, and the relief of finding her only family propelled it loudly ahead of her. She ran toward her uncle and threw her arms around his waist.

The man jumped back and pushed her off. He looked around at the other people and quickly said, "No! No! I no Oji!" He straightened his jacket. "I drive." He made a motion like turning a steering wheel. "I drive..." He tapped the sign with her name on it.

Miho stared at him, the information slow to sink into her mind. *Not Oji? My uncle sent a driver?* The brief happy lift Miho had felt, sunk. Miho said, "That's me. I'm Miho."

The man looked confused, so Miho said, "Watashi no namae Miho Mary Rivolo desu." (My name is Miho Mary Rivolo.) The man looked from the sign to her face then to the sign again. He pointed at her and raised his eyebrows in question. Then he shrugged and bowed slightly, "Yoroshiku."

Miho knew this meant, "Pleased to meet you." She bowed in return and also said, "Yoroshiku." The man lifted the card from around her neck, read it through and then gave it back to her.

"I drive," he said and motioned for her to follow him.

Miho hesitated. This situation went against what her parents had taught her. Miho knew that anyone they ever sent to pick her up would also say, "Thar she blows!" It was a funny joke, but also a way of knowing that it was okay to go with someone.

But how could her uncle know that? Kazuki Kiromoto had never been to visit them. He had never called. Miho thought that he had never even written a letter—at least not one that she ever saw. How would Kazuki Kiromoto know what she looked like or what secret password to give this driver?

Miho didn't have a choice. What else could she do? She had to trust that this man really had been sent by her uncle. *How else would he know my name?*

Miho didn't have a choice.

# 5
# Riptide

Miho sat in the back seat of the big black car and stared, wide-eyed at the city that swept by her. It was so big! They drove on and on, past an untold number of storefronts with signs she couldn't read. Occasionally a word, written in English, would appear. Miho couldn't begin to know why words like, "Much Cats" or "Freshy" would be on a store sign. She felt like she was being swept by a riptide away from the shore and into unfamiliar water.

Miho had been pulled from shore by riptides before. Her father had once drawn a picture of what a rip was. His drawing had little waves curling toward the beach. He explained that the motion of the waves often dug a channel in the sand and then the water would rush back out. You couldn't see it, but you would feel its pull.

Miho knew you couldn't fight a riptide. You would get tired before it did. You had to turn sideways and swim out of it. You had to swim parallel to the shore until the rip let you out of its grasp.

However, now, Miho didn't know where the shore was. She was being pulled into Nagoya and had no idea where she was, where her uncle was, or where this car would stop. She had no choice but to let this current sweep her into the unknown.

Finally, the car stopped in front of a very tall, very drab, gray building. Miho couldn't read the sign, but the driver, when he opened the door said, "This home Kiromoto-san." He lifted the card from her neck and tapped a line that was written in katakana. "Home," he repeated.

Miho understood this to mean that they were now at her uncle's address. Perhaps her uncle had been getting a room ready for her. Maybe he had been out buying food for a special, welcome-to-Japan dinner. Just as Miho toyed with another idea of what nice thing her uncle might be doing for her, the driver held out a key.

She took the key from his hand and looked at him. He gave her shoulder a little push and said, "Go. Go home."

*Go home? I would give anything to go home!* Miho realized—for the first time in her life—that home was not a place; it was a feeling. She had lived in many different countries and in many different houses. She had even lived on boats. But she always felt that home was where her parents were. Home was where love was. And she had lost the people she loved the most.

This realization hit her hard. Tears welled up in her eyes like high tide during a full moon. Miho crinkled her nose against them, but her breath started to hitch and the tears started to spill.

The driver grabbed her shoulder and ran her into the building. He pulled a hanky out of his coat and started to pat her face. "Sh! Sh! Sh!" he said. Miho looked up, thinking he was trying to make her feel better. But the driver was, again, looking around nervously at the other people in the lobby and pushing the elevator button repeatedly.

The elevator opened, he pushed her in, and began hitting the arrows to close the doors. When they shut, he sighed and looked relieved. He looked at Miho, who was swallowing her obviously shameful tears and was wiping her nose with the back of her hand.

They got off on the seventh floor. The driver walked ahead and Miho followed him down the hall. They stopped at a door that had 714 on it. The driver slid the key in the door and opened it slowly. "Ohayo gozaimasu," he called through the doorway. "Ohayo?"

Miho knew this meant, "good morning."

There was no one in the tiny apartment. The driver pushed Miho in and then handed her the key. "Domo sumimasen," he said, bowed quickly, then backed out the door and pulled it shut before Miho could even remember what 'domo sumimasen' meant.

The silence filled her ears and the reek of stale cigarette smoke filled her nose. Miho slowly set her backpack down, unzipped it, and pulled out Shinju. She pressed the old, gray dolphin to her mouth and nose, hoping to block out both the smell and the fear.

Miho looked around. It was a short look. The apartment was smaller than some of the boats she had lived on. The living room had a small sofa, a dirty ashtray on the floor and a TV on a stand, nothing more. The kitchen was really just a little alcove off the living room. There was a small hallway that had three doors. When Miho examined them, she found a closet, a bathroom and a bedroom. That was all there was. There were no pictures on the walls, no flowers in a vase, not even a telephone.

She sat on the sofa, squeezing Shinju tightly under her chin and wondering what she was supposed to do. She tried watching television, but couldn't understand the actors. She finally took out her portable CD player and fell asleep on the couch, listening to the lilting, other-worldly sound of great whales.

# 6
# Oji-SAN!

Something was burning and somebody was shaking her foot! She rubbed her eyes and squinted into the dark room. The man whose face was lit by the glow of his cigarette was still shaking her foot. "Oji?" Miho asked.

He threw his head back and laughed. However, when he stopped, he looked anything but happy. He squinted his red-rimmed eyes at her and then leaned over to flip the switch on the wall. The sudden light made them both wince a little.

He was wearing a suit, but was carrying the jacket and had the tie pulled loose. He swayed slightly and a bit of ash fell on the carpet. "Oji-SAN!" he yelled. Then he turned and went down the hall, bumping the walls a couple of times. He slammed the door.

Miho stared up at the ceiling. She should have known to use the term of politeness and honor. *Oji-san, Oji-san,*

*Oji-san.* She repeated this in her mind, making sure she wouldn't forget again.

Sleep was slow to come back. Her body felt wide awake and her ears had nothing to do but listen to the snores coming from her uncle's room and the city sounds, seven floors below. She talked to Shinju. She assured her that they would be okay. Miho slipped her headphones back on and finally, listening to her whales, slept again.

Again, somebody was shaking her foot. A thin, feeble light came through the room's single window. Miho sat up quickly and tore the headphones from her ears.

"Ojisan," she said.

Kazuki Kiromoto was now smartly dressed in another dark suit, a blue tie knotted snug against his neck and only a little redness still rimming his eyes. He stared at her and then pursed his lips as if he were holding back words.

"I go work now," he finally said.

"Ojisan," Miho got to her feet and blurted out, "what am I supposed to do?"

Her uncle looked around the apartment, as if some entertainment would magically appear. His gaze stayed on the kitchen. He reached into his inner coat pocket and pulled out a wallet. He extracted paper bills and handed them to Miho. "Make dinner," he said. Then he turned on his heel and walked out the door.

The click of the lock seemed to echo forever. Miho stared down at the bills in her hand. This had to be a bad dream. The kind of dream where you had to take a test but couldn't find a pen, or the one where you went to school and then realized you were in your pajamas or worse, your underwear! Miho wouldn't have been surprised if the room suddenly filled with people pointing and laughing.

She wanted to cry, but instead, stared at the scar on the back of her hand. She rubbed it a little and reminded herself that she'd beaten a shark! If she could do that as an eight-year-old, she could figure out how to make her uncle dinner. She got up and brushed her teeth. She put Shinju, the money, her Japanese phrasebook, her passport and the card she had worn on the airplane into her backpack. She took a deep breath, rubbed the scar on the back of her hand and, with the key safely in her pocket, went down the elevator and out into the city of Nagoya.

She stood for a long time looking at both the tops and the bottoms of the buildings around her. She knew from traveling in boats with her parents, especially through inlets and coves, that you had to be familiar with your landmarks.

What she saw were not the hills and trees and interesting rocks she would normally mark, but the A-1 Bento Box to the left of her uncle's apartment building and the shoe store to the right. These would have to do.

Part of Miho wanted to go striding off into the city. She wanted to do something dramatic to prove she wasn't as scared as she really was. But in her mind, she could hear her father's voice. "Never dive first, Miho." They had been standing on a rocky ledge near their new home in Alaska. "You should always swim in or jump feet first, because you don't know how deep the water really is."

She didn't know how big Nagoya really was, but she decided to swim around a little first. She walked the one block around Ojisan's gray box of a building. Then she walked two blocks. She became a little more comfortable.

All around her Nagoya swirled like a mad sea of people, cars, buses and subway centers. Almost everyone that walked past her looked twice. She thought it was because, although she was only ten, she was as tall, if not taller than many of the adults around her.

Miho saw a subway entrance with a map on it. She

stopped to study the map and although she couldn't fully read the kanji and the katakana on it, she could see the shape and size of the city.

Nagoya was near the sea! Her cheeks pulled into a little smile as she stared at the blue on the map. It looked like Nagoya sat at the back of a bay! "Ise Bay," it said in English. Miho studied the map more and decided she could walk to the water. *Over five blocks, down six, over three and down twelve. 5,6,3,12.* Miho repeated these numbers so she would know how to get there. *5,6,3,12. 5,6,3,12.*

An hour later, Miho regretted her decision. She could smell the sea on the wind, but was still looking at gray buildings and busy roads. She felt to go back now would be to have wasted all this walking, so she plodded on.

Finally, the buildings became smaller and the skyline shrunk until there was nothing ahead but docks and sky and boats and seabirds. Miho found a place to sit and watch the boats come and go.

For a long time she thought of nothing; she simply let her eyes fill with the light that bounced off the water. She listened to the shrill calls of gulls and the low guttural sound of diesel engines pulling boats from their slips. She longed to be on one of the boats, heading

out into the blue expanse. She wondered if she would ever be on a boat again.

A shiver ran through her and alerted her to the fact that the spot she was sitting in was now in shadow. The sun was slipping down the backside of the day and she was far from Ojisan's gray box!

She jogged up five blocks and turned left and had gone two more when she realized her mistake. She should have first walked 12 blocks back! She had done her numbers backwards! Miho turned around in a circle and didn't recognize...anything.

# 7
# So American

A feeling like the one she had at the airport stole over her. Her legs got heavy and her heart began to pound. *Think, Miho! Think! What would Mom and Dad tell you to do?* She had to swallow hard, once, to make sure the words "Mom and Dad" didn't crack her open.

But thinking of them, although painful, was the mental nudge she needed. She remembered that if you were in any kind of trouble, you should find an adult, preferably a policeman. She fished her phrasebook out of her backpack and looked up "Police." She found the phrase asking where the police station was, but instead of trying to learn to say it properly, she simply marked it with her finger and waited.

When a woman walked past her, Miho grabbed her sleeve. The woman looked startled, then annoyed. Miho pressed the book toward her, pointing to the phrase.

The woman, in turn, pointed over Miho's shoulder to a small box on the corner and then pulled away.

Miho walked toward it, wondering if it was a big phone booth. But there was, indeed, a policeman inside. Miho tapped on the window; she already had her finger held in the phrasebook.

"Konnichiwa," said the policeman and stepped out. Miho pointed to the phrase, "I'm lost" and then pulled out her card from the airport and pointed to the address of Ojisan's building. The policeman took the card and pointed at her. "Genkin?" he asked.

"Money! Yes, I have money!" Miho pulled the bills from her pocket and showed him. The policeman held up one finger to indicate she should wait. He stepped inside the box and picked up the phone. When he hung up he came out and stood next to her. She didn't know what she was supposed to do. He looked at her and said, "Amer-i-ka?" She didn't want to explain that she was both, or half, or gaijin, so she nodded.

A taxi pulled up and the policeman showed the driver Ojisan's gray box address. He took the money from Miho and gave most of it to the cab driver. Then he bowed a bit and said, "Sayonara." Miho bowed back and said, "Sayonara," and got into the cab.

All the way back she worried. *I don't have food and*

*now I don't have money! What will he do? He's gonna yell, for sure!* Miho began to tremble a little at the thought.

As luck would have it, when she walked through the lobby, a pizza delivery man, who was actually a teenager with headphones on, was waiting at the elevator. She followed him in.

As it began to rise she said, "Konnichiwa." The young man glanced at her and then looked back at the elevator doors, bopping his head to a beat she couldn't hear. Miho tugged his sleeve and pulled out all her money. She pointed at the pizza and waved the money a little. His eyebrows raised and he looked over the bills in her hand.

"Hai," he said and handed her the pizza. He rolled the bills up, tucked them in his pocket, and grinned. At the seventh floor, Miho got off and said, "Bye." The young man just grinned again and threw her a salute.

Miho hurried down the hall and was surprised to see three large boxes outside the door. They were hers! The boxes contained all her clothes, some books and toys from home! She had been so scared and worried about finding her uncle and then being in a strange apartment in a strange city that she had forgotten to be worried about her things.

She nudged the door open and pushed the boxes

through with her knee. She set the pizza on the counter and began to look through the cupboard for plates. The doorknob rattled and she looked up in time to see Kazuki Kiromoto's feet fly up into the air as he fell over her boxes!

He scrambled up, his face turning red and his eyes casting about until they fell on her and the pizza. "Konnichiwa, Ojisan," Miho said and remembered to bow a little.

Ojisan began to shake his head and his voice boomed out, "No! No! NO! Not Konnichiwa! Not afternoon! Kon-ban-WAH. It is NIGHT!"

He took two steps to the little kitchen, "This dinner? This?" He lifted the lid and held up a slice of pizza that, strangely, had pepperoni and corn niblets on it. He tossed the slice back in.

Her uncle walked in a tight circle around his apartment, lit a cigarette, drank in the smoke and muttered thickly in Japanese.

Miho tried not to cough from the smoke and decided she had better try to fix things. "Ojisan," she bowed again. "Thank you for bringing me into your home. I'm so happy to meet you and I..." She sifted through her mind as to what to say next. "I'm happy to meet you and I tried to find a grocery store and I got lost. I got lost and..."

"Silence!" He had stopped circling and now stood still, chewing on his bottom lip. He seemed to smolder like the hot, red tip of his cigarette.

"This is not good for me to have you here."

"Why?"

"Why? Why! See!" He started circling and smoking again. "You so American! Why this? Why that? Don't matter why! You like you mother! Why I have to be married? Why I have to listen to you? Yoko no say thank you, just why!"

The way he said it made Miho angry. He spat her mother's name out like it was the pizza he obviously didn't want. Without thinking, she took two steps toward him. She was almost as tall he was and he took one step back.

"Don't talk about my mother that way!" Miho yelled. She clenched her Hokusai hand into an angry fist.

From the hall came a rattle and a gurgle and then, with a wet whoosh, water began to gush out of the bathroom! Ojisan yelled, but at least it wasn't at her. He pulled his cell phone from his jacket pocket and began yelling into it. He pulled towels from the closet and tossed them to Miho.

She began to mop up the water. It seemed to be

boiling up out of the toilet. She was grateful for the distraction. Focusing on the water cooled her anger. Ojisan forgot about her as he got busy yelling into the phone. *Maybe he'll forget to keep yelling at me!* Ojisan opened the apartment door and stood in the hallway, waiting. Miho kept mopping and wondered how on earth this man could be related to her happy, loving mother.

When the building repairman came in, Ojisan grabbed Miho by her shirt collar and simply said, "Come!" They left the watery mess in the apartment and headed down to the streets of Nagoya.

# 8
# Tomorrow We Go

Ojisan took them next door to the A-1 Bento Box. He pushed Miho into a chair and marched to the counter to order. His deep, seething anger was so great; Miho imagined she could see steam rising off his head. He came back with two boxes containing different foods in little compartments. He tossed a pair of chopsticks on the table and sat down.

He was muttering in Japanese under his breath and shoveling food into his mouth. He didn't look up at Miho. Finally he stopped, laid his chopsticks across the box, and pressed the heels of his hands into his eyes. When he looked up at Miho, he looked five years older.

"I apologize. I still angry with my sister."

Miho's eyes widened. This must be why he never came to visit or called or anything.

"Why?" Miho whispered, wondering what her mother could have done that was so bad.

Ojisan's mouth pressed tight again and his cheeks reddened. Miho realized what she had said, ducked her head and began prodding at her bento box.

"No why!" He pressed the heels of his hands into his eyes again. "I businessman." He finally said. "I have no wife. This not good for me. Not good for you." He began to poke at his bento box too.

They sat this way for a while, each poking at their food and their thoughts.

Ojisan sighed heavily and said, "Tomorrow we go to Goza." He put his hand up just as the word "why" started to escape Miho's lips. She clamped her mouth shut. "It is O-bon. O-bon is festival for the dead. Three days, you pack clothes." He paused, "No ask why. You sleep—tomorrow we go. "

That was the last thing he said to Miho. They went back to the apartment in silence; Ojisan went into his room and closed the door. Fresh smoke, if cigarette smoke could ever be called fresh, seeped out from under his door.

Miho lay wide awake with worry and wonder and jet lag. She worried about how she could ever live in this gray box with this stinky, angry uncle. She worried that she would always be a tall gaijin, unable to hear or speak Japanese properly. And, she wondered about Goza. She let her mind dwell more on Goza because wondering about something completely unknown was easier than worrying about what she already knew.

She saw a telephone book and retrieved it, hoping there was a map that could show her where Goza was. In the back of the book, she found it. Ise Bay dropped away from Nagoya in an almost teardrop shape. At the bottom, on the southwest end of Ise Bay, a thick peninsula of land pushed out, the Ise-Shima Peninsula.

The peninsula stretched out into the Pacific Ocean, and all along its curve there were small bays and inlets, and towns with names like Toba and Ise. As the peninsula curved back around toward the mainland, it made an extra little hook. Miho turned the map sideways. There, curling over, much like her Hokusai wave, was a strip of land. Inside that strip was Ago Bay and at the tip sat Goza. Miho couldn't stop smiling. Her wave wish made at the docks today had come true! She was going back to the sea!

# 9
# Goza

Ojisan stood next to Miho on the train heading south. He was trying to read a newspaper. But the train was so crowded with people heading home for O-bon that he and Miho had to stand and balance and wait for a seat to open up.

Miho listened to the clickety-clack of the train running on the rails, but kept her attention on her uncle. Any time his eyes looked away from the paper, Miho asked a question.

Clickety-clack. Clickety-clack.

"Ojisan, why do you have to go to Goza for O-bon?"

"Because parents there."

Clickety-clack. Clickety-clack.

"Ojisan, I thought my grandparents were dead."

"Yes, that is why we go for O-bon. They house there."

Clickety-clack. Clickety-clack.

"Ojisan, do you mean they are buried there, or that their actual house is there?"

"Their house. My house now."

Clickety-clack. Clickety-clack.

"Ojisan, why do you live in Nagoya if you have a house in Goza?"

Clickety-clack. Clickety-clack. Clickety-clack.

Miho waited for her answer.

"Ojisan," she began again.

"Stop! Ojisan, why! Ojisan, why! Miho…" he looked past her and searched for words. He scowled and said, "You should be name, Shizuka! Maybe that help." He pushed his paper back up in front of his face.

*Shizuka?* Miho fetched her phrasebook from her backpack and looked up Shizuka. It meant "quiet." She got the hint. She leaned around the people seated next to her. Slivers of pale blue kept peeking around the hills and buildings that bordered the rail line, as if the sea were teasing her. It was maddening. Miho imagined she could smell the briny air and hear the call of seabirds; really it was stale smoke clinging to Ojisan that filled her nose and the demanding wail of a baby two rows up that filled her ears.

People got on and off at each stop. They were all going home for O-bon. Her uncle took an available seat and finally Miho too, could sit down. She continued to study her Japanese phrasebook, reading the words and whispering the phrases back to herself. Miho didn't mind studying out of school.

Most of her life she had been home schooled. Her family spent so much time traveling and on boats, it was rare she got to go to a real school. Her parents set lessons and goals and even gave her tests.

But this was a real-world test! If she was ever going to not be "gaijin" she would need to speak the language!

The time passed quickly as Miho practiced how to say hello and goodbye, please and thank you in all the different ways the Japanese did. It was important to know the difference between the familiar way, the way you would say something to a friend, and the polite, honorific way. She began to understand why her uncle had been upset at her saying, "Oji," instead of "Ojisan." She wouldn't want him calling her "kid." When you added "san" to any name or title, it showed respect.

A lot of people got off at the town of Ise. At a station named Toba, the train nearly emptied. Ojisan sat across from Miho, eyes closed and head rocking gently with the train's movement. Miho studied his face and saw there the same rising cheekbones and full upper lip as her mother's.

Miho knew that she had the same high cheekbones and mouth. She had the smooth, straight, jet black hair her mother did. From her father, however, she inherited slightly pointed ears and a lanky build. Miho was well on her way to having the long legs and arms and thinness of her father. She also had his blue-green eyes.

Miho looked at her uncle and looked at the handful of people sharing their car. *Like being tall wasn't enough, I have these crazy green eyes! Maybe that's why the lady at the airport said I'll always be gaijin.* Miho frowned at the thought. *I can't change my eyes!* She bent back over her phrasebook and studied harder.

At the next stop Ojisan's eyes popped open. He looked across at Miho and said, "Kashikojime."

"Nani?" Miho said, testing out the word for "What?"

"Kashikojime." Ojisan said, rising to pull their suitcases off the top rack. "This end of line—no more stations."

Miho wondered how they would get to Goza if this was the end of the line. To her great delight, she found one got to Goza by ferry! When they boarded, Miho started to run ahead and then turned back to her uncle. In her best Japanese, she asked if she could please go to the front. She held her breath, hoping she hadn't said anything bad by accident.

The smallest flicker of a smile, hardly a twitch really, passed across Ojisan's face and made his cigarette jump. He simply said, "Hai."

Miho ran to the bow and held the cool rail. She couldn't help but send back a little "*thank you*" to the winking, sparkling waves in Ise Bay that had granted her wish to be on a boat again. She thought of one of her father's favorite poems.

> *The sea! The sea! The open sea!*
> *The blue, the fresh, the ever free!*

Loud vega and slaty-backed gulls flew alongside the ferry as it began to cross Ago Bay. Miho felt the cool, salty air pass over her skin and shivered with delight. She took deep breaths and felt herself relax a little.

Scattered throughout Ago Bay were small islands of all shapes and sizes. *Ago-wan.* Miho reminded herself of the right word for "bay." She could see other places where the mainland poked out into Ago-wan; hills rolled away from the water and beyond, shrouded in distant blue haze, old mountains squatted.

Her eyes gathered in what she could see of Goza as they approached. It wasn't small, but it definitely

wasn't a big town. There were fifty or so boats along the shore and the smell of fish reached out to pull the ferry to shore.

Miho was, for the first time in weeks, feeling comfortable with where she was. Fishermen and deckhands yelled back and forth to each other as they tied their boats to docks. Small trucks and motorcycles pulling carts, puttered away, loaded with all manner of sea creatures suitable for eating: fish, crab, small squid, shrimp. Miho had been in many places like this one, where the smells of salt and sea and sweat mingled with diesel and dying fish. It was wonderful.

Miho scampered to catch up with Ojisan. He was striding off the pier with great purpose, puffs of smoke trailing out behind him like an old steam engine. He walked as if he couldn't wait to get away from the bustle of the docks. They walked uphill on the single road that ran the length of the small peninsula. Miho was breathing hard by the time they reached the top. Ojisan was breathing harder and sweating. Of course, he was wearing a dark suit, carrying two suitcases and had a stinking cigarette dangling from the right side of his mouth.

As they crested the hill, Miho stopped dead in her tracks. The hill rolled down to the Pacific Ocean and became a wide, sandy beach. Waves could be heard, bringing their tales of the vast deep to the shore. Pelicans flapped in a slow lazy line just off shore and terns wheeled and dipped into the blue. Small lanes branched off the main road and connected the houses that were scattered all along the hillside. Ojisan turned right down a lane, toward the tip of the peninsula. Miho could barely see the shingled roofs and latticed shoji—wood and paper screens—beyond each wooden or bamboo fence that lined the road. At last her Oji turned, opened a tall gate and fished a key from his coat pocket.

# 10
# You Ama

"SHOES!" Ojisan barked, as he stepped out of his own loafers and slid his feet into slippers that sat on a low shelf in the small entry room. Miho did the same. "Always shoes," Ojisan muttered and began to slide back walls. Miho was amazed at the way the small rooms opened up and air began to move through the house.

In the third room, there was a cleverly made wall of built-in drawers and cabinets. Ojisan crossed this room to the far corner. Miho followed to see what he was doing.

On that wall was a shelf and on the shelf there sat a collection of objects. Miho recognized a black and white photo of a beautiful, young woman with her chin tilted slightly down and her eyes turned coyly up. It was her grandmother. Also on the shelf was a smaller picture of her grandfather in a smart looking military uniform, a statue of a fat little Buddha, a smooth, pink conch shell, and a bowl with sand in it.

Ojisan was muttering and pulling his lighter from his pocket. *Oh no. He's gonna stink up this beautiful place!* Miho took a deep breath, thinking it would be the last of the clean, tangy sea air that would be allowed in the house. But Ojisan didn't light a cigarette. He lit a stick of incense and placed it upright in the bowl of sand. He took a step back and pressed his palms together. He made a deep bow and held it for several seconds. Miho did the same.

She looked around the house and was utterly charmed. The floors were covered, not with carpet riddled with cigarette burns, but with tatami—flat, woven mats. Many walls were latticed with wood and a thick yellow paper. Though there were few glass windows, the light came through the paper and the rooms were bright. Ojisan was now sliding half of a wall back and the house opened to the sea breeze! He slid another wall back to open the space further. He then crossed the room and levered half-sized panels up. The light and the wind now swept through the house and made it feel as open as the deck of a ship. He walked to the far end of the room and slid another wall back. He beckoned to Miho. "You sleep here." She peered around him into an almost empty room.

"Sleep?" she said, unsure if she heard him right. His English was pretty good, but his words were often rounded and clipped and the 'r's' were hard to hear.

"Hai, nemurimas." He put his hands together and tilted his head on them to indicate sleep.

"Ojisan, there's no bed."

"So American," he muttered as he walked across the room and slid back a door revealing a closet. On the top shelf there was a fat roll. "You sleep futon. This Japanese. Every day, put futon out in air and then put back here," he slapped the futon. "Every day." He squinted his eyes at Miho, as if daring her to ask 'why.'

He began to pat his pocket in a way that told Miho he was looking for his stinky cigarettes. She sighed, waiting for the click of the lighter and the swirling stench to once again fill her world.

But once again, Ojisan didn't light a cigarette. Instead, he put it, unlit, in his mouth and said, "Come." She followed him through the main room and out the front door. Once on the lane, Ojisan lit his cigarette, inhaled deeply and said, "You must learn to get dinner." He said this in Japanese, but Miho understood the words. He set off down the lane.

Just as Miho started to walk after him a strange feeling

stole over her, making her legs weak and compelling her to turn toward the sea. Her eyes scanned the sharp edge of the horizon. Then, in this strange new place, she saw something familiar. The smoothness of the water was broken by the rising and falling of rounded backs and small, gray fins. *Dolphins! White-sides? Common? Spinners?* Miho couldn't tell from this far away, but she immediately began to count the little puffs, the blows of the sleek mammals, coming up for a breath of air. She counted about forty of them and then tore her eyes away to run after her uncle.

"Ojisan! Ojisan!" He turned and looked surprised that she hadn't been trailing along in his puffs of smoke this whole time. "Ojisan, look—dolphins!" Miho pointed out to the pod of dolphins. They were still moving parallel to the shore.

"Hmmm. Maybe dinner dolphin." He kept walking.

Miho stared after him wide-eyed. *I must have misunderstood!* She ran to catch up again. "Ojisan! You don't eat dolphins!" Miho laughed, hoping this would clear things up.

"Hai! Hai! Iruka very tasty!"

Miho stopped walking again and felt a little woozy. *Eat dolphins? Eat the ones that sing and play and talk and tease?* Miho had spent so much time watching dolphins, listening to her parents and her parents' friends talk about dolphins, that she knew they weren't food; they were friends!

She wanted to ask Ojisan why anyone would want to eat a dolphin, but he was turning into a small market. "Ohayo!" the woman behind the counter called. Then she squinted at the door, squealed a little and came out from behind the counter. "Kiromoto-san!" She gave a quick bow, never taking her eyes off Miho's uncle.

Ojisan nodded crisply in return. He tossed out a quick greeting and turned down the first aisle. The storekeeper began to follow him, peppering his back with Japanese too quick for Miho to understand.

Miho remained in the doorway. Sitting all the way across the small store, next to another open door, was an elderly man. He was leaning forward on a tall walking stick and looking intently at Miho, so she bowed and said, "Ohayo."

He pushed against the stick to lever himself out of the chair and then shuffled over to Miho. His head was topped white, like an old, but great mountain. The sunlight coming through the doorway gleamed through his thin, snowy hair as he looked her up and down. His face was so deeply wrinkled that Miho could barely catch the glint of his dark eyes.

The buzz of the chattering woman came up the aisle, propelling Ojisan ahead of it. His plastic basket only had a few items and he rounded the corner and set off down the next aisle, his shoulders hunched against the barrage of talk behind him.

"Hmmmmm." The old man hummed and continued to look at Miho. Then he nodded and shuffled back to his chair. He used the walking stick to slow his descent.

The storekeeper and Ojisan came back to the counter. Ojisan bowed slightly to the old man. The old man again pushed against his walking stick, rose, and spoke for the first time.

"Kiromoto Kazuki." The old man's voice was as strong as his small body seemed weak. The voice had a weight to it that commanded the attention of Ojisan, Miho, and the woman behind the counter.

"Kazuki-san," the old man continued, directing his resonant voice to Ojisan. He started speaking slowly, but then sped up. Miho couldn't pull out any words she knew, but she knew he was talking about her because as he spoke, he looked away from Ojisan and fixed his gaze on her. When he was done, he turned to the woman behind the counter and uttered a few more words. Then he sat back down and nodded his head as if to say, "There! I'm done speaking. You may all go back to what you were doing."

When they left the store, Miho asked Ojisan what the man said.

"He no say anything important."

"If it isn't important, you can tell me," Miho countered.

Ojisan stopped walking and gave her a strange look. He began to pat his jacket, seeking his cigarettes, but then stopped. His hand dropped to his side in a defeated way and he looked out over the water, squinting against the lowering sun.

"He say, 'You Ama.'"

# 11
# I Am Gaia

It was all Miho could do to hold her tongue as they walked back. Ojisan didn't seem inclined to elaborate on "you Ama." Instead, he handed her a bag of rice and showed her where the rice maker was kept. This was something Miho knew how to do. She had been making rice since she was a little kid. She watched Ojisan stir-fry the vegetables he had bought and heated miso, a type of broth that they sipped out of small bowls. They sat on the floor at a low table and ate in silence.

Three times during their meal Miho asked what Ama was, but Ojisan remained silent. After Miho had cleaned the dishes and put them away, she smelled his cigarette smoke coming from outside. She followed the trail and found Ojisan across the road, standing on a large rock, looking out toward the blackness of the night sea.

"Ojisan," Miho began, but he held up his hand.

"Come," he said and set off down the road again.

Miho walked behind him, her mind popping up questions the whole time. They followed the road until it rolled downward and curved toward the backside of the hill, toward Ago Bay. *Ago-wan,* Miho corrected her thought.

Ojisan stopped and lit another cigarette, then pointed across the water. Miho could just make out the smattering of islands that dotted the bay. "In past, this water make wealth for Goza. This water and Ama— Ama are women." He stopped and took a deep pull on his stinky stick. The glow from the tip lit his face and showed the creases around his eyes.

"You Obasan—grandmother—she was Ama. Her Obasan too. Ama are women of the sea."

Miho felt like her heart had stopped. *Women of the sea? Did they live in the sea? Were they some kind of mermaid?*

Ojisan continued. "Ama dive with just breath." He patted his chest. "They find the best treasures in the sea: pearls and awabi. Ama only Japanese women to make lots of money!" He smiled a little. "Ama also find good dinner: oyster, seaweed, crab. My mother such good Ama."

Even in the dark, Miho could see a deep sadness wash over him. He continued to talk. "Not safe, being Ama."

He turned and looked down at Miho. "There shark, there dive sickness, some Ama don't come home."

Miho waited. And waited. Ojisan spoke again, quietly, "Haha (Miho knew this meant "my mother") was Ama sea took."

Miho started feeling cold all over. Her mother had never talked about family too much. She only said that her parents had passed on before she met Miho's father and Miho had never thought to ask for more information. Now, on the eve of the festival of the dead, *O-bon*, thoughts of her unknown Japanese family began to crowd her head.

Ojisan turned toward Miho, the glow from his cigarette glinting off small tears at the corners of his eyes. However, he smiled broadly for the first time since Miho had met him and patted the top of her head. "You and I same, Miho. No mother, no father." He stamped out his cigarette. "You lucky, no sister." And with that he turned and walked home.

Miho lay on her futon, listening to the endless rhythm of the waves caressing the beach and turning over Ojisan's story yet again. She turned it around and around, looking at her family on one side, the sea on the other, her mother, her uncle and even her father. *Did he know about Ama? Was my mother Ama? That old man said I'm Ama. What does that mean?*

It could have been all the questions. It could have been jet lag. Either way, Miho could not sleep. She could only think of her grandmother, her mother and the ocean—the great mystery that seemed to tie them all together.

Miho finally slipped from her futon and tiptoed to the kitchen to get a glass of water. She only wanted to smell the sea air. She really had no plans to do anything else. She went out to the veranda and sat cross-legged on the dark wood. In the dark, there were no children squealing, no radios playing, just the music of the Pacific Ocean reaching this Japanese shore. *This might seem like a strange place, but at least the music is the same!*

That thought made Miho feel a little better. She tipped her glass up and found it empty! Her drinking water was now standing beside her, tall and shimmering; not spilled, but holding the shape of a drinking glass!

Miho looked at the empty glass in her hand to make sure she was seeing what she thought she was seeing! She got to her feet and began backing up from the oddity before her. The column of water began to quiver and shift and form itself into a new shape.

The water now had short legs, a long tail, a long lithe body, short ears and quivering snout. When one of the short front legs raised and began to wave, Miho knew what she was looking at...the otter!

Miho took another step back, right off the edge of the veranda! She landed with a thud and quickly got to her hands and knees. She raised her eyes just over the edge to see if the weird water was still doing otter-like things.

Not only was the weird otter-water still there, it had dropped to all fours and was scampering toward her! Miho scooted backward faster than a crab. The water ran right off the edge of the veranda, balled up, and began to roll toward the front gate!

Miho's mouth was hanging wide in disbelief. The water flattened out and squeezed right under the gate. Miho jumped to her feet and ran to follow it! The silvery ball was now rolling like a liquid tumbleweed down the road. At the corner it paused long enough to rise up, assume its otter shape...and wave.

When Miho closed in on it, the water balled back up and began to roll down the hill toward the beach, toward the dunes...toward the sea! Miho ran faster to keep up with it.

Across a parking lot, over a curb and out into the sand the ball rolled. It zipped up the dune and Miho scrambled on all fours trying keep up. When she finally reached the top, the ball of water was gone.

Miho scanned the wide beach. The wind stirred and Miho shivered, feeling the hair on the back of her neck rise. There it was, this time for real, fur and all—the otter. As before, on the day Miho would rather forget, the sleek otter stood on its hind legs. As before, it waved its paw.

Miho always thought that if she hadn't followed the otter, she might have met the same fate as her parents. She trembled with that thought. She desperately wanted to be with them, even if it was at the bottom of the sea or in the belly of a shark.

Without thinking about how absurd it was to talk to an otter, Miho yelled, "This is all your fault!" She now shook with anger, remembering the puttering of the motor, taking her parents away as she, the stupid daughter, turned to follow the otter.

"You are right," the otter said, and dropped to all fours.

*It talks!* Miho took a staggering step back and slipped down the back of the dune. She slid a ways on her bottom, sand piling up in her pajama shorts. The otter trotted along the top of the dune. Again, it rose up on its hind legs. Miho could see the moonlight reflected in its small dark eyes.

"Oh dear," the otter said. It sounded like the laughter of the little pipers that ran up and down the beach. "You will need to be much more careful if we are to get anything done."

Miho was at a loss for words, Japanese or otherwise.

"Come," the otter said, using Ojisan's command. It turned and disappeared over the dune.

Miho got up, wondering if she was having a futon-induced dream. She scrambled up and over the dune and saw the otter jumping along through the deep sand to the water's edge. Miho followed.

"This is a special place, where the earth meets the sea," the otter said; its voice had a lightness, a bounce to it, like a sparkling stream.

Miho remembered her anger and placed both her hands on her hips, "This is all your fault! Why? Why didn't you let me go with my parents?" The question seemed to rip out of her. It was a question that had been digging at her heart for months, but she hadn't said it out loud.

The waves, which had been lapping with a gentle rhythm at the sand, rose up. The otter jumped back as a dark hill of water crested over into thick white foam. Miho ignored the water swirling around her ankles.

"Why?" the otter said. Again, it sounded like Ojisan, a bit perturbed at being questioned. "You chose! That is why. That is how it is. Every day some things live, some things die. That day you lived; your parents died. I did not do this. I simply came to you. And, I must say, it has taken me a while to find you again!"

Miho was beyond mad, she was furious! She was so enraged that her ears filled with a rushing sound and, without thinking, she kicked toward the otter, sending wet sand and water flying at it.

The otter shook hard, like a dog. The moon glinted off the sand and water flying off its thick fur. Miho kicked again and searched for words to express the deep loss she had been carrying, like her own ocean of grief.

The otter shook again and said, "Okay, if you want to play water games."

The sea around Miho's feet drained away. Along the whole shoreline, the sea retreated as if it were running away from the bizarre scene of a ten-year old arguing with an otter. Miho stared at the newly bared sand and the plethora of creatures flopping and hopping, wondering where their world went. Then Miho realized what the retreating sea meant.

She only had time to look up from her feet and see

the moon shining through the crest of an enormous wave. It was beautiful and terrible. Miho had bodysurfed waves as long as she could remember. Her body knew what to do when faced with one too big to handle—she dove.

She dove into the monster and began to kick hard, hoping to kick her way through its power and emerge on the other side. But this wave was much too strong. It pulled Miho up into its foaming, forward edge. Miho felt the forward-pitching energy and thought, *into the washing machine.*

She was lifted and dumped into the swirling, churning madness of this wave. It pushed her against the bottom and, just as a washing machine churns clothes, turned her over and over. Miho held her breath and waited to feel the bottom so she could push upward. This was not the first time she had been dumped by a wave.

But her breath began to run out and still she was being ground and spun on the grit and gravel of the shore. The big wave rolled her all the way up to the base of the dunes and then left her, gasping and dazed. The wave pulled back and a smaller wave crashed and ran up to Miho as if, on behalf of the otter, to say, "There! You kick me, I'll kick you back!"

Miho sat up, pushing her hair out of her face and

feeling utterly defeated. The ocean resumed its gentle, rhythmic lapping. The otter was there beside her, dark eyes glinting out from the light-colored fur. "Are you ready to listen now?" the otter asked. "This is harder for me than you."

Miho wondered how that could be, considering that she was wet and scraped and exhausted and the otter looked just fine. "Who are you? What do you want?" Miho asked.

"Tonight, I will tell you who I am, but as for what I want, that will have to wait." The otter began to waddle in a slow circle around the bedraggled Miho.

"I am Gaia. I am the whole of the earth. I am every rock and raindrop. I am the wind and the waves. Do you understand?" The otter paused its circular pacing to look at Miho.

Miho said, "Watashi wa wakarimasen." (I do not understand)

The otter sighed and kept walking, looking at the sand and speaking in a voice that sounded like the endless rising and falling of the tides. "I am Gaia. I am the very sand you sit on and the air you breathe. I am the great sum of all the parts."

Miho shook her head, trying to make space for such a statement. She was exhausted, partly from her ride in the rogue wave and partly from allowing her grief to swell to the surface.

"Listen," Gaia said. Her voice had a glint and a gleam, a moonbeam tripping across the water. "Listen. It is the way you will learn. Listen to your teachers."

And there, so low it was mostly a vibration Miho felt through the wet sand, came a single note of whale song.

Miho jumped to her feet, eyes scanning the place where the black of the sea met the black of the sky. As expected, a great "whooooosh" came across the water. Miho saw the rising steam where the hot breath of a great whale met the cool of the night. A moment later a large, broad tail showed itself above the water.

Miho was wild to be able to see better. *What whale is this? A right? A humpback?*

In her mind, Gaia's voice, sounding like the very sparkles made by the tips of waves in the sunlight said, "You still have family. Where your heart is, so is your family. They are calling you. I am asking you—come, woman of the sea, and help me."

# 12
# O-bon

Miho stood shivering in the moonlight and waited for the whale to blow again. But it didn't. Miho began to wonder whether she had heard a whale at all. The colder she became, the more she wondered if she hadn't imagined this whole strange episode.

She climbed over the dune and began to make her way back to the house where Ojisan slept, hopefully unaware she had ever left. At her back, the ocean continued its fine, measured lapping. Perhaps it too was unaware that she had ever come and gone.

Outside the house, Miho began to brush the sand from her body and wondered how she could possibly get back into her bed, *futon,* like this. She decided to concentrate her efforts on her feet so as to not dirty the floor. Once inside, she went directly to the shower.

The warm, fresh water felt as if it were washing the

pain of the evening down the drain. She didn't think of her parents. She didn't think of Gaia. She didn't think. She let the water clean her and clear her.

BANG! BANG! BANG! "Miho!" Ojisan was pounding on the door! "Miho! Why you up? Why you shower?"

Her first thought was to yell back, "No Why!" But her second thought was better.

"Jet lag!" she yelled toward the door.

There was a small space of silence. She could almost hear Ojisan muttering in Japanese. Miho had an image of him sleepily patting his pajamas, looking for cigarettes, and she smiled.

"You go sleep more!" Ojisan yelled through the door. "Tomorrow O-bon—need sleep!"

Miho finished up and climbed back into her futon. What would O-bon be like? It was a festival for the dead, but who wanted to be festive about such a thing? Miho only had time to turn that thought over once, before she fell into a deep, untroubled sleep.

Ojisan woke her again by shaking her foot. "Miho. Miho. Be up, we need to prepare for O-bon." He left her room.

Miho dressed quickly and found Ojisan hastily setting out breakfast. "After breakfast," Ojisan said in Japanese, "we clean house and then we go get our family." Miho was sure she misunderstood, but decided to follow his lead instead of asking why.

Throughout the rest of the morning, Ojisan and Miho dusted the corners, polished wood and shook out every tatami mat in the house. As she cleaned, she tried to convince herself that the jet lag and the new home and the new uncle were making her a little loopy. She didn't really have a water fight with a talking otter— that was definitely a crazy thing to believe. She must have dreamt the whole episode. She tried to convince herself, but the scrapes on her elbows, knees, and palms were no dream.

In the afternoon, Ojisan went out behind the house. Across the small, neglected garden sat a low shed. He began to dig through it and Miho could hear what she was sure were Japanese curses. He pulled out what looked like a wooden tub and a sort of short metal crowbar. He handed the bar to Miho and went back inside with the wooden tub on his shoulder.

He placed the tub on the floor under the shelf in the corner that had her grandmother's picture on it. He motioned for Miho to hand him the metal bar.

"What are these for, Ojisan?" Miho asked, hoping that it wasn't too much like a why question.

"This," he motioned toward the tub, "is oke. And this,"

he waved the bar, "is tegane." He mimed poking and prying and tossing something into the tub. "Okasan's Ama tools."

Miho wanted more details, but he was already up and off to the rear of the house. He came back with a small case. From it he pulled two medals, hanging from short, brightly colored ribbons.

"These from Chichi (father)." He laid them on the small shelf.

"Why are you putting them out?" Miho asked, her curiosity pushing away the hesitancy to ask why. Ojisan didn't seem to mind.

"The dead come back for O-bon. Must put out the things they loved in life." He headed to the kitchen area with no more explanation.

Miho didn't hesitate. She went to her room and pulled the portable CD player, the CDs and the big photo album from her backpack—her mother's recordings and her father's pictures. She stood for a moment, staring at the objects, amazed that this was the way she could hold her parents. She swallowed the tears that threatened and went back to the main room.

Ojisan had brought out a small table and set it next to the items. He returned to the kitchen. Miho took her parents' things and laid them on the floor next to the oke. Ojisan came back with two sets of bowls, cups and haishi, chopsticks.

He saw Miho staring down at her objects and went back to the kitchen. He returned with two more place settings. He poured sake into each of the four cups and rice into each bowl. Then he carefully piled up some tangerines and placed a wrapped sugary treat at each place setting.

Ojisan and Miho ate a very late lunch in silence. She kept looking into the room with the lonely table set for four dead people. She wondered what else would happen during O-bon. Ojisan sighed and looked very weary.

"Now we must go to temple, to grave. You have nice clothes?"

Miho wished he had told her this before she left Nagoya. "No. Just shorts 'n stuff." She stared at the table, wondering if this would make her uncle mad and make him say, "So American." But he just shook his head and rose from the table.

The first afternoon of O-bon was very hard for Miho. Goza was filled with families. Grandparents and grandkids, parents and aunts and uncles gathered together and filled Goza's temple yard.

Miho felt tall and underdressed; most of the people, even Ojisan, were dressed in yukata, summer kimonos. She felt tall and stupid; she didn't understand a word of the long ceremony at the temple. She felt tall and family-less; it was just her and her Oji, who didn't hold her hand or talk to her to tell her what was going on.

He didn't talk while they weeded around the family grave either. Miho could, however, hear the families around her. The word "gaijin" reached her ears more than once. When she did look up, people would look at her, see her gaijin-green eyes and smile politely...too politely. Little kids stared and stared. Miho felt like an alien—a tall alien.

The only good part was after Ojisan went to the

temple and came back with a paper lantern, already lit. For the first time, he really looked at Miho, looked right into her eyes.

"I'm sorry you lost your parents," he said in Japanese. "I know you are sad and I don't help too much. Let's try to be happy during O-bon. Happy we are all together now."

They walked home in silence, their lantern one bobbing light among many blinking down the roadways. As each family reached their home, they hung the lantern outside the gate. Ojisan did the same.

For a while, Miho and Ojisan sat on the veranda, facing the sea and watching the other families bringing home their lights, their dead. Miho was sure they were both lost in thought about those they loved. Miho was also keeping her eyes wide open for the strange creature that had come and turned her life upside down.

# 13
# Enso

The second day of O-bon, Ojisan again commanded, "Come" and headed out the door, pulling a cigarette from his shirt pocket as he did.

Miho followed him and wondered if the strange things that had happened—the otter, the wave, the whale—could have anything to do with O-bon. She wondered if the strange things would stop after the festival. For the first time, she realized Ojisan would most likely go back to Nagoya after the three days. *After all,* Miho thought, '*He businessman.*'

The center of Goza was filled to the brim with people dancing, drumming and singing. Miho had no idea what was going on and Ojisan seemed to have forgotten all about her. It was obvious that many of the people knew him. Calls of "Kazuki-san!" came floating across the crowd and she would see Ojisan push his way through the crowd to meet and talk and laugh with the originator of the calls. More than once, Miho saw him tip a bottle to his lips.

This continued all day. Miho began to get hungry and tired and a bit bored. She decided to head down to the beach. She glanced around to see where Ojisan was—she should ask permission, after all. He was far across the square with his arm slung over another man's shoulder, laughing in a big, full-bodied way that reminded Miho of her mother. Miho stuck out her tongue in his direction and then headed toward the beach.

As she walked, she saw a wizened little figure on the beach, face to the ocean and something in hand. It was the old man from the store! He seemed to be holding still, yet moving, flowing. Miho wondered if it was a trick of the sun and the waves that made him look like that.

She left her shoes on the crest of the dune and walked to the water's edge. Miho sort of hoped the old man would see her and come over to tell her more about what it meant to be Ama.

The waves were small, as she suspected they usually were in Goza. *At least until you get an otter mad at you!* Miho thought, before she could stop herself. It was simpler to think that the events of the past evening were nothing more than a dream or a fancy of her half American, half Japanese, fully tired mind.

She stood, enjoying the feeling of the ocean sucking the sand from under her feet and watching the wee little sandpipers run back and forth to the surf's edge. They picked away at the small crustaceans that each retreating wave revealed. Miho envied their simple life. There was no such thing as being half a sandpiper.

She looked down the beach to the old man. He held what looked like a tall paintbrush. He had both his spotted, gnarled hands wrapped around the handle and used his whole body to pull the brush this way or

that. He occasionally took an easy, graceful step into or out of his work. He looked like he was dancing.

Miho walked closer, wondering what he was painting and wondering if she should say something to announce her presence. But she didn't have to. Without looking up from his work, the old man said, "Konnichiwa."

Miho stopped in her tracks. How did he know she was there? She returned his greeting and added a deep and long-held bow. She sensed that this man both deserved and demanded respect.

He finished and stepped back. But he didn't take much time to admire his work; he simply turned toward Miho and said a quick but long sentence in Japanese. Miho had to shake her head and say, "Wakarimasen." (I don't understand.)

"Hmmmmm." The old man stroked his chin and regarded her, eyes twinkling from within his deeply creased face. "No spoke Engrish for…" He drew his hands out wide, "long time." He smiled, pleased with his effort, and the smile seemed to warm the air around them. Miho smiled back, happy to have someone besides her uncle to talk to.

"Watashi wa namae, Miho, desu." Miho said, introducing herself in Japanese.

"My name, Taro Tomikoro."

"What is this?" Miho asked, indicating the shapes he had brushed into the sand.

"Sho-do. It mean, Way of Brush."

*Sho-do,* Miho liked the sound of that word. "What does it say?" she asked, grateful that this adult didn't seem to mind questions.

He laughed, a surprisingly deep, rich laugh for a frail, little man. "Can tell kanji meaning, but Sho-do say more about Taro Tomikoro than kanji I make."

Miho didn't understand what he meant and thought this was because his English was very choppy. But she couldn't take her eyes off the large brush. Making kanji in the sand was something she had done before, but only with a stick, never with a giant paintbrush.

"Can I try?" Miho asked, hoping it wasn't a rude, gaijin request.

"No try," the tiny, weathered man said. Miho sighed and looked at her feet.

"No try," he repeated. Miho looked up and he was holding the brush out to her. "Must do, no try. I show."

Miho took the brush from Mr. Tomikoro. The old man took his leathery hands and moved Miho's hands around until she had the brush gripped in a way that suited him. He stepped back and then raised his hands to shoulder level, indicating that she should do the same.

Miho felt a little silly; she looked like she was going to plunge the point of the brush deep into the sand. She waited for him to tell her what kanji to make.

"Stand, like this." He planted his feet shoulder width apart and softened his knees a bit. He made a fist in front of his belly. Miho waited. "Breathe," he said.

*I am breathing!* Miho thought, but exaggerated her breath a bit so Mr. Tomikoro could see it. Her shoulders began to heat up as she held her arms out.

*When is he going to tell me what to do? Maybe I am just supposed to start. I can draw the kanji for "ocean;" should I start with that? Why isn't he talking? This brush is heavier than it looks! What does he want me to do next?*

Miho's mind continued to chatter this way and she occasionally looked to her right to see Mr. Tomikoro standing there, still as a statue, watching her.

*This is silly! What am I learning? Should I just draw something?*

She started to lower the brush, her shoulder muscles instantly letting out a little cheer of relief.

"BREATHE!" he barked.

Miho's arms popped back up.

*Why do Japanese men like to yell so much? My dad hardly ever yelled, only when I did something really bad. Boy, I hope he doesn't smoke like Ojisan. He doesn't smell bad like Ojisan. Man! My shoulders are killing me! What IS this? Is he making a joke on me 'cause I'm "gaijin?"*

Miho tried lowering her arms just a smidgen, to bring some ease to her shoulders, arms and hands.

"BREATHE!"

Miho's arms popped back up.

*Breathe! Breathe!* Miho's thoughts felt like they were banging up against the sides of her head. She knew Mr. Tomikoro was waiting for something before he would show her more. *Okay, breathe, Miho. Just breathe. How do I breathe? I can feel the air on my nostrils and the sea in the back of my throat.* Miho stopped thinking about the brush and focused more on her breath. *My belly rises every time I inhale. Okay belly, inhale. Okay ribs, squeeze and push that air out. Belly in, ribs out. In. Out. In. Out.*

Miho stopped wondering about the Sho-do lesson. The complaints from her shoulders seemed further away. *In. Out. In. Out.* She kept her gaze fixed on the horizon, that knife edge where sea and sky had their conversations. *In. Out.*

Mr. Tomikoro spoke in a voice she could barely hear above the murmuring of the sea caressing the beach, "Make circle."

*Circle? What does that mean? How big? How fast? Do I*

*still hold the brush like this?*

Miho lowered the tip of the brush into the sand and did her best to make a circle. The brush seemed to get pushed and bumped by the sand. *Maybe I should go faster! Slower? Oh, no! It looks like an oval! It's flat!* Miho stopped and kept her eyes down on the flat, wobbly circle. She knew, without asking, that it wasn't good...Sho-do.

When she looked up, Mr. Tomikoro's face was blank, but there was a hint of a smile glinting out of his deeply creased eyes. *Like wave wishes,* she thought.

He reached out and took the brush. He didn't take a noticeable breath or do anything special, but the very air around him seemed to still. Without looking directly at the sand, he swiftly drew a circle. It was smooth and complete and somehow had as much energy in the blankness within, as the darker line that defined it.

"Enso," he said, and swept his hand in the shape of a circle.

He flapped his hand toward Miho. "Breathe... Enso...Breathe...Enso. You do, no try. Hai?"

He turned and knelt down to retrieve his walking stick lying in the sand beside him. Miho stared at him, waiting for something more like a real lesson. He flapped his hand at her in a way that told her to get going on this 'Enso.' Then he turned and headed back toward the

dune. She could hear him saying in an almost sing-song voice, "Breathe…Enso…Breathe…Enso."

Miho watched his retreating back and then began to attempt another Enso. She looked at her second attempt and thought, "Ugh!" Before she could look at it any longer and figure out what she did wrong, a big wave came up and swept the kanji away.

Miho discovered that each time she drew Enso, a wave came to erase it. If the tide had been rising, Miho would have understood. But the tide was going out, the ocean retreating. Still, one long finger of water continued to crawl up the beach…just to scrub her Enso away.

# 14
# Why Why Why

It was nearly dark by the time Miho pulled herself away from the enchantment of the sea and sand. She didn't want to go back to the festival just to listen to songs she couldn't sing. She was hungry! She trudged up the hill to Ojisan's house and found a bag of wasabi-covered dried peas in the cabinet. She hardly noticed the hot fumes that filled her head (which really was the fun part of this snack), and kept staring at the four bowls. *Where are they all now? Heaven? Do they talk to each other? Maybe they were here for O-bon. Did Mom and Dad see my terrible Sho-do, that sloppy Enso?*

Miho was still nibbling and pondering when she smelled the acrid smoke of Ojisan's cigarette. Ojisan came through the door a moment later. He had sweat stains on his shirt, a grin on his face, and a nearly empty bottle in his hand.

"Oh-ho, Miho!" he motioned to her with the hand

holding the bottle. "Where you go?" He giggled. "An Engrish poerm! Oh-ho, Miho! Whah you go!" His mouth seemed to have trouble making the words.

He took a drink and then patted his shirt, looking for cigarettes. Miho could tell this was a motion he had done so many hundreds of times his hands did it even when he wasn't sure what he wanted.

"It like, I have..." his smile faded and his eyes narrowed, "new sister." He swayed a little. "But you, sister...worse, sister."

He tottered over to the table and fell to a seated position with a thud. He began talking to the two bowls on his left.

"I do soooo good for Yoko. She have everything. I even find husband. But this one!"

He turned to address the two bowls on his right. "How I find husband for gaijin? This all you fault!" He looked up to regard Miho with his limp stare. "How I find husband for you? You don't even talk good!"

Miho thought this was the stupidest thing anyone had ever said to her. Husband? She was ten years old! He should be worried about getting her to school! And besides, he talked worse than she did!

"Ojisan, why are you so mad at my mother?"

Ojisan staggered to his feet, narrowed his eyes and

inhaled sharply. Miho realized her question and held her breath, waiting for the yelling to start.

But Ojisan didn't yell. He closed his mouth and turned back to the empty bowls at the table. "See? See? She just like Yoko! Why! Why! Why! She going to do same thing! Make me work, work, work and then go away and be American! Bah!" He spat toward one of the bowls. "You say you like all her 'why, why, why.' Stupid American."

Ojisan lowered himself to the floor and tipped the bottle to his lips. He seemed to have forgotten all about Miho.

Miho walked as quietly as possible over to the table and folded herself down to the floor. "Ojisan, did you take care of my mother?"

"Hai." He shook his head sadly. "I leave school. For while, I stay in Goza with Yoko. But I need go to Nagoya for more money job. I work hard. I thought since parents gone, my beautiful sister need something wonderful. I pay for her school."

Ojisan tipped the bottle again and wiped his mouth with the back of his hand. "Yoko do so well in school she want more school, in America, in California. I tell her no, time to get husband, get married. I find such good husband for Yoko."

"My dad?" Even as the question popped out of Miho, she knew how wrong she was and wished she could stuff the question back into her mouth.

But Ojisan seemed too tired to yell. He patted his shirt pocket for his cigarette pack and pulled it out. He peered into the package and, finding it empty, crushed it up in his fist.

"Yoko shame me. She say no to my friend and go to California. She tell me she don't need me. I work so hard for so many years and she go anyway. Now!" Ojisan seemed to snap to attention for a moment. "Now, look what happen! She run away from Goza, from Ama, from place she should be and look what happen anyway!"

He looked at Miho, but his eyes seemed blurry and he couldn't hold her gaze. "Now I have new Yoko. I have, 'why, why, why' here again. But, Tomikoro-Sensei say you Ama—maybe you stay. Maybe you stay."

Ojisan dropped his chin to his chest. Miho waited for him to say more. She felt like a heavy jacket had been draped over her shoulders. Ojisan's story made her think about her mother, but in a different way than just being her mother. Miho had more questions and waited for Ojisan to look up, but he didn't.

His chin stayed on his chest and his breathing sounded deep. Miho wondered if she should get him up and tell him to go to bed. She decided he was quieter this way, so she got up and went to her room.

# 15
# Listen

Once again, sleep was slow to come. The only sounds she heard were the night birds chattering to themselves in the treetops and the waves making their endless landings on the shore of Goza. Miho waited for sleep.

She focused her attention on the rhythmic whoosh and hiss of the waves below. The sounds of the sea had been her lullaby most of her life, and it always helped her go to sleep. Miho waited for the waves to take her off into a restful place where she didn't have to wonder about her mother and her grandmother and why the sea seemed to want the women in her family.

Miho waited, but sleep didn't come. The wonderful wave sounds that normally lulled her to sleep now seemed to be calling her. The whoosh and hiss started to sound like "MeeeeeeHoooooooo." She finally got up and left her room.

Ojisan was sprawled across the floor cushions, the empty pack of cigarettes still crushed in one hand and the other hand across his eyes. His jaw hung open and he was snoring gently. Miho didn't think he would wake, but tiptoed across the tatami-covered floor anyway.

Miho followed the call of the sea down to the sandy dunes. The tide was high and the foam of the waves crept far up the beach. Miho sat on top of one of the dunes, listening to the wind hiss through the sea grass and listening even harder for the sound of whales breathing.

"You do not have to wait for the whales to wander by, you know."

Miho was so startled by the voice that she, once again, fell back and took a tumble down the backside of the dune! She scrambled to her feet, shaking sand from her hair and shaking it out of her shorts. Before she looked up, she said, "Gaia?"

"Ahhhh! She knows my name! This little one must be listening!"

Miho finally lifted her eyes. On top of the dune was the dark outline of the otter. *Well, I guess I'm not crazy,* Miho thought.

"Come!" the otter said, the command sounding not so much like Ojisan, but somehow more like her mother. "I will teach you how to listen even better."

The otter's rump disappeared over the dune and Miho sighed. Part of her felt that this was absolutely nuts, thinking you could hear an otter talk and then following it down to the sea. But then again, this was what her family had always done—listened and followed the minds in the water.

Miho scrambled over the dune and found the otter hopping and splashing about in the white, sparkling remnants of waves that crawled their way up the beach. "I see why you humans are always flocking to my beaches—this kind of tickles!" The otter dropped and rolled a bit in the sand.

"Okay, otter. I'm here and I'm listening. But if all you are going to do is recommend vacation destinations, I'm leaving."

"Oh my dearest, I would not waste this much energy to crunch myself up into this tight little body, only to chat with a child about the wonders of beaches! Oh no. I am here because I have heard you and I know you have heard me.

You heard me every time you went to sleep listening to the waves come to shore. You heard me when you turned your ear toward the horizon and heard the breath of the whales. You heard me when you sat on your boat and listened to the sea birds cry and call. I am Gaia. I am the whole of the earth. And, the earth is the sea, the river, and the rain."

Miho took a moment to turn all those words over in her mind and then asked, "What do you mean, 'the earth is the sea, and the river and the rain?'"

The otter tilted her head and looked both cute and a bit frightening at the same time. "Swim with me and I will tell you. Trust me and I will teach you. I will teach you to talk to the dolphins and understand the whales." The otter turned and slipped its sleek body into the water with barely a ripple.

That was all Miho needed to hear. She kicked off her shoes and dove into the surf. The tide had turned and the pulse of the waves was heading back out to the deep. Miho fixed her eyes on the little round head and began to swim.

It was hard to see. The moon was only half full and the lights of Goza did not crawl too far from shore. Miho was swimming hard, but Gaia was pulling further and further ahead. Finally Miho stopped and began to tread water.

"Gaia! Hey! I can't swim that fast!"

Gaia's head disappeared and a moment later popped up next to Miho. "Oh! I see! I guess those long arms and legs would slow you down. Hmmm. Well!" Gaia said, her voice sharp with the certainty of decision. "Tonight, I shall simply have to swim slower. But I will have to find you some help. The water is wide and we simply can not have you puttering along like a manatee now, can we?"

"But why, Gaia?" Miho couldn't hold back the question. "Why do I have to go fast? Why are you talking to me? Why didn't you just talk to my mother? She would've listened." Miho swallowed hard and tried not to look at the image of her mother's dark eyes and bright smile that danced in her mind.

Gaia sighed and began to float on her back, her webbed front paws folded across her chest and otter toes poking from the water. Miho wished she had her own thick pelt to keep her warm and keep her afloat. They rose and fell over the swells.

"I am Gaia. I am the whole of the earth. However, I can no more control every part of myself than you can control the fifth cell in your pinky toe."

*Pinky toe? My pinky toe?* Miho imagined her feet churning and dangling into the night sea and tried not to think of the many sea creatures that might find such a toe a tasty novelty.

Gaia continued. "Your whole life you have been

listening—listening to the whales, to the waves, to the streams, and the patter of raindrops. You have made these sounds part of your own thinking and that is why I need you now. I need your help."

"But why? Why can't you just help yourself?"

"Could you help yourself if someone cut off your hands?"

Miho thought of her hands churning and dangling in the night sea and, again, tried not to think of those same sea creatures that would come back for her hands after they had snacked on her feet.

Gaia's voice grew louder. "Could you help yourself if someone filled your lungs with smoke?"

Miho thought of Oji and the fact that he chose to fill his lungs with smoke, many times a day. She frowned at the thought and then wondered why Oji couldn't help himself stop.

"You humans are doing so many things to me, things that are beginning to cripple me, hurt me. These pains are growing deeper and more widespread and to me, each of you is smaller than the fifth cell of a toe. You are more like an electron in that cell. You are so very small, but you are also part of me. If I am hurting, then you are hurting too. If I die, then you will die too."

The waxing moon glinted off Gaia's dark otter eyes

and Miho saw that they welled with tears. Miho's own eyes moistened. She knew the deep pain of death. And yet, underneath the idea of death was the expanding and contracting notion of being part of Gaia and Gaia being part of her.

Gaia's voice skipped softly over the waves. "If you help me now, you help yourself too." They bobbed in the black water as Miho considered Gaia's words. She felt so very small in the vastness of the sea. She had felt this small before. Under the water, she rubbed the raised Hokusai-scar and reminded herself that she could be small and still be brave.

"OK. I don't completely know what you are talking about, but my..." Miho had to swallow hard to continue. "My Dad always said that you could only really see nature if you were patient."

"Ahh, my dear, this is true. But to be one with the water, you can't hope to see. Eyes are no good to you; you must learn to listen. This is why I bring you out at night, so you will let go of vision and trust your ears." Gaia turned and continued to swim slowly to the west.

She finally climbed out onto a rocky beach, shook, and sent sea water spraying in all directions. Miho wished she could shake too. She would warm up quicker. "Find a large rock, my dear, one about the size of your head," Gaia said. Miho looked around the beach and saw a rock meeting that description. She went over and gave a grunt as she hoisted it up to hip level. "Like this?" she asked.

"Yes, now bring it into the water."

"But Gaia, I can't swim with a rock!"

"You don't need to swim; you need to sink!"

Gaia was already out past the low, foaming break of waves. Miho shuffled over the stones and back into the water. The rock felt a bit lighter in the water, but she had to squeeze it to her belly to keep from dropping it. "Now," Gaia continued, sounding very much like a schoolteacher, "take a deep breath and sit down on the bottom. Place the rock on your lap so you can sit still, and then listen."

Miho held the rock and dropped to the bottom. The pebbles and stones on which she sat made a gravelly growl as they rolled to and fro. The waves themselves made a sort of low growl and hiss, as if they were alive.

On top of the big, obvious sounds of water and shore dancing together, Miho heard little snaps and pops. Miho knew these to be snapping shrimp, clacking their claws to stun their prey. Underneath the sound of the waves rolling the rocks was the far-off pulsing thrumming of a ship.

Miho was out of air, so she braced her feet against the rock and pushed up to the surface. Her lungs drank in sweet night air and she turned to see Gaia, floating toes up. "So?" Gaia asked, the question sounding like the pause before a storm.

"I heard the waves and the rocks and some snapping shrimp and a ship. But, I'm not sure where the ship is, the sound kinda comes from all around."

"Again," Gaia commanded.

"Why?"

The sharp look Gaia shot at Miho was followed by an early breaking wave that knocked Miho in the head and sent her rolling off her rock. "Again," Gaia said, her voice so soft it seemed to only be a hint of sea spray.

This time, Miho didn't ask why. She primed her lungs and sank again. She noted all the things she had heard before and then opened her ears and her mind to more.

There seemed to be a very high *twitter, twitter, snap! Twitter, twitter, snap!* Miho sensed that further down the beach, the waves were bigger and hitting the rocks with a bit of a clap. The patter of water, rolling back off the rocks into the sea could also be heard. Now that she had been here a while, she realized what a noisy place this shoreline was!

Then it came, a sound so deep and low that it rattled her bones more than passed through her ears. *A whale!* It was a whale sending out a "ping!" A ping is a single boom that washes through the ocean, seeking another whale and Miho knew this sound! She again, braced her feet on the rock and popped up into the night air. "Gaia! There is a whale out there!"

"What else?" Gaia asked gently.

"Gaia, there is a whale out there! Can I see it? Will you teach me to talk to it?"

"There is more to the water than whales!" Again, the quick look that Gaia gave her was followed by a singular, early breaking wave that slapped Miho in the face and knocked her from her rock.

Miho understood. She shook the water from her ears and said, "I heard something that twittered twice and snapped once. I'm guessing that further down the beach the rocks and the waves get bigger, 'cause I heard them too."

"Better," Gaia said. "Many fish signal and talk, but most people do not hear. You must learn to hear if you hope to learn the way of water. I am Gaia and I am water. You, my dear, are water too. Learn the way of water and you will learn all my secrets. You are the first; everything has come from the sea and is still connected to the sea." And with that, Gaia rolled in her round, otter way and disappeared beneath the inky surface.

It was a long walk back to Ojisan's, but Miho was kept busy with the many questions that sloshed to and fro in her mind. *I am water? Is that like being Ama? What did she mean that I would learn her secrets?* Such questions came and went like so many waves.

Inside Ojisan's, Miho found that her uncle had rolled onto the tatami-covered floor and was now face down, breathing deeply. Miho got into dry clothes and pulled little stuffed Shinju from her backpack. She kissed her one-eyed friend and fell onto her futon. Sleep came at once, like the one big ping from the whale, and took her deep.

# 16
# Heart of Japan

Miho was roused by the conflicting sounds of happy, chirping birds outside and low, pained groaning inside. She found Ojisan on one knee, with one hand on the table, trying to press himself up. She ran to grab his elbow and help him.

His eyes were squinted so tightly that she couldn't see them and a sweaty smell clung to him like a fog. A low burp roiled up out of him, and Miho waved her hand to send the sour smell away from her face.

He shuffled toward the kitchen and gulped down some aspirin. He started toward his room, stopped, and turned to Miho. "We go home today."

Miho was surprised. She thought O-bon was three days long. Surely there was more to do today. Besides, she couldn't stand the thought of leaving this big open, airy house and going back to the tight, smelly confines of the apartment in Nagoya! Miho mustered her best Japanese and said, "Excuse me, I must have misunderstood. O-bon is only two days, yes?"

He held the wall as if the very act of being vertical was extremely difficult. He cleared his throat and said, "O-bon three days, but not necessary. Go today."

Miho looked at the swaying, stinking uncle and sensed that he hadn't forgotten; he just wanted to run away from Goza. He meant to go back to that hot, gray city. Who knew how long it would be before he would want to come back here; judging by the dust when they arrived, he didn't come often.

"Ojisan," Miho bowed briefly, as a precaution. "You look sick. We shouldn't travel today." Miho could just imagine what the dipping, rolling ferry ride would do to him!

"Noooo," he growled. "Work tomorrow. Must work!"

"Tell them your new niece is here from America." She fished for another reason. "Tell them your American niece got sick from sushi and you must stay here until she can travel."

"You think lie okay?" His voice wavered and Miho sensed that he wanted to yell, wanted to think of her as a lying American girl.

"Ojisan." Miho bowed a little lower this time. When

she rose, she walked forward and reached out for his hand. He flinched when she took it, but his eyes finally opened fully and looked into her own. "You're not well. How can you feel better on that ferry rolling back and forth? You might feel even worse on that rocking train." He belched.

"You go sleep some more." Miho still had his hand and led him toward his room. "You can visit some friends this afternoon and I will do what needs to be done to finish O-bon and...and, I'll cook dinner! Just call your job. If you want, I can pretend to throw up in the background."

Her Oji snorted, and then laughed out loud. Miho smiled back. This was the first time they had shared a smile. "OK. OK. I call, I sleep." He pulled his wallet from his back pocket and poked her in the chest with it twice as he said, "You cook."

He slapped the wallet into her hand, turned, and headed to his room. The door slid shut and Miho heard one more short laugh. She looked at the wallet and considered the possibilities. She was going to get to stay in Goza one more day! She wanted to make the most of it. Miho toyed with the idea that she could somehow convince her Oji that they should live here all the time.

*But first, this is the last day of O-bon. What do I do? What do I cook? And how do I buy it; I barely speak the...* And then she remembered that there was one other person she knew who could speak some English.

Miho showered and changed and slid Ojisan's wallet in her back pocket. She slid his door open a crack, just enough to see that he was snoring softly, curled up on his side and looking almost like a child.

She thought of another thing she could do to make him happy and get him to stay in Goza. She grabbed his crumpled, empty cigarette pack off the floor, shoved it into her front pocket, and headed out into the bright, blue day.

Small, round clouds had risen from the sea and were now marching inland. Boats dotted the horizon and clusters of families already peppered the sandy beach. Miho walked down the road drinking in the tangy sea air and thinking, *I want to stay, I want to stay.*

She walked to the store where Mr. Tomikoro first proclaimed her "Ama." As before, the little man was settled into a chair opposite the door, leaning forward onto the walking stick. The same woman was behind the counter, chattering away on the telephone. She glanced at Miho, then turned her back and faced the wall as if to say, "I don't see you; therefore, I don't have to serve you."

Miho walked right up to the old man and bowed deeply. "Ohayo, Tomikoro-san." He bowed his head in return. Miho dug through her mind for the right Japanese words and then gave up. She needed help and thought his English was probably better than her Japanese. "Sumimasen," Miho said, meaning, 'excuse me.' "My Japanese is not very good, but I need some help today. Can you help me?"

He said, "Hai," and pushed himself up from his chair. Miho was surprised. She hadn't even told him what she needed help with! The woman behind the counter saw the old man rise and hung up the phone. "Chichi," the shopkeeper began.

Miho knew that "chichi" meant "dad"—she was Mr. Tomikoro's daughter! The two had a brief exchange of words that flew like birds over Miho's head. His daughter shot Miho an angry look and retreated to the room behind the counter.

Miho began to explain the challenge of her situation. "You see, I never lived in Japan before. My parents…" Her thoughts and her voice stopped like they had hit a wall. *How do I explain 'Lost at Sea'?* She swallowed hard, took a deep breath, and continued. "My parents…died. Well, now I have to live with my Oji, Kazuki Kiromoto.

He lives in Nagoya. I don't like Nagoya; it is noisy and hot and smells funny."

She took another deep breath. "Anyway, I think Ojisan drank too much last night and he's sleeping. He wanted to leave today, but I told him to sleep and I would take care of whatever I need to do for O-bon. Except, I have no idea what you do on the third day of O-bon."

Mr. Tomikoro looked at Miho without saying anything. A smile twitched the corners of his mouth. He pivoted around his walking stick and took small steps toward the back door that stood open next to his chair. He motioned her to follow.

Beyond the door, Miho was surprised to find a beautiful, small garden. There was a tree that looked like a maple, a little pond, and several large rocks that made you want to sit down for a spell. The back of the garden was a living wall of green bamboo. There were flat stones inlaid into the earth. Miho followed Mr. Tomikoro along this path to a single story building to the left.

Miho watched Mr. Tomikoro remove his shoes and step over the high threshold. As Miho slid her shoes off, she saw him bow low and long. When she stepped over the threshold, her breath caught.

The room had six small desks and one larger desk at the far end. At the other end, were long, low shelves. It was obviously some sort of classroom. But what stole Miho's breath was the arrangement of items directly across from the door.

There was a space tucked back into the wall. Deep blue irises were set in vases at the bottom. From the top, there hung a long piece of paper with four jet black kanji symbols. The strokes that had made the kanji were not perfect or precise, but bold and energetic. Below them, lying sideways in a cradle of dark red wood was a sword. It was as if those kanji symbols could leap off the wall and wield that sword! Miho felt like she had entered the heart of Japan.

# 17
# Sho-do

Mr. Tomikoro retrieved some items from the low shelves. As he walked back, he motioned for Miho to sit. He swiped the dust off the surface of her desk. He set down a dark-gray rectangular block of stone, about the size of a 16-pack of crayons; a squared-off well was carved down into the block. Next, he set a black, rectangular stick by the stone. Mr. Tomikoro then went to the front of the room, retrieved a small teapot and filled it with water from a corner sink.

He shuffled back and poured a bit of water into the well in the block. With the black stick he began to pull water up from the well and rub the stick up and down the slope. The water began to blacken!

"Why..." Miho began.

Mr. Tomikoro put his hand over her mouth. "No question. No Engrish," he said.

He handed her the black stick and made the rubbing motion. Miho understood and began to wet and rub the stick, making the water in the well ever thicker and blacker. She still wasn't sure why she was doing this. Was this part of O-bon? But she rubbed and rubbed. Mr. Tomikoro went to the back of the room and brought up two small rocks and some small rolls of paper. He unrolled a piece and used the rocks to hold it in place.

"Motto." He made the rubbing motion again.

Miho kept rubbing and wondering. Finally, Mr. Tomikoro produced a small brush and dipped it into the well, now filled with a deep, dark black. He drew a single line down the edge of the paper. "Motto." He made the rubbing motion again.

Miho kept wetting the stick and rubbing it, watching the dark ink slide down into the well. She knew what she was doing now. She was making ink to do Shodo! Mr. Tomikoro was going to teach her Shodo!

He tested the ink again. Satisfied, he said "Watch," in Japanese and made five lines come together in a kanji that looked like this: 永

"Ei," he said, pointing to the kanji. "Wakarimashtaka?" he asked. Miho knew he wanted to know if she understood the meaning of this kanji.

"Mizu?" She guessed. She thought it looked like the kanji for water.

"Machigata."

Miho knew this word from her classes at the Consulate. Machigata meant wrong.

Mr. Tomikoro closed his eyes. His mouth turned down and the creases deepened in his forehead. Miho waited and resisted the urge to talk. She could hear the wind moving through the tree in the garden and the distant, rhythmic hiss of the ocean.

"Ahhhh!" Mr. Tomikoro exclaimed, his eyes flying open and filled with delight. He pointed to the kanji. "E-tern-ity!" He began to speak, and Miho had to focus intently to understand his Japanese. She heard, "one, two, three, four, five." Watching Mr. Tomikoro do the kanji that meant "Eternity" again, she understood it was important to do the strokes for eternity in that particular order. *"Ei,"* she corrected the thought to Japanese.

He handed her the brush and a fresh sheet of paper. She dipped the brush in the ink and began. Her first attempt had big blots of ink at the end of each stroke. The second had wavy lines where there should be none. The third try looked better, but simple and dull.

She sighed. This was harder than learning cursive!

Why did Mr. Tomikoro want her to write, "Eternity?" A noise distracted her, and she looked up to see her new teacher come into the room with an armful of cut grasses and bamboo.

"Work! Work!" he said in Japanese and Miho bowed her head back over her work, determined to make Eternity. "*Ei*," she again corrected her thought.

As she did the five strokes over and over, she began to think about O-bon and her parents and how, although they were gone, she would carry them forever with her—in her memory, in her mind, in her heart. Forever. Ei.

Miho took a fresh sheet of the grainy paper and thought of forever, eternity, *Ei*. She sat back from her latest attempt and smiled. She looked up to call Mr. Tomikoro and was surprised to see that he had fashioned the pile of grasses and bamboo into two small boats! Each was about the size of a shoe box, fat in the middle and twisted up into a curved point at one end.

Miho stood and almost called out, "What are those for?" But she remembered that he had said no questions, no English. She remained standing as Mr. Tomikoro walked slowly to her desk. He picked up and examined each sheet of practice paper. He finally picked up her last one, smiled, and began to nod.

He took that piece of paper with him back to his desk, rolled it up and tucked it into one of the boats. Then he came to retrieve the items from Miho's desk. He motioned for her to follow him to the sink where he showed Miho how to properly clean the brush and the stone.

Miho watched the water run down the drain. It started off black with ink, but slowly, the water swirling down the drain began to clear. Finally, the last hint of gray left the water. The brush was clean and you couldn't tell that the brush had ever been steeped in the inky blackness.

When they were done, Mr. Tomikoro handed her the little boat that had her paper rolled up inside. "For tonight," he said. "You ask Kazuki-san."

Miho cradled the delicate little boat and followed him through the garden and back inside the store. He set his boat on the counter and smiled at her. Miho took a step back and bowed and said, "Domo arigato," the polite way to say 'thank you very much'. She started to leave and then turned back and added, "...Sensei." This was the Japanese word for teacher. His smile grew wider.

She turned to leave again and then remembered her front pocket. She pulled the crumpled empty cigarette package out and put it on the counter. She looked at Mr. Tomikoro, shrugged her shoulders and said, "Ojisan likes those."

She walked back to the house feeling hopeful. She had her O-bon boat, even if she didn't know what it was for and she was going to make a good Japanese dinner—no pizza this time! She knew she could make her Oji like her better.

# 18
# Eternity

Miho dropped off her grass boat and checked on Ojisan. He was still snoring like an outboard motor. She headed over the hill to Ago-wan. The sun was high and fierce and sweat trickled down the back of her neck. Even the steady ocean breeze did little to cool the afternoon heat.

She went directly to the area where fishermen set up stalls in the shade of a long pavilion. As she got closer, the smell of fish and the sounds of talk and laughter filled the air. She walked slowly down the row, looking at the wide variety of sea life set out in large trays of ice. Some of the day's catch still swam in buckets of water.

A young man with a wide smile was arranging several large fish in his ice. She decided she would try to buy her fish from him. "Sumimasen," Miho said. He looked up (And he did have to actually look up; Miho was taller than he!) He looked surprised, then covered his surprise with a polite, "Konnichiwa."

"O kudasai," she began; that meant, "I would like." Miho pointed at the fish and octopus she wanted.

He wrapped her selection and handed the packages to her with another smile and a quick sentence in Japanese. Since he spoke fast, most of the words were lost on Miho. Again he spoke, even more quickly and a little louder. People around them were looking, and Miho could feel her neck and face getting hot. She knew that they all knew she was a stranger, gaijin.

She wanted to run away, but made herself pay, bow slightly and say, "Domo," before she turned to escape the fish market.

Miho hurried back up over the hill and didn't slow down until she was at Ojisan's and had the fish safely in the refrigerator. Then she got herself a large glass of water, went to the front of the house, and sat to gaze out at the sea.

She watched more fishing boats make the return journey around the tip of Goza, into the safety of Ago-wan. At the beach, many families had laid out blankets; the laughter of children playing in the foaming waves mixed with the cry of seagulls. Part of her wanted to go down to the surf and meet those kids. But she knew how easy it was to lose track of time when you were playing in the water. Better to stay close to the house.

She watched a small flock of pelicans take turns folding their wings, plunging down into the blue sea and bobbing back up. They tilted their long beaks high to swallow their catch. How could Ojisan live in Nagoya?

She leaned against the door frame and closed her eyes. The puffs of warm air lifting up from the beach felt like a caress on her face and the sea smells made her feel so at home. The combined laughter of kids and gulls was like music, the sea providing the steady beat. Miho dozed.

When she rose, she went to the kitchen determined to make such a wonderful meal that Ojisan would never want to leave. For the next hour Miho worked hard in the kitchen. It was a test of her chopping and stir-frying skills and, as she adjusted her grip on the knife, she wondered if cooking weren't a bit like Shodo.

Ojisan's house filled with wonderful smells. As Miho dumped the last of her preparation into a serving bowl, a frumpy Ojisan appeared. He seemed a bit more rested and was looking from her to the table with a mixture of confusion and surprise. Before either one of them could say anything, a voice called through the door.

"Kombanwa, Kiromoto-san!" Sensei stepped over the threshold. He immediately frowned at Ojisan and barked a few quick phrases at him. Ojisan looked down at himself and blushed. Miho suspected it was a bit of a reprimand to Ojisan because her uncle frowned a bit, bowed quickly, and turned to head to the bathroom. When he emerged, he was clean and smelled a great deal better.

He also was patting his shirt pocket and glancing around the room. Sensei motioned to the small bag he had set on the counter. Miho fished out the new pack of cigarettes and took them to her uncle.

Now Ojisan really looked surprised! He looked over her shoulder at the table filled with bowls of rice, fish, and vegetables. He rubbed his eyes and looked back at the cigarettes, then back at her. A smile crept across his face.

Sensei gave them both a wink and turned to go out the door. He paused to pick up Miho's small boat. "Kiromoto-san," Sensei began. Miho figured the rest of what he said was something about bringing the boat to the ocean that evening. Ojisan went to Sensei, thanked him, and bowed as he took the boat.

"Itadakimas," a sort of Japanese grace, was all her Oji said during the meal. Miho was also silent. She knew better than to ask what the boat was for, or how he knew Mr. Tomikoro, or when they would go back to Nagoya, or if he liked the food, or if he ever tried to quit smoking, or any of the other questions that swept through her mind.

After dinner, Ojisan stood at the front door with the grass boat tucked under his arm. "Come," he commanded and they set off down the hill. The sun had left the sky. The horizon was lit from below with an astounding array of red, yellow, and orange. Great flocks of seabirds were silhouetted against the fiery sunset as they came to land for the evening. Below, the beach was filled with the same families Miho had seen at the cemetery and at the dancing celebration. Most had paper folded into square boats, but some had grass and bamboo boats, like hers.

The same priest that had sung his song at the temple was there, chanting and holding a lantern. An assistant was with him, and as each family approached, the assistant would take a small candle from a box at his feet and light it from the lantern. One member of each family took the boat and the candle, then waded out past the point where the small waves tipped and broke and rolled to shore. The candle was placed in the boat and then the boat was pushed out toward the horizon.

By the time Ojisan and Miho got their candle, the sea was dotted with at least two dozen floating lights. Ojisan handed the boat and candle to Miho and said, "We must send our family away again, until next O-bon." He nodded toward the ocean.

Miho kicked off her shoes and waded in. Around her were other people, some with tears in their eyes, pushing their little boats off into the deep. Miho wondered if anyone else there had really seen their family disappear in a boat as she had. She set the candle in the flat bottom next to the rolled paper that said, "Ei...Eternity." She took a deep breath and pushed the boat toward the flaming horizon.

It bobbed off after the other little lights. Miho stood in the water and watched it drift away. It was as if Goza disappeared and she were back at the rocky cove in Alaska, watching her mother waving and calling to her to get a tape recorder if she found the otter.

Her heart felt like it was cracking open; the sadness that spilled forth was like the black ink that she had squeezed from the brush earlier that day. She kept her eyes on her own little light and wished the ache could somehow begin to lessen, to clear like the water from the brush.

*Ei.* She reminded herself. *Eternity. They will always be*

*with me, even if my boat is swallowed by the sea like their boat was. I am Ama and I will be in the sea with them. Always.*

She came back to shore where Ojisan stood, frowning down at her. He patted her back and simply said, "Come." They trudged back up the hill to the house. Ojisan stopped to huff out the light in the lantern hanging from the fence, and they went inside the house.

It did seem emptier, as if people had left it. Ojisan took his mother's tools back to the shed and put his father's medals away. Miho took the dishes to the kitchen. She gathered the CD player and the photos from the table and took them to her room. She kissed them before tucking them into her backpack.

Ojisan watched her from the doorway. "Tomorrow we go home," he said. Then he repeated himself in Japanese and added, speaking very slowly so she would understand, that she should be ready in the morning.

Miho nodded and said, "Hai."

# 19
# Teachers Are Everywhere

Leaving Nagoya had been so exciting, but returning to it…wasn't. However, there was a bright spot in the leaving. As Ojisan locked the front gate, Mr. Tomikoro came walking down the road. He had a book tucked under his arm. Ojisan bowed and said good morning to the old man. Miho stared at the ground.

When she looked up, she did her best to tell him, in Japanese, that they were going back to Nagoya and that she couldn't learn more Shodo. Sensei laughed and handed her a book.

Miho couldn't read the title, but inside there was page after page of kanji and many ways to draw the beautiful figures. She smiled and thanked him in the most polite way she knew.

"There are teachers in Nagoya," Tomikoro-Sensei said in Japanese. "Teachers are everywhere. Not just Shodo teachers. Watch. Listen."

Sensei glanced at Ojisan, who was puffing impatiently and looking out at the ocean. The bent old man held his staff and leaned forward a little to be close to her ear. "I think I see you soon!" He straightened up and winked. Ojisan turned and commanded, "Come!"

Miho bowed quickly, said goodbye, and hurried off after her uncle. She looked back twice. Both times Sensei was still standing, leaning on his staff and watching them go down the road.

~~~

The first day back in Nagoya, Ojisan muttered about Miho getting lost. She told him that she could read a compass and a GPS and maps pretty well. When you are on a boat in the open ocean, there are no street signs or landmarks to tell you where you are! Her father often let her try to figure out their position and help choose the heading to return home.

Ojisan only grunted at this information. But that evening, he pulled a surprise from his pocket. It was a cell phone! He flipped it open and showed Miho that not only was it a phone, it was a camera, could take video and, best of all, it had a GPS positioning system in it! He had programmed the phone with both his work and cellular numbers and the exact position of the apartment building. Miho couldn't get lost as long as she had the phone with her.

"So, there it is," Ojisan said, fishing a cigarette from his pocket. "Now you can go to store and find way back."

Miho used that phone as both a teacher and a guide. She went out in the morning and sat next to people talking at bus stops, stood behind them in lines and followed them through the market. She palmed her phone and captured short videos of people talking. Back at the apartment, she could play the videos over and over and use her Japanese/English dictionary to figure out any words she didn't know.

She knew that it was probably wrong to take videos of people without them knowing, but she also knew that most of the bus stops had video cameras in them already. In a city like Nagoya, someone was always watching. She learned much more about speaking Japanese from those candid conversations than she did from the boring workbooks she had. Sensei was right; there were teachers everywhere.

Using the GPS, she could venture out into the city and find her way back. She was thrilled to find a large green park about 10 blocks from Ojisan's apartment. It had a big pond, a little creek, and lots of trees and grass. The park felt about 10 degrees cooler than the rest of

Nagoya. The summer sun was turning the city into a cement oven and Miho preferred the cool grass, water, and fresh air to the air conditioning in the apartment.

She also sat by the pond and wondered about the otter, about Gaia. She watched the reflection of clouds bob across the pond and worried. How would she ever find out what Gaia meant by talking to the whales if she couldn't get back to the sea? What could she do in Nagoya? Learn to talk to the turtles that crawled up on the rocks to sun themselves? Miho doubted they had much to say.

Throughout the week, the temperature climbed to mind-boggling heights. Ojisan's shirt was soaked with sweat as he came through the door. The heat made everyone move slow and become very grumpy. One evening, over dinner, Ojisan was grumbling about needing an apartment with two bedrooms. He said Miho couldn't sleep on the couch forever.

"Ojisan," Miho said, seeing an opening, "The house in Goza has lots of room. We could live there and you wouldn't need to get a different apartment."

Ojisan only frowned at her and said, "Goza!" with a snort, as if it were the silliest idea in the world.

That night, as she washed the dishes, something happened that made her desire to get back to Goza even stronger. She was watching the stream of water fall from the faucet and thinking about the strange creature that had come into her life when it happened.

*"Learn the way of water,"* Gaia's voice echoed through her mind, *"and you will learn all my secrets."* Miho stood, unmoving, transfixed by the sight of the silvery, bubbling water running from tap to drain.

*"Could you help yourself if someone cut off your hands?"* Miho held out her hand and looked at the scar. She curled her hand around the column of water that was falling into the sink. She drew her hand back out and uncurled it.

There on her palm sat a perfect cylinder of clear, cool water! She stared at it, not believing her eyes. *"Eyes are no good to you. This is why I bring you out at night, so you will let go of vision and trust your ears."* The memory of Gaia's words continued to echo in her mind.

Miho leaned down, turning her head and bringing her ear close to the cylinder. She listened—and then listened harder. "Come, woman of the sea," Gaia's voice whispered, and this time, it wasn't in her head.

Now Miho couldn't believe her ears! She leaned in closer wondering if Gaia would tell her *how* to get back to the sea.

"Miho!" Ojisan snapped. "Stop playing—do dishes!"

Miho jumped and spilled the strange bit of water down the drain. She tried this a few more times in both the kitchen and the bathroom, but was not able to grasp a column of water, much less hear it talk to her.

Toward the end of the week, the city grew even hotter.

"Sumimasen," Miho said, being as polite as possible. She had learned a lot from her video lessons. "I'm probably wrong, but it might be much cooler in Goza. The breeze from the ocean would feel wonderful, don't you think?"

Ojisan started to frown, but Miho could see the idea catch hold. Before he could say anything, there was a knock at the apartment door. A messenger handed over an envelope. Miho watched as Ojisan read the short letter inside. He dropped it on the counter, fished out yet another cigarette, and began to circle the small apartment. Finally he stopped and looked at Miho.

"OK. We go to Goza, but only for weekend."

Miho couldn't help herself. She let out a yell, rushed across the room, and squeezed her uncle around the waist. He held his arms over his head and tensed up. When she stepped back, she could see that his face had gone red. He stuck his cigarette back in his mouth and said, "At least there is good fish in Goza."

Miho could hardly sleep that night. She whispered to Shinju that they were going back to Goza, going back to Sensei and maybe another Shodo lesson. They were going back to the sea!

# 20
## *Lagenorhynchus obliquidens*

On the train, Miho asked her Oji how he knew Mr. Tomikoro. "He was my Sensei," he said in Japanese.

"You studied Shodo?" Miho asked, also in Japanese.

"No. Well, yes. Everybody studies some Shodo. But what I learned from him was Jujitsu, some Aikido and Kendo. I was pretty good too. Once I thought I would compete, then teach, but...everything changed. I could not support myself and your mother teaching; I was not ready to be a teacher anyway."

Ojisan looked out the window for a moment and then pushed his newspaper up in front of his face. Conversation over. Miho thought about how much she and her uncle had in common. Both of them had their lives pushed into a new direction through no action of their own. Both of them had lost people they loved. Miho wondered if Ojisan was sad to hear about her mother.

When they boarded the ferry, a man called out to Ojisan. He smiled broadly and the two men bowed, shook hands, clapped shoulders, and finally laughed and embraced. Ojisan introduced Miho. She said politely, "Yoroshiku." The two men fell to talking in the way grownups do, so Miho left them inside the air-conditioned ferry and went out to the deck. She was much happier listening to the chug of the engine and the crying of gulls than the talking of two grown men.

She looked westward, where the peninsula came to a point and Ago-wan became the great Pacific Ocean. In the distance, she saw the rolling and flashing of dolphins! Miho counted them. She was happy to see that they came into the bay as well as cruised the ocean shoreline. She would have that much more opportunity to watch them, to get to know them.

When they docked, Miho asked Ojisan if she could stay to watch the dolphins. He shaded his eyes with his hand to see the pod now passing between the ferry and one of the many small islands that dotted Ago-wan.

"Hai. Hai," he waved his hand impatiently and went back to talking to his companion. Then he stopped and cupped his hand around his mouth to call to her in English, "Miho-san, can you make nice dinner again?"

"Only for you, Ojisan!" she called back. He laughed and waved and turned, chuckling, back to his friend. They set off up the hill and Miho set off walking parallel to the bay. Her eyes were fixed on this group of 40 or so dolphins, but her heart couldn't help but note that she and her grumpy uncle had just shared another smiling moment.

Miho had to walk fast to keep pace with the pod. Their dorsal fins were deeply curved, a deep, dark gray on the leading edge, fading to a light, almost white, gray. Miho could also see long streaks of the light gray along their dark backs. Mr. Hernandez had taught her a long time ago that if you saw those light-gray "suspenders" you were seeing Pacific white-sided dolphins. They were what he studied. Miho liked looking at his books of photos. Most science-type people called white-sided dolphins "lags" because they had a long scientific name that started with "lag." The lags had rounded black-lipped snouts, white bellies and those lovely streaks of light gray down their dark bodies.

She smiled, remembering Mr. Hernandez. He would be happy to see that there were at least two babies in the group. The babies took many more breaths than the adults. They poked their small rostrums, their snouts, up out of the water, splashing a great deal more than the adults did with their smooth, practiced rolling breath.

Miho walked far to the east of the docks and began to climb the hill in order to see better. She was soaked with sweat. The air coming off the water was more sticky and humid than cool and refreshing. She wished she were in the water with the dolphins.

The dolphins turned further north into Ago-wan and Miho lost sight of them as they rounded another one of the many small islands that poked up in the bay. Instead of returning back toward the ferry landing, she decided to go up over the hill here to the east. She took out her phone and took a GPS reading. She liked knowing exactly where she was and looked forward to finding out the exact position of Ojisan's house.

The ringing of her phone jolted her out of her thoughts. "Miho! Where are you?" Ojisan barked as soon as she had answered.

"Sumimasen. I'm coming now, Ojisan."

She hurried back to the path that ran down the ocean side of the hill and turned onto one of the many small roads that ran between the homes and businesses of Goza. Miho continued west and jogged until she came to the familiar gate. She pushed her wet hair off her sweaty forehead and went in.

In the doorway, leaning on his staff, was Sensei! She

smiled, said, "Konnichiwa, Sensei," and held her bow for a respectful amount of time. Ojisan came out of the house, pulling his cigarettes from his shirt pocket. "Tomikoro-Sensei wants you to go with him."

He said something to Sensei that Miho thought was about her being back in time to make some dinner. Sensei didn't say anything, just went through the front gate and down the road towards his daughter's store. Miho followed.

"Sensei," she ventured. "Was my Oji always so grumpy and mad?" She hoped her Japanese was good enough that he understood.

"Kiromoto-san, majime," Sensei replied.

Miho didn't know what "majime" meant. "Wakarimasen," she said, and wondered how many more times she would have to say she didn't understand. Sensei thought a moment and then scrunched his eyebrows together and made a serious face.

"Serious?" Miho guessed.

"Hai! Hai!" Sensei turned to go through the store and Miho followed. "No questions. No Engrish," he reminded her as they removed their shoes and stepped over the high threshold. The long classroom was stifling hot, as if the sun had baked all the breathable air from it. Sensei sent her to the back of the room to retrieve the items they would need. He filled the teapot with water.

Miho began to prepare her ink. Sensei stood silently and watched. Twice he dipped the brush and drew an experimental line before he was satisfied with the quality of the ink. Miho spent her time working on both enso and ei. Her Shodo, to her anyway, was better. She smiled. Sensei nodded and told Miho to clean her tools. Again, she watched the water run dark to start with and then begin to clear.

After she had returned her tools to the shelf and they were outside, Sensei stopped her and tapped her in the chest. "Energy inside, ki, flows on paper. Way of Brush start in you, Miho."

Miho nodded as if she understood, but the idea was almost as confusing as an otter telling you that it was the whole of the earth. Miho walked back to Ojisan's with one too many ideas bouncing around: the ink, the otter, the boat that went to sea with the candle in it, the one that went to sea with her parents in it. Her head began to throb.

By the time she arrived, her head ached so badly she could hardly see straight. Her eyes began to water as she conveyed this to her uncle. He gave her some aspirin and told her to go lie down. Mr. Masuaki, Ojisan's friend from the ferry, had invited him out to dinner anyway.

She was happy to stay behind. Miho didn't want to spend her evening listening to the two men talk and having to say "excuse me" every time she dared to say something. She felt a little better, curled up on her futon with her little, gray Shinju tucked under her chin. She heard Ojisan leave and slept a little bit, but the hiss of the waves woke her. Again, they began to sound like they were calling her name. Again, Miho rose and went to the front room, where the opened walls allowed the now cooling ocean breeze in to freshen the house. The sun was diving down toward the horizon and Miho decided to go find Gaia.

# 21
# Mujo-kan

Miho walked the beach, looking for the otter while thinking about her ki and her Shodo. She stopped at the east end of the beach where the sand turned to rock and the rock climbed the hill. Miho looked up and decided, since she hadn't seen Gaia, she would do some more Goza exploration.

She walked up from the beach and trekked eastward and upward through town. The peninsula rose much higher where it began to hook into the mainland. The hill grew steeper and rockier. Miho sweated and panted as she neared the crest. Just over the top, she heard the sound of running water.

She pushed into the woods and found a marvelous spring. The water bubbled right out of the rocks and began a flashing, sparkling journey down to the sea! *All water flows to the sea, Miho.* Her father's voice flowed from her memory like the water flowed from the rocks. *The ocean covers 75 percent of the earth, and all water wants to get back there. It can be lifted up into the clouds in Fiji, rain in Colorado, flow through California, and back into the sea.*

Miho thought of the wonderful book that Sensei had given her. She remembered the word and the kanji she wanted: "Mujo." It meant "flow." Another good word was, "Mujo-kan," the "feeling of flow."

Miho sat for a while and let the sound of that phrase, "Mujo-kan," flow right over her. She liked it. She sat and thought, *Mujo-kan* and stared at the flickering, clear water as it made its journey back to the sea. *I'm like water,* Miho thought. *I always want to flow back to the sea! Mujo!*

The day continued to wane and the breeze continued to cool. She thought of the way water flowed so effortlessly over and around the hard, dark rocks. *Mujo-kan.* Her vision filled with the glimmer and gleam of the stream as it ceaselessly flowed. *Mujo. Yeah, I'd really like to be the water and flow to the sea whenever I wanted.* A shadow darkened the clear water in front of her. Miho looked up to see Gaia, standing on her hind paws and waving—waving goodbye.

Miho felt pushed! She went headfirst into the stream and began to roll down the hill. She was falling, bouncing, panicking. *Wait,* she thought. *I'm not falling;*

*I'm...I'm...flowing!*

She was flowing down the hill—sliding around rocks and under logs! She felt no jostles or jolts, no rocks hitting her, just...*mujo*. She and the water picked up speed and for an exhilarating moment, they were airborne!

Miho sputtered and spat the suddenly salty water from her mouth. Looking behind her, she saw the stream ending in a short waterfall, spilling into the sea. She looked around and found herself in a cove surrounded by large, dark volcanic rock. The persistent ocean had tossed the thinnest sheen of water over the rock so many thousands, maybe millions, of times; the cooled lava that had once been dark and jagged was now smoothed and shaped.

Miho paddled over and found a low place in the rocks. It was set back into the rock and made a simple stone chair. Miho pulled herself up out of the water, plopped herself down and rubbed the remaining water from her eyes. She took a deep breath and gazed out to the horizon, looking for anything familiar.

The waves were just big enough to occasionally cover her legs, like a liquid lap blanket. The sun had started its evening descent behind her, behind the hill, into Ago-wan. A few fierce golden rays found a path through the trees and sent shimmering ropes out over the water. Miho squinted and saw movement, shattering the gold that was reaching out across the water. The otter head moving toward her sent hundreds of light-tipped wave tops out on either side.

Miho waved her right hand, relieved to see Gaia.

"Ohayo, my dear."

"Ohayo, Gaia-san," Miho said and bowed a little from her seat in the rock. Gaia rolled onto her back; her leathery toes poked from the thick bushy fur of her feet. She tilted her head toward Miho.

"You like this seat?" Gaia asked.

"It's cool, like a mermaid chair. When I was little I used to build mermaid chairs, mermaid houses, mermaid dining tables...all kinds of things. Sometimes under water, sometimes on shore. I figured, people come to visit you when you have a place to meet them, and I wanted to meet the mermaids."

"I saw you. I can tell when anyone is fully engaged with all the toys I create. Sometimes it is a bird song, sometimes it is a cool breeze, and sometimes..." Gaia paused and tilted her head a bit so that her dark, glittering eyes fixed on Miho. "Sometimes it is a wish made at the tip of a wave."

Miho was startled. She wanted to ask Gaia how she knew that. She wanted to ask if Gaia answered the wishes. But Miho was becoming more Japanese every day, so she held her tongue and waited to see what else Gaia would say.

"If you are going to help me, you are going to have to be able to travel through the seas and the rivers, through the rain and the snow. I felt you tumble down the mountain and know now that you will be able to fit in with new friends and learn from new teachers."

With a small "plunk," Gaia rolled her body into a ball, dove, and shot off into the ever-deepening gloom of the little, rocky cove. Inside, Miho was frantic with questions. *What friends? What teachers? Snow?! What on earth does Gaia have in mind for me to do?*

But Miho, becoming better at watching her mind do loop-de-loops, decided not to run off ahead of what was really happening. She sat in the hard, wet mermaid chair and waited.

Her feet dangled in the water, rising and falling with the swells that came and swept across her lap. A buzzing began in the soles of her feet, almost as if they were falling asleep. The buzz climbed up and down her lower legs. The fast vibrations grew in intensity until a black-lipped snout broke the water—this dolphin had been using its echolocation to find her!

Her heart quickened as she looked at the dark, round and thoughtful eye of the dolphin looking back at her. The dolphin bobbed with its head above the water and flipped a few chirps and pops toward her.

Miho straightened her body and slid into the undulating cove. She felt her whole body being prickled and tickled by the tiniest of sound waves. Five more dolphins popped up! She heard their puff, draw and click of exhalation, inhalation, and blow holes snapping back shut. Miho was surrounded by their bobbing dorsal fins, dark eyes, and rostrums! She was certain they were the same Pacific white-sided dolphins she had watched earlier that day.

The lags began to squeeze up against her. Their taut, hard bodies pushed in close until she had no choice but to throw an arm over the wet, sleek back of the dolphin on either side of her.

The dolphins began to breathe in unison, making extra-loud exhales and inhales. Miho thought of Sensei commanding her, "Breathe!" She began to breathe with the dolphins, pumping her lungs. The dolphins on either side of her bunched the muscles under their tight, smooth skin. Miho took an extra-deep breath and down they went!

The small group went about ten feet down and then curved back up toward the surface. The Lags didn't do their usual rolling breath. They popped almost straight up and waited until Miho had exhaled and inhaled, then took her down again.

This time, they went even deeper! Miho felt the pressure of the sea above her, pushing in on her ears. She let go of the dolphin on her right to squeeze her nostrils and blow inwardly. "Pop!" went her ears and she felt better. She now used both hands to grasp the dorsal fin she still held.

She felt her air beginning to wane and also felt the buzz of the dolphins behind her, scanning her body.

They went rocketing up toward the lighter blue of the day above. It was difficult and amazing, so amazing that she was almost breathless!

Again and again the dolphins took Miho down into ever darker, colder water, then brought her back up when she needed to breathe. She quickly learned that breathing more like a dolphin worked much better. She rolled her belly up and turned her chin over her shoulder as they approached the surface. With her mouth facing skyward, she was able to take another breath faster and the group put on some real speed!

Miho didn't have time to wonder where they were, how far out to sea or how deep. She was fully focused on breathing with the group. After a time, the dolphins began to spread out into a line—Miho in front, holding tightly to the hard, curved dorsal fin.

They were down deep, where only a glimmer of light made the water deep gray instead of pitch black. Clicks and squeals and buzzing dolphin-talk zinged around her. The ongoing chatter was a mystery to Miho. Suddenly, the dolphin she was holding jerked downward, pulling its dorsal fin out of her hands!

Her forward momentum instantly slowed and panic began to bubble up in her. She couldn't possibly kick her way to the surface in time for her needed breath!

Did Gaia drag her out here to make her "lost at sea?" Her heart pounded.

However, the dolphin that had been behind her pushed up and shoved its dorsal fin into one of her grasping hands. Instantly, they went zipping to the surface for a breath. They continued on, toward the horizon.

Again, the dolphin she held jerked away and the one behind her caught her up and took her to the surface. Miho began to relax and even let go when she found her ride start to pull away. She noticed that many times when she surfaced to breathe, the others were still below. Miho realized that they were taking turns carrying her up.

She began to trust in the next dolphin catching her up and taking her to the life-giving air above. She felt better as she picked up the rhythm of their handoffs. (Could it be called a 'handoff' when it was a fin she was holding?)

They were flying through the ocean! Occasionally one of her companions would leap clear of the water, twist, and land with a SMACK! The sun in the west dipped into the depths and sent a golden sidewalk out over the water. They raced along this golden path, and Miho's mind reeled with the magic of it.

She was part of the group. The happiness that grew inside her chest felt so big that it was like an air-filled buoy that would always bring her up to the surface. The sun had left the sky and now there was very little difference between being in the shallow or the deep. It was all dark. Miho had to pay closer attention to the pressure in her ears and on her body to know when to breathe.

The lags slowed their pace and the group began to cruise gently along the surface. Miho swiped at her eyes and craned her neck to take in the stars above. She could also see lights blinking along a hillside about a half-mile to her left.

*Goza…they brought me home!* Sure enough, they curved inward toward the little rocky cove where Gaia sat, waiting in the mermaid chair.

# 22
# Baka-da!

Gaia was laughing in that unseen, but deeply felt way. "Even in the dark, your eyes shine like the sun!" the otter said. "Did you enjoy your ride?"

Miho searched for words to describe how she felt— a word for a feeling that was higher than happy and also deeper, like happiness that had gone into her bones. All Miho could do was nod her head and smile.

Gaia's chuckles seemed to blend into the lapping and gurgling that the waves made upon the rocks. "I hoped that you could keep up with your new teachers."

"Gaia," Miho began. "Why do you call them my teachers?"

Gaia did a few quick otter-rolls in the surf, as if she was buying time, thinking of an answer. "The minds on the land and the minds in the water are so similar and like minds can teach each other. You are so small in these great oceans that for you to be able to do your work, your mind and their minds need to come together. I am making that so. Come along, my dear. I think it is time to leave the water for today. Your uncle is sure to miss you by now."

And with that, Gaia rolled once and then dove. Miho stood, staring out at the place where Gaia had been. She struggled to find room for both the happiness and the ache. The big space that the happy ride had made in her chest now filled with a deep ache of love for her mother and father. But the ache wasn't as dark as before. It was as if the ride through the water had washed it a bit clearer. The ache was only gray.

The smoke from Ojisan's cigarette reached Miho before Miho reached the house. Ojisan was pacing the road out front, pulling so fiercely on his cigarette that it glowed like an angry red eye in the dark. When he heard Miho's footsteps, he turned and threw the cigarette to the ground. As he mashed the butt into the dirt he demanded, "You say you have headache! Where you been?"

Miho struggled with the translation, but knew by his tone, his posture and his angry red face—he wanted an explanation for her absence. "I was playing at the beach." Miho said, her voice so small it seemed like the onshore breeze would carry it up over the hill and dump it into Ago-wan.

Her uncle took two surprisingly big steps for a small man and grabbed Miho's shirt collar. "Uso bakkari!" he barked. *He thinks I'm lying,* Miho thought, shocked she understood his words. Ojisan continued in English. "I been to beach," he said, his voice low and gravelly. "I been to beach and you no there."

Miho's heart was pounding. "I was swimming, Ojisan...I swear! I was out in the water!"

Ojisan walked purposefully into the house. Miho, dragged by her collar, stumbled up over the doorstep after him. He pulled her through the house and then pushed her into her room. "Baka-da! You stupid girl! Sharks come in dark! Boats no see you in dark!" He looked up at the ceiling and said, "Why I curse with 'nother water girl?" He leveled his gaze back at Miho. "Pack. Tomorrow we go back to Nagoya...for good! You no swim there!"

And with that, he slammed the door. Miho stared at the door and felt the meaning of his words sink in. *Back to Nagoya? Back to the big, loud, smelly city and the little, quiet, smelly apartment?* Miho's heart sank.

She had seen the change in her Oji this weekend. He had smiled. She had heard him laughing with his friend. He had even joked with her a little. Miho sensed that Goza made him feel better. But could she ever talk him into coming back again? She put her things into her backpack, pulled her futon down off the shelf and pulled ratty gray Shinju into bed with her. She rubbed the matted stuffed dolphin's back and returned her mind to the feeling of going fast and furious through the sea. And, on that memory of flying along with her new teachers, she slept.

# 23
# Rising Storm

Miho woke to the sound of laughter. She rubbed her eyes and sat up. Her arms, shoulders and back felt like lead, proof of the adventure Gaia had sent her on. The ache was comforting in a way, a physical reminder that what had happened was real. Miho stretched her shoulders and told Shinju they absolutely had to find a way to stay in Goza!

In the main room, her Oji was sitting at the table with Sensei and the man she had met at the ferry the day before. Both were listening intently to her teacher. Sensei finished what he was saying and there was a brief pause before they all erupted into yet another burst of laughter. Ojisan saw her, smiled, and waved her over to the table. "Miho, did I tell you that Mr. Masuaki was Sensei's best student? He still does Shodo, in Kyoto."

Miho smiled at the man and then turned to Ojisan. Again, she did her best to be a polite, Japanese girl.

"Sumimasen, (excuse me) I must have been mistaken. Aren't we leaving this morning?" Miho asked.

Ojisan was already turning back to the conversation between the two other men. He waved his hand at her. "We go last ferry. You have whole day; go be water girl."

Miho wanted to hug him. Not Ojisan, but the man who obviously made her uncle want to stay longer. Another day to find Gaia and maybe another chance for a crazy ride! She bowed to the group of men and said in her most polite Japanese, "It was very nice to see you again." Miho changed, grabbed her backpack, and set out.

By the time she arrived at the rocky cove with the mermaid chair, the day was already on fire. Great clouds were rising off the ocean and piling up. The air felt thick and heavy and one could almost taste the building electricity. Miho knew it would rain that day or the next.

The tide was out and the mermaid chair was high up out of the water. Miho climbed down to it. She stopped to explore a few small tide pools along the way. The retreating ocean had left a sampling of creatures in small pools in the rock. She watched a pair of starfish make their slow way across the bottom of one and counted

five spiny urchins in the bottom of another.

But, fun as it was to poke around tide pools, she was there to find an otter—to find Gaia. She sat in the mermaid chair and watched the sea. The swells were high. Here in the cove, there was no gradual rise to a sloping beach. The waves smacked into the dark rocks with slaps and booms and shots of foam that rose high in the air.

Miho loved that no two waves ever dashed themselves on the rocks in the same way. She gripped the rocks and laughed at the flying foam. She thought of her father; he would undoubtedly say the "Young Sea" poem.

*The sea is never still.*
*It pounds on the shore*
*Restless as a young heart,*
*Hunting.*

Miho wished her father were there to say all the cool lines that went between that opening stanza and the last few lines that Miho could still remember.

*Let only the young come,*
*Says the sea.*
*Let them kiss my face and hear me*
*I am the last word*
*And I tell*
*Where storms and stars come from.*

She squeezed her eyes shut, trying to remember the name of the poet. Sandbag? Sandflea? She shook her head. Her father always said it, but she couldn't remember. When she opened her eyes, she saw a school of something, maybe sardines, passing by; a raucous cloud of black-tailed gulls hollered overhead. The gulls took turns diving into the school and lifting back up with a flopping, silver fish caught fast in their beaks.

The fish seemed bunched up on the surface, actually

making the water look like it was boiling. When Miho saw a fin break the water, she knew why. The dolphins were back! They were working together below the waves. The dolphins became a team to herd the fish into a ball, push the fish ball to the surface and make it easier to catch and eat them.

Miho stood on the rocky seat and waved out toward the water. She cupped her hand around her mouth and yelled, "Ooooohaayoooooo!" She clapped her hands and kicked off her shoes when she saw the black and gray dorsals turn toward the cove. The white suspenders along the sides of their bodies confirmed that these were her friends from the day before.

She took a deep breath and dove into the cool of the ocean. The five white-sided dolphins crowded around her. She knew what to do! Miho grasped the fin of the one closest to her and, with her hands and arms and back screaming with the soreness from the day before, she found herself pulled off into another wild ride.

In less time than it had taken her to walk to the cove, Miho found they were bending around the end of the peninsula and into Ago-wan. She thought of all the boats that came in and out of the bay and began to worry that they would be seen for sure. But the pod traveled deep into the bay, weaving around the many small, tree-clad islands. They slowed and eventually stopped, bobbing on the surface. Miho looked around and thought, *Why are we here?*

"Why. Why. Why. You like this word," a voice said, sounding as clear and fine as the ripple of sun on dolphin skin. Miho spun around and there, reclined on her back as if nothing were easier, was Gaia. "I think you are wondering why you are here," Gaia said, curling and uncurling her little otter toes a few times.

"Well, yeah. Why here? Why in Ago-wan?"

"There are many things to see here. We will not have to contend with the swell or the boats. It is much easier to see where it is quiet."

"Huh?" Miho could not understand why it would be easier to see where it is quiet.

Gaia curled her fuzzy body into a ball and disappeared into the dark water of Ago-wan. The dolphins rolled and dove as well. Miho treaded water, cupped her hands around her eyes and tried to peer into the inky depths. Just as she was wondering if she were supposed to follow, Gaia bobbed back to the surface.

She floated on her back and Miho saw that there was something concealed under her dark otter paws. "Use your eyes, dear one. Tell me what you see." She moved her paws and Miho saw an oyster balanced on her fuzzy chest.

"It's an oyster, Gaia." Miho said, wondering if this were some kind of trick question.

"Look closely," Gaia said, her voice low, almost a whisper. "Look at every detail, every ridge, every curve, every tiny chip. Keep looking until you think you can describe this oyster perfectly." Miho squinted against the glare of the sun bouncing off the water and stared at the oyster until her eyes began to blur.

"Now," Gaia continued. "Close your eyes. Can you see the oyster with your mind as well as you can see it with your eyes?"

Miho closed her eyes, focused, and pictured every detail of the oyster. She peeked once to see if what her mind remembered was really the same as the oyster that was still nestled in the thick, gray otter fur. It was.

"I see it, Gaia."

"Good! Now, keep your eyes closed, keep that image in your mind, and duck your head underwater."

Miho almost asked why. But she did as Gaia said. She was rocked back as something struck her in the head! She was struck, but there was no pain. It wasn't like being hit by a hand or a ball. It was...a pulse. It was a force, a wave, an...image?

In her mind, the idea of the oyster she had been

looking at was replaced by a whole other kind of image. It was still the oyster, but it now shimmered before her in three dimensions. It had no color, but was so very real! She could see every ridge and dent of the shell, better than she could remember it.

Her eyes flew open, but all she saw was the retreating dark of Ago-wan and the green circle of light above her head. Miho kicked to the surface. Gaia was bobbing there, her dark eyes flashing with the reflected sunlight. "Well?" Gaia asked.

"Gaia…I saw it! But it wasn't like seeing or remembering, it was…"

The largest dolphin popped in front of her, cutting off her sentence. He placed the rounded end of his snout close to her face and Miho felt another pulse, this one softer. The oyster image that floated up in her mind was also softer, fuzzier. The dolphin turned and dove and Miho was left swimming with questions. "Gaia, is that sonar? I know sonar helps them see underwater, but did he just *give* me the image?"

"Clever girl! I knew you would know how to listen. The ocean you know is only the skin on the top of a bigger, wider, darker world. In this world of water, your eyes are no good to you. I have given you the power to see with your ears."

A dorsal fin was pushed into her hand. She reflexively grabbed on and took a deep breath. She was pulled down far enough to have to squeeze her nose and pop her ears. The dolphin came to a stop, hovering in the deep.

One by one, the other four dolphins swam up to her and blasted her mind with the image of the oyster. They looped and swooped, repeatedly passed her by, and pulsed her the image as they had gathered it—except, they had all "looked" at it from different angles. It was like seeing something in a movie, where the camera swung around the object in a circle. Miho felt dizzy from the experience.

And then, the last image she was given was something she hadn't seen. It was as if the outside of the oyster had been made transparent, and what she "saw" instead was the fleshy, lumpy center. In the folds of the oyster's meat was a round object. A pearl!

Miho was running out of air and began to exhale. The dolphin took her cue and with one powerful flick of its tail, shot them to the surface with great speed. Miho caught her breath and saw Gaia doing something very otter-like. She balanced a flat rock on her chest, the oyster set upon the rock. In her otter-paws, she clasped a larger, round stone and was bashing away at the oyster.

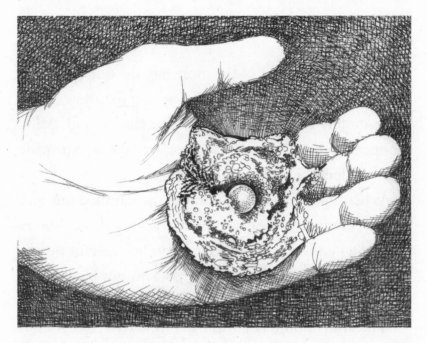

The oyster's shell fell away with a final crack.

Gaia tossed the oyster meat to one of the dolphins and then held out her paw. In it, sat a shining, whitish-gray pearl; it was enormous, almost like a marble! Miho took it from Gaia. "This is how all pearls used to come from my depths—one-by-one. Now, little Ama, let your teachers help you find some more. This is a good way to learn to use your new eyes."

And with that, Gaia dove and disappeared into Ago-wan. The dolphins circled Miho until she was sure that Gaia wasn't returning. She slapped the surface of the water with her hand and one of the smaller white-sides pushed its dorsal fin into Miho's grip. Down they went.

For the remainder of the morning, the dolphins took her to the bottom of Ago-wan looking for oysters and then sending Miho pictures of what they found. Miho scooped up the few that had pearls in them and made a little pile on a rocky outcropping.

When she needed to warm up, she climbed out into the hot summer air and set about cracking those oysters open. She ended up with four large, wonderful pearls. She stuffed them deep into her pocket, got back in the water and then looked up to a very distressing sight.

The afternoon ferry was halfway across Ago-wan— the afternoon ferry that Ojisan said he wanted them to be on! She was very, very late and he was sure to be very, very mad! She looked from the ferry to the shore, her heart racing. She didn't know how to tell her dolphin friends that she needed to go, and fast. The largest dolphin rolled up alongside her and gazed at her with his large dark eye. He seemed to be waiting.

Since Miho didn't know what else to do, she slapped her hand on the water. In a flash a dorsal fin was in her hand and she was being pulled. She could tell the dolphins were going back the way they came, around the end of the peninsula. But Miho didn't have time for that.

She let go and began to kick straight for shore. The dolphins came back and again tried to pull her westward. She again let go and swam toward the docks. Finally, the dolphins didn't try to take her around. But they were smart; they stayed down, under the water and out of sight as they sped her toward the shoreline.

It grew noisier as they got closer to the boat traffic. The group of lags finally peeled off and headed west, toward the outlet to the sea. Miho kicked hard toward shore and came out of the water on a rocky spit of land.

She hurried toward the ferry launch, wondering if Ojisan would be there, waiting, angry. Maybe he was so mad that he left without her! Miho's heart was pounding with possibilities. She pulled the four large pearls from her pocket as she walked, rolled them in her palms and wondered if Ojisan might be a little less angry when she showed him what she had found.

It didn't take long for Miho to see that Ojisan was nowhere around the ferry or the pier. She did see two men talking and gesturing toward her, probably wondering what a little gaijin like her was doing all alone, down by the docks. She couldn't help it. She stuck her tongue out at those men and then ran up the hill.

The heat of the day was now like a weight on the world. The clouds had piled high and the gusts that came off the sea were wet and weighty. Miho could hear thunder rumbling to the south. A summer storm had been brewing over the cauldron of the ocean and was now speeding toward shore.

When Miho arrived at Ojisan's, she was surprised to see he was not there! The house was darkened by the storm clouds. She looked all over, worried that he was so mad he had left her. She called his name and felt her throat beginning to tighten with fear. Her eyes threatened tears like the sky threatened rain.

It crossed her mind to call him, but then another thought hit her like the first crack of thunder that announced the storm's arrival. Her backpack, with her phone, was still down by the mermaid chair!

Not knowing what else to do, she went out the front door and ran down the road to Sensei's. As she ran, fat drops began to patter the dry, packed dirt of the road, sending up little puffs of dust. Miho ran faster, hoping to get to the store before the storm unleashed the fullness of its energy.

She stepped through the doorway just as the rain let loose with a hiss behind her. Sensei was on his feet, talking to two men: The same two men she had stuck her tongue out at. They turned and one of them yelled something in Japanese. Miho was pretty sure it was, "There she is; that's the girl!" The other man shot out his left hand and grabbed her by the upper arm! He was yelling too. Miho twisted and pulled and began some shouting of her own!

"Hey! Get off me!" she yelled. Lightning lit the scene in a crazy way and thunder crashed its way through the small store. Miho could feel the man's hands begin to dig into her pocket...the pocket that held the pearls.

Miho slapped at his searching hand and pulled against his tightening grip. Another crack of thunder ripped the air, as if to accentuate her distress. There was a flash of light. And a flash of wood.

There was another crack, but this one was not thunder. It was the sound of Sensei's walking stick striking the man who held her! The stick streaked past her face and connected with the man's ribcage. The man let go of her arm and spun away from her. She saw the long, worn stick flash by again, this time striking the man in the side of his neck.

He hollered, grabbed his neck, and stumbled back into the rain-filled doorway. The other man, the one who had yelled, turned and swung a fist at Sensei. Her teacher pulled back just enough so that the fist barely

missed his chin; his face was calm and his step was sure.

Sensei then grasped the punching man's arm and with no perceivable effort, pulled the man past him. With a flick of the old man's grip, the punching man flipped over his own arm and landed with a thud, legs piled up against Sensei's sitting chair. Miho was reminded of the day she first saw him on the beach. Sensei moved without effort, like a flowing dance.

Sensei was still facing the door, but took a gentle step back and placed the end of his walking stick against the downed man's cheek. Miho was breathless. There was another flash of lightning and it lit Sensei's wonderful, lined face just as he gave Miho a wink.

# 24
# Like Ama

The man in the doorway was still holding his neck, but began to shake his other fist and yell again. Miho could understand enough to know he was yelling about her. She heard the word "Shinju." She knew without a doubt, from all the nights she talked to her little stuffed dolphin, that Shinju meant "pearl."

A shadow came up behind the man. Another flash of lightning made the shadow look twice as big. The man let out a yelp when the shadow reached out and grabbed his shoulder. It was Ojisan!

He tugged the man out into the driving rain and then stepped through the doorway. His wet hair was pasted to his face and the anger that danced across it, ten times more terrible than the rising storm outside. Miho could hear the wind picking up to a howl and was certain that her uncle's yelling would soon join it.

Sensei took a step away from the downed man,

letting him up. He used his walking stick to give the man's behind a sharp smack and sent him out the door to his companion. He barked something at their retreating backs. Miho had seen enough movies to know this must be Japanese for, "And don't come back!"

Ojisan and Sensei stared at each other over Miho's head. The storm grew. The air darkened even more, as if all the unsaid words between the two men were swirling about. Miho held her breath, feeling as if some decision were being made.

Finally, Ojisan looked down at her and asked, in a voice that was more menacing than the thunder that continued to rumble and tumble over the hill, "Miho, do you have pearls in your pocket?"

"Ojisan, I swear I found them! I went to the mermaid chair and there were these dolphins and…"

"SILENCE!" her uncle boomed. Miho almost expected a flash of lightning to follow his command.

He leaned toward her face and hissed, "Baka yamero-yo." Miho scrambled for the translation. *Stop acting stupid?* Ojisan's voice again lowered to that dangerous place. He spoke in slow, careful English. "This question require yes or no. I no ask for STORY! Do you have pearls?"

Miho's bottom lip began to quiver as she dipped into

her pocket and drew out the four, large shiny pearls. She heard Ojisan inhale sharply. He looked over her head at Sensei and they had a quick exchange of words. He turned back to Miho. "You take these? You take these from the market, yes?"

"No! Ojisan, I found them! I found them...like Ama."

His face grew red and Miho couldn't tell if he was at a loss for words or if there were so many words piling up that he couldn't speak them all. He reached out, scooped the pearls from her palm and dropped them in his shirt pocket. He continued to glower at Miho and said, "I miss work...again. I hope I have job still! This all your fault."

"But Ojisan, I was ready to go this morning. You wanted to stay. This is your fault too!"

As soon as the words left her mouth, she wanted them back. She was arguing with the man who had made it very clear that this was not a very Japanese thing to do. She squinted her eyes against what was sure to be a tirade.

But Ojisan didn't yell. He shook his head and looked at her Sensei. He spoke in Japanese, slowly and carefully, so Miho was sure to understand each word. "I'm going back to Nagoya tomorrow. She is staying here. You want

Ama. You have Ama. You want a student. I give you a student. I will come back next week. I will come back only to sell this house and be done with the sea. You decide if she stays in Goza or returns to Nagoya."

And with that, Ojisan turned on his heel and went out into the rain. Miho was stunned. She kept going back over his words, making sure she had understood them correctly. She looked up at Sensei, who was leaning on his walking stick...smiling.

His smile broke into a grin and the grin gave way to a chuckle. He shuffled back to his chair, used the stick to ease his way down, and then sighed. "Shodo, ashita," he said, which meant, "Shodo, tomorrow."

Miho was incredulous. She was getting her wish, staying in Goza, and yet she was miserable. Ojisan didn't want her anymore! She stared at Sensei, wishing he would say more, tell her what to do. But he didn't.

Finally, Miho bowed, said goodbye and headed out into the misting rain. Although the storm had passed over Goza and had gone streaking across Ago-wan, the sea was still in a frenzy. The pounding waves filled Miho's ears as she plodded back to the house she had grown to love as much as any home she had ever known.

This was the house where her mother had grown up, the house where she had learned to love the whales.

Goza was the place where Miho herself had met Gaia and had the most exciting time in her young life, traveling and listening to dolphins. Would she end up here, or back in the hot, crowded city?

Miho did not eat. She did not sleep. She sat in her room with Shinju under her chin, listening to the ocean continue to tell the story of the storm to the beach. *I am the last word. And I tell where storms and stars come from.* She sat and went back over all the events of the past four months. Her life was so different. She couldn't have known it would change so much.

When sleep finally pulled her down, her father's voice rose like a whisper of memory, *"The only thing for certain about the sea, is that it will change when you least expect it."*

# 25
# Kimo

The smell of cigarette smoke yanked Miho awake. She flew through the house, out the front door and through the front gate. Fog cloaked Goza. Miho could just make out the silhouette of her uncle, walking eastward, his cigarette a hot, glowing spark in the cold, milky fog.

There was a moment when Miho thought about running after him. She thought about crying and begging not to be left alone. But she remembered that she wouldn't be alone. She had lessons with Sensei and she could spend all the time she wanted with her white-sided friends. And there was Gaia, who although small, seemed bigger than any grownup she had ever known, even her tall father.

Eating breakfast alone was strange. She fetched Shinju and set the little dolphin across the table, with her good eye facing in, of course. "Do you think he would get in trouble if people knew?" Miho asked. She was fairly sure adults were not supposed to leave children alone. "Maybe he is coming back tonight. Maybe he is just trying to scare me."The dolphin's round, plastic eye stared at her, but no answers came.

"Well, I'm NOT scared!" Miho declared. "I've been alone lots of times." She marched out the door with purpose and went down the road to the store and her teacher.

The sea had resumed its normal, low lapping of the beach, looking innocent, as if it hadn't flung such wild weather at them yesterday. Miho glanced quickly at the horizon, wondering if the pod of lags would be back today, wondering if she could call them back.

Sensei was not in his chair when she entered the store. His daughter gave a tight, polite smile that faded fast and then jerked her thumb toward the back door. Sensei was in the garden, looking at the lotus flowers that floated in the little pond. Miho said "Ohayo," and bowed.

Sensei rose and asked in Japanese, "What do you need?"

Miho thought maybe she misunderstood his words and asked him to repeat them, slowly. He did and Miho considered his question. What did she need most?

Parents! But he couldn't help with that. She finally decided what she needed most to get through the next few days was courage.

She told Sensei in English. He thought and then said, "Aaah, Kimo!" They went into the classroom and Miho began to prepare her ink. As she pushed her charcoal stick back and forth, she thought about courage. She watched the Hokusai scar on the back of her hand. It was proof that she had been brave before.

But Miho knew she hadn't really had courage; she had been very scared when she faced that big bull shark. She had been scared, but she had acted anyway. But that had been in a quick moment. What about now?

Sensei drew the kanji for courage, *Kimo.*

He said, "Shodo will become you. Make Kimo, be Kimo. Repeat, repeat, repeat Kimo kanji, you become Kimo."

Miho considered this as she practiced the lines. Once Sensei came and placed his hand over hers, showing that you could push down into the paper and lift back out at certain times. Shodo was not just two-dimensional, like writing; it went into and out of the paper too.

She made Kimo over and over and over again. She

did it until she didn't really care what it looked like, just that she felt brave as she made it. Time slid by like a stream and she didn't notice. She felt safe and sure in that classroom and she wanted to build as much courage as she could.

When Miho's nose picked up the scent of food, her stomach let out a tremendous growl. She was surprised the morning was gone! A tray had been set in the doorway, a tray with two bowls of steamed rice and vegetables. Miho didn't know what surprised her more, that the entire morning was gone, or that Sensei's crabby daughter had done something nice.

They ate in the garden. Sensei didn't talk, so Miho kept quiet too. The courage kanji swam behind her eyes. She reminded herself that it wasn't "courage," it was "kimo."

Sensei rose, leaned on his staff and spoke slowly, so that Miho could follow his Japanese. "I think you have enough courage to last all day," he said. "What does this Ama girl want to do with the rest of her day?"

Miho smiled. "I would like to go to Ago-wan and look for the..." she stopped short, realizing she didn't know the Japanese words for "Pacific white-sided dolphins." She doubted Sensei would know their scientific nickname, lags. "...look for my friends," she finished instead.

"Hai," he said. "Come to your uncle's for dinner."

"Domo, Sensei," Miho said, wanting so much to hug him. But she knew this was not the Japanese way. So she bowed politely and left through the store.

Later, as she clambered down the cliff, she was happy to see her backpack, still safe behind a rock. She squatted down and was surprised to hear a small "Beep!" come from inside!

It was her phone, flashing a text-message at her. "Are you OK?" the message said. It was from Ojisan! She spent the next few minutes figuring out how to get the tiny keys to say, "I am fine." She almost hit "send," but decided to add one more thing, "Miss you."

She stared at the phone after she sent the message. There was an idea bubbling around the back of her mind, like something she had forgotten. But when the idea failed to bubble up, she put the phone back into the pack and climbed down to the mermaid cove.

The day had grown hot, so instead of sitting in the chair, looking at the water, Miho dove right in. She floated on her back, watching small, high cotton puffs of clouds race across the sky. Her ears were underwater and she practiced listening. She was amazed at all she could hear.

There was the smacking of the waves against the rocks, the ever-present, distant chug of diesel engines, the snapping of creatures with claws (Miho didn't yet know how to tell the difference between shrimp, lobster and crab), and...whistles!

She sat up and scanned the horizon. The pod of lags was coming! Not only were they coming, they were taking turns leaping high out of the water and there were so many more than Miho had seen before. They swarmed into the cove and her skin was alive with the feel of their echolocation. And there was Gaia.

The whiskered face popped up next to her and the otter promptly rolled onto her back, paws poking from the sea. The whole strange combination of creatures bobbed in the waves.

Miho said, "Ohayo, Gaia-san."

"Ohayo, my dear. Are you ready for more language lessons?"

"Yes! Hai!" She almost added, "Yahoo!" Ever since Gaia had mentioned talking to the minds in the sea, she had waited for this moment. She would be able to continue her mother's work.

A large dolphin appeared on either side of Gaia. They rolled on their sides and turned their bright, alive eyes on Miho. Gaia said, "First you must listen, learn.

Only when you understand their ways, will you be able to speak." Gaia dove and resurfaced on Miho's other side. "You must hurry. Things are happening and you will be needed elsewhere."

And with that, the otter rolled and vanished. *Why does she do that?* Miho thought. She turned to the dolphin on her right, and said, "She says something incredible and then splits before I can ask a question."

The dolphin tossed his black-lipped snout in the air and let out a chirp. Miho knew he didn't understand a thing she said. "Well," she thought aloud, "Gaia said, listen first." She made an arching motion with her hand and took a tremendous breath. They dove.

For the next fifteen minutes, Miho was completely focused on getting into rhythm with the group. There were so many of them! She found herself grabbing dorsals she hadn't seen before. She knew that the lags she had been with the day before must have, somehow, told the other ones what to do. Each fin was different, nicked here, notched there, and with varied amounts of black, white and gray. This was the way people like her parents and Mr. Hernandez did their research, learning the individual marks of each whale or dolphin and giving them a name or number.

When they broke the surface for their fast grab of

air, Miho saw the flash of white stripes in the air. They traveled fast and many of the group leapt clear out of the water as they snatched their life-giving breath. Mr. Hernandez had told her they breathed this way when they were moving fast. There was less resistance by leaving the water completely than by rolling through it. "It's all about the hydrodynamics," he had said. He had waved his hands around in that animated way of his as he talked about drag and timing and the marvelous design of dolphins. Miho had only understood about half of what he said, but loved the way he got excited when he talked about it.

And now she was experiencing it firsthand. *If Mr. Hernandez could see me now!* The distraction of indulging her memory caused her to miss the next dorsal grab and she was left bobbing as scores of lags whizzed by her.

A small, high, "poof" startled her. It was one of the babies! The little lag seemed so small after being with the big strong adults. It swished its head from side to side and Miho could feel the sonar. It was "looking" at her. Miho smiled and wished she could say, "Hello" or "Ohayo" in some dolphin way.

Its mother came up on the other side of Miho and also floated on the surface. Miho realized what an honor it was for a female dolphin to allow another creature to come between her and her child. She barely had time to snatch a breath when a larger, hooked dorsal was thrust into her hand.

Finally the group slowed down. Three adults surrounded Miho; the rest peeled away and dove. It seemed the lesson was about to begin. She clasped the notched dorsal of the one next to her and down they went, down into the sun-dappled world below.

They hung about 10 feet down. Miho felt the familiar knock in the head as an image of a dolphin was passed to her. Then she felt three quick smacks and heard a kind of click, whistle combination. The three images were each of a dolphin, its tail in a different position—as if swimming.

Up for air, then the exercise was repeated. And again. And again. And again. Then, just when Miho was beginning to wonder what this lesson was meant to teach, the lesson changed. She received one quick image and the click-whistle combination, together. In her mind's eye, she saw the dolphin swim. She understood. This was a sort of dolphin verb, an action. That particular image, combined with the click, whistle meant, "Swim!" They went up for air.

Then the dolphins sent her "dolphin" and a "whistle, buzz, click." She shook her head no. She didn't know how else to say, "Wakarimasen" or "I don't understand."They sent her the same combination and then did something unexpected. They raced for the surface and all four of them, Miho included, went rocketing up into the air!

She let go of the fin and yelled, "Whoooah!" before she tucked her chin to turn her descent into a dive instead of a belly smack. She got it! She understood! Whistle, buzz, click meant, "Jump!"

The lags taught her image/click combinations for, "turn," "slow," and "fast." She understood! But she still had no idea how to speak. Could she take a sonar scan, turn it around, and send it back out with the right clicks or whistles?

She tried. Miho scanned the dolphin with the notched dorsal fin and when the image returned, she took that picture and sent it back out. The reaction was immediate. All three of her companions raced to the circle of light above and burst into the air, buzzing, laughing. She had done it—she spoke!

# 26
# Hurry

When the group returned Miho to the cove with the mermaid chair, her brain was full to bursting. She had learned to listen. She had begun to learn to speak. And, she had figured out it was a lot like Japanese. The dolphins' combination of image and sound presented an idea that was much like kanji—a shape that had, folded within it, multiple other words or ideas. Perhaps, as she learned from Sensei, she would be better able to learn from her dolphin-sensei. *Notch,* she thought. *That's a good name. What else do you call someone with a notched dorsal fin?*

Miho collected her backpack and headed back to Ojisan's. Good smells from within the house reached her before she reached the gate. She removed her shoes, slid on her slippers, and stepped over the threshold.

Sensei was already seated at the low table and motioned for her to sit. His daughter Tomiko appeared carrying several serving bowls. She also carried a scowl on her face. She set the bowls down and pivoted back to the kitchen. Miho followed and helped deliver the rest of the food to the table. After they all said, "Itadakamas," the room became silent and stayed that way. But unsaid things swirled around. Anytime Miho caught Tomiko's eye, she had a tight, small smile on her face. Miho could tell it was a mask of politeness.

When they were done, Miho didn't ask, but just began to clear off the table. Tomiko and Sensei had a low, quiet conversation. Miho pretended not to understand, but she did.

"Why do you care about this gaijin?" Tomiko hissed.

"Why do you not care? She is Ama. She is Goza," Sensei said.

Tomiko opened her mouth to speak and then closed it again. She obviously knew the rules of being Japanese better than Miho.

"You have never been an outsider," Sensei said. "It is difficult. It takes courage."

Miho was surprised that she understood the conversation so well. It was as if Gaia had opened a new pathway in her mind. She felt more open to language and all the ideas and feelings it carried. Sensei finished by saying something along the lines of, "If you don't have something nice to say, don't say anything at all!"

As Miho washed the dishes, she heard Tomiko leave. Miho couldn't decide whether or not she was happy she had understood their conversation. Although it was cool that she could understand the Japanese, she didn't like them arguing about her. Miho thought of Sensei as her friend as well as her teacher. She had felt adrift for so long; she just wanted a place to come ashore, to be on solid ground.

When she had the last dish cleaned and put away, she went out to Sensei. "Thank you for having dinner ready. Please tell Tomiko-san I am grateful and would like to repay her for such a kindness. Tomorrow, you will be my guests and I will make the dinner."

Miho clamped her hand over her mouth. The words had simply tumbled out, in Japanese, without her knowing all the words or planning what to say. It was as if some language switch in her brain was flipped into the "on" position.

Sensei laughed, rose, and went out into the night, still chuckling.

Miho was left standing in a quiet and empty house, thoroughly confused and just a little bit afraid. She focused her mind on the courage kanji and got ready for bed. It was hard to believe that this was only her first full day alone in Goza. So much had happened and she really hadn't been alone at all!

She pulled her futon down and Shinju out. She whispered to the stuffed dolphin all she had learned that day. She taught Shinju what real dolphins say to mean "swim" and "jump." As she taught her small, stuffed friend, it solidified everything that she had learned.

That night, her dreams were a swirling, crazy creation, made out of all the things her young mind was struggling to understand. She dreamed her mother spoke Dolphinese and told her about a big rogue wave that was coming, coming, coming. Miho, clutching her stuffed dolphin, ran along an unknown shoreline, looking for the dream-wave so she could warn her parents. She ran into Sensei, who was laughing and pointing to the sea. "You Ama," the dream-Sensei said. But he turned to leave before Miho could ask any questions.

While she was looking at Sensei's retreating back, the rogue wave came up behind her. But it didn't crash over her head. White, curling Hokusai wave fingers reached over her shoulder and plucked her stuffed dolphin from her arms! Miho raced after the wave that was now drawing back into the endless ocean. Tears streamed down her face as she watched her beloved companion

get caught in a riptide. She wanted to yell out as she watched Shinju get swept away from the shore. But in that dream way, her voice didn't work. The small, gray shape was a mere dot in the vast, dark blue.

But then the real dolphins came. They came and sported and leapt and laughed until she waded into the surf with them. In their dolphin language, they told her they were happy to have her with them, that the sea needed a voice in the world.

They began to cheer, "Here she comes! Here she comes!" Gaia arrived. Miho begged the dream-Gaia to give her a tail and a dorsal fin and the lovely white stripes so that she could truly be part of her new family. Gaia shook her round, whiskered face and pointed back to shore. There stood Ojisan, his hand shading his eyes, peering toward the horizon.

"You have family, my dear. He is Ama too. Listen and learn and take your tale to him. Hurry. The sea and the rivers and the rain are my very blood and there is poison within. Hurry. After you learn, you will be able to meet the others and the real work will begin."

Miho sat up fast and hard. Sweat ran down her spine and dripped into the small of her back. Her breathing was fast and ragged, and her heart thrummed with a deep ache. She had Shinju clutched in one fist.

Looking down at the raggedy creature, Miho said, "We gotta hurry, Shinju. Ojisan will be back this weekend and I think something is gonna happen. I gotta be ready. I…" but Miho couldn't think what it was she had to do. "I gotta learn," was all she could think of. She rolled over and lost herself to the sound of the endless waves crawling to Goza's shore.

# 27
# Shinju

The sun rose large and fierce. The earth quickly reached its limit to absorb heat and was radiating it back to the sky as Miho made her way to Sensei's Shodo lesson. There was not a puff of wind and the sea barely rippled. The only waves reaching Goza were the ones made by the moon's endless tug on the rim of the earth.

The weather seemed to match the sense of prelude that Miho's dream had generated. Something was coming. She felt it in her bones, and it seemed as if the sea felt it too.

As before, Sensei was in the garden. As before, he asked her what she needed. As before, she said, "kimo." She felt that no matter what happened, courage would come in handy. Without courage, any other quality would be useless.

So again, her brush endlessly followed the strokes of

the kanji and a resolve began to form in her belly. She dipped and drew her brush across the rice paper and drew the sense of courage deep within her.

She was startled when Sensei placed his gnarled hand on her wrist. "Enough," he said in Japanese. She looked up at his lined face and the seriousness she saw there looked like...courage. She didn't ask why it was enough. She knew.

"Hai," she said and took her things to the sink for cleaning. As she methodically removed the blackness from her brush and stone, she saw Sensei out of the corner of her eye. He was holding up her last kanji with one hand and stroking his chin with the other. After a time, he smiled, nodded, and took it to his desk.

Again, lunch was on the step of the classroom. Again, Sensei and Miho ate in silence, looking at the lotus flowers, both lost in their own thoughts. When they were done, Sensei rose and said, "I am looking forward to the meal you will prepare for my daughter and me." He raised his eyebrows slightly.

Miho understood this to be his polite way of reminding her. "The pleasure is mine, Sensei. All will be ready at 6 pm." Again, she was surprised at the easy way the polite, honorific, Japanese flowed from her. "Sayonara," she said and bowed and left.

This time, when she went to the mermaid cove, the lags were waiting for her! She laughed and waved and started to call out, "Ohayo." But what came from her mouth was a squeal and a click!

The dolphins were ecstatic and the cove exploded with leaping, twisting, rolling gray, black and white. Miho was shocked, but only for a moment. Perhaps the way Japanese was becoming natural, so was Dolphinese. She dove.

That day, the pod took her to a bay further down the coast. As they traveled, Miho began to understand the endless whistles, clicks, squeals and squeaks around her. The lags were doing what a group of people would do as they walked along together. They made observations of what was around them and they chatted.

Images flew from side to side as they streaked along. They showed each other the jellyfish and the boats and the debris they detected. At one point, an image of a shark, a tiger shark, shot about the group and everyone rearranged so that the babies and their mothers were in the middle.

Three young males sped off to the west and when they returned, they shared the images, the story, of how they bullied the shark away. Miho laughed and the lags around her laughed back. They seemed as happy to have this new creature to speak to as she was to be able to hear.

Miho didn't want to go too far that day. It was important that she have plenty of time to make dinner for Sensei and Tomiko. Miho managed to show the baby's mother, (who Miho began to think of as 'Star' because of a small five-pointed blotch of white on her dorsal fin) an image of the setting sun.

Miho did her best to follow the image as it was passed around the group. It moved lightning quick, and there were many other squeals and buzzes and commentary. She just couldn't follow. But it didn't matter; she had made herself understood. The pod delivered her back to the mermaid cove long before the sun hit the horizon.

When they arrived, the pod slowed and rested. Miho floated on her back, because it was the easiest thing for her. She heard a sound that somehow got translated in her mind as, "Why?"

The baby she had met the day before was beside her. It too was resting, but belly down, because its blowhole was positioned on its back. Miho's mouth and nose, on the other hand were most definitely on her front! And that is what she told the little gray dolphin.

The young Pacific white-side hadn't yet developed the distinctive white suspender stripes down its sides and was instead, a pearly gray, like stuffed Shinju. Miho began to think of her as another Shinju. To show this new Shinju why she floated on her back, she puckered her lips and blew skyward. Shinju blew from her blowhole.

Miho rolled face down in the water and blew bubbles into the deep. Shinju rolled onto her back and let out a very nice bubble stream. They did this, all the while looking into each other's eyes. Shinju's mother circled around them and occasionally brushed her pectoral fin against one of them.

Miho had an inspiration. She did the fastest clicking

she could, almost a buzz, and saw the sound return as an image of the little Shinju. Then she held that image and sent it back as more clicks with her best attempt at the whistle, click for "jump."

Shinju took off like a rocket ship to the surface and not only jumped, but did a complete flip in the air! Her new little friend understood! When Miho spoke again, she did her best to say, "Swim and find oysters with pearls?" She knew that most of them didn't understand, but one young lag did. He thrust his dorsal fin into Miho's hand and tugged her down.

She could clearly hear the intense buzzing of his sonar and did her best to see the returning image. He honed in on an oyster and pulled Miho directly to it. She tugged the oyster from its moorings and they shot to the surface.

Shinju swam over to her so Miho ducked under to speak. She did her best to send the image of the rocks ahead of them and the click/whistle combination for swim. Shinju pushed her small dorsal into Miho's hand and tugged her to the rocks. Miho was so happy she could talk to her new friend! She climbed out and pounded open the oyster. Inside there was, indeed, a pearl. Miho tucked it into her pocket and then turned to face the cove.

Bobbing in the swell were twenty or thirty of these amazing creatures. Miho's heart swelled up with love and gratitude. She was part of a group; they didn't care that she was gaijin. They were teaching her, talking to her, and listening to her. She never doubted that she would be brought up for her next breath. This family would care for her in the dark, cold world of the open ocean.

# 28
# Gaijin Green

Part of her wanted to sit in the marvelous stone chair, watch the tide pull out, and relive all the amazing events of that day. But Sensei would be coming. Sensei AND Tomiko! The last thing Miho wanted to do was give that woman another reason to frown at her. After all, she did provide Miho with a meal the day before. This was the polite way to return a kindness.

Miho ran all the way back to Ojisan's house. She showered off the salt water, changed into clean clothes, and hit the kitchen. The rice cooker was humming and the wok was popping with bits of ginger and shrimp when her guests arrived.

Surprisingly, they both complimented her cooking! Miho felt her cheeks grow hot. She also thought of the pod of dolphins that did their leaping, sporting dance in celebration of her ability to talk to them. It was turning out to be a pretty good day.

When they were done, Tomiko even said, "Gochisosama," something her father used to say to her mother. It means "it was a feast," and is a compliment to the cook! Tomiko said she had to return to stock the shelves. It was the first time Miho had considered the hard work that was involved in keeping a store like that. She thanked Tomiko for coming and then had an idea.

From her pocket, Miho pulled the single pearl she had found that day. She handed it to the open-mouthed woman. "I am grateful for all the kindness you have shown me," Miho said, her eyes respectfully downcast. "You are generous to share your father's time with me. I am in your debt."

Tomiko shut her mouth, shook her head and swallowed. She closed the pearl in her fist and said, "You are always welcome in my home." Then she blushed, bowed quickly, and left.

Sensei smirked in that small, still way of his. Miho began to clear the table and wondered if he would leave too. "So, what adventure did you dive into today?" the old man asked.

Miho was taken aback. How did he know she had dived anywhere? "Na wakarimasen," she said, her old, familiar, "I don't understand." He just shook his head and left, humming a little tune. Miho really didn't understand him sometimes.

That evening, as she washed her face, Miho discovered something strange. When she lifted her dripping face up and looked into the mirror over the sink, her eyes were dark brown!

Miho leaned in closer and saw the brown-ness fade, returning her eyes to their old gaijin-green. She did this again and again, wondering why her eyes would look different after being in the water. *It must mean they're different in the water!* she thought.

Miho filled the sink, made sure the cap of the toothpaste was on tight, and then pushed the tube to the bottom. She then put her face in the water, eyes open. She could read every word! It was as if she were wearing a diving mask.

Now that she thought about it, while she traveled with the lags, she could see remarkably well, when there was enough sunlight! Miho tried a few more times, confirming this new skill, watching the mirror each time she came up.

Part of her wished her eyes could stay dark brown, and then maybe she wouldn't look so foreign. But then again, the green was a gift from her father. She was grateful that it would be with her always.

The following hot, sweltering day was much the same. Sensei asked her what she needed. She said courage. But he told her no, that courage was hers— what else? She thought about her strange life, the way she was learning two new worlds, two new languages. So she finally told him she needed 'understanding.'

Old Mr. Tomikoro raised his eyebrows and told her this was a very wise answer. "Satoru satori," he said quietly. Miho thought it was good she had courage, because the symbols for understanding were complicated! *It looks like it should be easy, but it isn't!* She pondered this as she tediously followed the strokes. Not one, or two or three, but a total of ten spread out into two different figures!

悟

As she labored through another attempt at "understanding," Miho realized this was what her life was about now: understanding why her parents were gone, understanding this new country, understanding her uncle, understanding the way of the brush, understanding Gaia, and understanding the way of water and the minds within it.

She worked at the strokes until a whiff of food

tickled her nostrils. The whole morning was gone! As they ate in the garden, Miho began to grasp just how much she didn't understand: why Sensei's daughter was living with him, why Ojisan was also alone—until now anyway. She didn't understand why there were no Ama in Goza or how Sensei knew she was Ama. She didn't understand how Sensei decided when her Shodo was good or bad. She may have courage, but working on understanding had left her feeling sort of stupid.

Miho sighed.

"What is it you want to ask?" Sensei asked. Miho didn't answer right away; she was too surprised that he knew she was bubbling with questions. She thought about the best one to ask him at this moment. Questions about his daughter seemed too personal and questions about Ama would only lead to questions about Gaia and water and a host of other things.

"How do you know when the kanji I have made is good?" Miho asked in Japanese.

"This is a good question. Of course, all the lines must be correct or it would say something else! But when the kanji shows outside what you are on the inside, this is a very a good thing."

"How does it do that?" Miho asked, sensing this was a good time to be direct with her questions.

Sensei held out his arm. With his other hand he slapped his head, his heart and his belly. "What is here and here and here," he said as he slapped, "is energy. What you think and feel comes out here," he said, grasping his outstretched hand in his other fist. "Same with sword."

*Sword?* Miho tried to understand, tried to understand the connection between her brush and the sword that sat in its position of honor in the classroom. "Do you know how to fight with a sword?" Miho asked.

"Hai. And feet and hands and, most important, mind and heart."

"Why is mind and heart most important?"

"When you fight with mind and heart, you find there are very few times you need fists or sword." And with that statement, Sensei rose and bowed and headed into the store. Lesson over.

As she walked back to Ojisan's, Miho thought how to take her shodo lesson, satoru satori, into the water with her. It was strange; she was just a kid and people like Mr. Hernandez had been studying this species of dolphins for decades, but she might already know more about them. Miho couldn't wait to get out to sea with her friends!

Inside Ojisan's, her phone was beeping. The text

message said, "Be there Friday night. You OK?" Miho set to work on the tiny keys and typed, "I'm great! Miss you. Will have surprise on Friday."

She didn't know it until she typed it, but she had thought of a way to keep Ojisan in Goza. He said he worked in Nagoya because that was where the money was. But with her flippered friends and her newfound skills, Miho could find just as many, if not more, pearls and abalone than her grandmother ever had!

She hit 'send' and then walked quickly eastward, through Goza, to the mermaid cove. Today, she had a mission. She wanted to find so many pearls that Ojisan would want to stay in Goza forever. After all, the only time Miho had ever seen him smile was here, by the sea.

Again, the white-sides were waiting for her. She dove in and tried to share an image of what she wanted to find. But a dorsal fin was thrust into her hand and off they went. This time they went east, into the open ocean.

Miho soon found out why. They met up with an enormous group; the horizon practically boiled with the breaking dorsal fins! As Miho's small group joined in, she was lost in the energy and conversation that flew around her.

Not only did images of what was around them constantly swirl by, but so did images of things that had happened, or maybe they were things to come—Miho wasn't sure how you told the difference. She saw the births of babies and the unfortunate accident between a big male and a boat. She saw the location of great feeding grounds and then heard something that really shocked her.

The lags began to talk about humpback whales! They were imaging the whales leaving. Miho understood her new friends were wondering if the great-winged whales had started the journey to their Alaskan feeding grounds yet. Then they began to sing the humpback songs! Miho knew these songs! She had heard them so many times they were as familiar as the poetry her father liked to recite.

The lags had pitched the songs up a lot, but they were humpback songs, nonetheless. She longed to know how to ask questions. What did the songs mean? Why did they share them? Did every whale and dolphin in the ocean know and share the songs?

But it was like gossip in a grocery store. Soon the chatter turned to something else. After a time, the group split into several smaller groups and headed off in different directions. The calls that flew between the groups were about schools of fish and great ships and sunrises and sunsets. Miho thought that perhaps they were all setting out to find good feeding and would reconvene later to share information.

Miho found her hand grasping a familiar, star-marked dorsal fin. Shinju's mother! Miho sent her images of oysters and pearls and soon the group turned north. Miho continued to dive and rise and breathe with the group, but didn't know how to ask where they were going or what they were doing. It was almost like being lost in Nagoya!

Soon, they swam along an unfamiliar shoreline. There were no houses or boats or any landmarks for Miho to confidently remember where they were. Star and Shinju took Miho to a rocky outcropping. Miho climbed out, grateful for some time in the sun, out of the chilly water.

Notch was the first dolphin to show up with an oyster clasped between his black-lipped jaws. Sure enough, there was a pearl inside! Miho longed to know how to say, "Thank you." Notch sped off, but as he did, a youngster with a strange zigzag to her white striping came, also with an oyster. *Lightning,* Miho thought. This was a good name for the speedy little girl with the odd stripe.

As Lightning returned to the depths, three males came. Miho noted the differences in their dorsal fins and dubbed them Curly, Larry, and Moe. She had seen them before; they were the ones who had chased off the shark. They were always together and always clowning around.

This odd parade continued until Miho's pockets were stuffed with pearls. She was now dry and sweating in the afternoon sun and happy to get back into the cool, blue Pacific. She showed a picture of the mermaid cove to Star and they set off.

All the way back, Curly, Larry, and Moe took turns leaping over her just as she turned to breathe. More than once, they made her laugh and she got a mouthful of water. When she stopped to regain her breath, Shinju was always beside her. She talked to the little gray dolphin in English, just as she did to her stuffed dolphin at home. When they were underwater, Shinju, in turn, talked to Miho in Dolphinese. They were becoming friends.

It was hard to leave her friends in the cove. Miho knew she only had tomorrow and part of the next day to convince Ojisan to stay in Goza. She wanted to find enough pearls so he could quit his job in Nagoya. It was at that moment she realized she didn't even know what kind of job he had, or if he liked it or not. *Understanding*, she reminded herself. It could be more important than courage.

Miho ate alone, with the stuffed Shinju sitting across from her. She spread the pearls out on the table and told her one-eyed friend about the massive crowd she had been a part of today. She told her about Lightning and Curly, Larry, and Moe and how the real Shinju liked to stay next to her. She told her old friend how her new friends passed around the songs of whales and how they had helped her find all these great pearls.

Miho cleaned her dishes and found a black lacquer bowl to put the pearls in. Then she fetched her phone and set it up in front of the bowl. She started the video recorder, ran around the table, and crouched down so that she was peering over the top of the bowl at the camera.

"Konbanwa, Ojisan! When you come back to Goza, I'll have even more of these! I have some friends that are very good at finding them and they let me keep them all! I can't wait until you come back. We can sell all these and maybe stay here always! I hope you're OK too. I'll see you Friday. Um, OK…" She paused, knowing what she would say if it were her parents, "…love you. Bye."

She ran around and turned off the video. She sent the clip to Ojisan and then she started to worry what he might say back. So she turned off her phone and went to bed.

# 29
# Curly, Larry & Moe

The next day, Miho was eager to get back to the dolphins. So eager, in fact, that Sensei stopped her shodo and asked her what she was doing. "Satoru satori," she said.

He shook his head. "You make the lines, but where is your head?" Miho looked at her work. It did seem… thin. It lacked a depth and solidness that should come with "understanding."

She rose and gathered her things. "I am sorry, Sensei. I have to go. I have something I have to finish before Ojisan gets back tomorrow." He nodded, not asking for more information. Miho thought he was the coolest grownup she had ever known.

She cleaned her materials, grabbed a quick bite to eat at Ojisan's, and then hurried to the mermaid cove. The dolphins were not there. Miho was disappointed. She looked out at the ocean. The wind that had traveled so many hundreds of miles across the water was whipping her hair back off her face and bringing the wonderful salty sea-smell to her nose. Ships dotted the horizon, and the call of sea birds punctuated the rhythmic slap of the swells coming into the mermaid cove.

She closed her eyes and turned her face to the sun that had not yet reached its midday zenith. The heat on her face was like a familiar hug and a good reason to relish diving into the still-shaded cove.

When Miho surfaced, there she was...Gaia! The otter bobbed over the swells and rubbed her paws together. Miho's disappointment dissolved as she stroked over to Gaia. "Konnichiwa, Gaia-san," Miho said and did her best to do an otter-like roll.

"Konnichiwa, Miho-san," Gaia said and did a real otter roll. Miho wished she could be so sleek in the sea, like Gaia, like the dolphins.

"I see you have been listening and learning."

"I have! Gaia, I..." Miho began, but Gaia held up one paw to silence her.

"I can tell you are learning and understanding more, having fun too, eh? But you need to be able to listen even deeper. If you are ever to go into my real depths, your deep listening is vital. Vital, do you understand what vital means?"

Miho chewed on the word. She knew that vital organs were the ones you really needed to live. "Vital are things you need for life, right? Like your heart and lungs and stuff?"

"Yes, precisely. Miho-san, your ears must be keen. Today you practice. Listen. Listen deeply."

And with that, Gaia tucked herself into a gray, rolling ball, dove, and was gone. Miho stared at the ripples where Gaia had been and wondered what she should practice.

*Listen, Gaia said. Deep listening.*

Miho floated and thought about what she had learned from the lags. She could hear the pictures they sent her. She was able to speak, but probably sounded like a baby to them. She had just started to understand how to do sonar scans. Since sonar required the hardest listening, Miho decided to practice that.

She looked down and could see through the gray-green of the water only to her knees. The mermaid cove would have to do. She dove and kicked hard to the bottom. She had just started to scan with her feeble sonar when she had to come up for air. It was frustrating to be so pokey after the speed she had shared with the lags. She went under again.

She was surprised to find her mermaid cove covered

with oysters! As her scanning improved, she was excited to find there were a dozen or so that had pearls hidden within—she would be able to stay in Goza for sure!

She was just getting the last of the pearl-containing oysters when three lags came streaking out of the gloom and almost gave her a heart attack! She was so startled she dropped the oysters and had to kick to the surface for air.

It was the Three Stooges, and they all had their heads out of the water. All three were whistling and chattering. Miho quickly got her breath and dove so she could better understand them.

Shark! They all talked at once, showing her the big tiger shark. Curly said, in Dolphinese, "Get out of the water!" Mo bombarded her with a command she didn't know and Larry let out a warning squeal that made them all shut up and turn.

The shark was approaching! Mo again gave the command she hadn't understood and a tremendous sound blasted out from the three dolphins. The shark swerved. Miho knew what this was. Mr. Hernandez had told her about the dolphin's ability to stun prey with their sonar.

The tiger shark swerved away at that pulse, but it began to turn back! Part of Miho, her body, wanted to kick to the surface and get as far away from the shark as possible. The other part, her mind, remembered what her mother had taught her about acting like prey. She held her position.

The shark picked up speed and angled straight toward her! She curled her Hokusai hand into a fist. But instead of cocking her arm back to deliver a punch, which wouldn't have been very powerful in the water, she brought the fist to her mouth.

The dolphins had their rostrums to help direct their sound, Miho had her Hokusai hand. The four of them pulsed their sound waves toward the shark. Miho would have laughed if she didn't need to hold her air. It looked like the shark swam into a glass wall. Bonk! He floated for a moment, dazed. The Stooges let out what had to be the dolphin equivalent of a cheer. High fives all around!

Miho kicked to the surface. She looked down and saw the shark turn and swim, although a bit crookedly, back out toward deeper water. Curly, Larry, and Moe followed her up. She did her best to thank them.

Miho scanned them. Just as she could see into the oysters, she was able to see into her friends as well. She could see their bones, their organs, and even their beating hearts. The ability to see inside meant there

was no lying in the world of dolphins. Each could see a faster heart rate or churning stomach.

Miho didn't know her dolphin anatomy that well, but when her buzzing scan hit Curly, she saw what could have been his stomach or liver. It had odd bumps all over it. Some were quite large and had fingers reaching out toward other...vital organs.

She didn't know what to do about this information, except swim over and wrap her arms around her new friend. She stayed there for a moment, feeling his heart beat against her chest. She didn't know what else to say. It had been a long day in the water, and her mind was a muddied jumble of English and Japanese and Dolphinese. A simple hug would have to do.

# 30
# Call Me

Miho ate a fine dinner of steamed oysters and sat with Shinju nestled under her chin. She stared at the two lacquer bowls filled with shimmering pearls. Would this be enough? Would Ojisan see that she could be a good Ama like his mother? Maybe she could be even better, because Gaia had given her the power to see right into those oysters! She was sure her Oji would know how to turn those pearls into money so they could stay in Goza.

In the back of her mind, a thought began to repeat, like a steady drip, plunking into a sink from a leaky faucet: *Gaia said hurry. She wants you for something. What? What? What?* Drip, drip, drip went the thought. And, like a dripping faucet, Miho soon tuned it out and focused on her immediate challenge.

What else would Ojisan want or need to stay here in his hometown? Perhaps Sensei would know. Besides, she needed to restock the pantry so she could make her uncle a great, "Welcome Home...Hint! Hint!" meal.

She set little Shinju aside and went out into the night. The ocean breeze was whisking the day's heat away, and the waves were hitting Goza with a bit more energy. Miho knew that the day's wind had whipped up the sea and all that energy had to go somewhere. She stopped to look out at the water. She thought about how the ocean gathered energy from the wind and turned it into waves.

*If there are wave-wishes from the sun, can there be windy-wave-wishes at night? Sure!* She thought hard on the image of her uncle saying, "Of course we will stay in Goza!" She sent her wish out to the breaking waves, where the wind's energy was released once again.

Tomiko was just starting to lock the door when Miho arrived. She shook her head at Miho. But Miho steepled her hands under her chin and made a face that meant, "pleeeeeease?"

With a roll of her eyes and a pursing of her lips, she cracked the door. "Go away! I'm tired. I've been working all day. Not that you know anything about working hard—spoiled, silly, hafu."

Miho was shocked! Then she realized Tomiko was assuming Miho didn't understand her fast, rude

Japanese. But she did. She had...*understanding*. She paused to think, so she wouldn't be rude back.

"I am sorry you think that a gaijin, like me, is spoiled or silly. I am neither. But I do wish to speak to your most honorable father, my Sensei. If it isn't too much bother, could you tell him I am here?" Miho cast her eyes down and bowed. She should have bowed out of respect, but she did it to hide her smile.

Tomiko's eyebrows shot up and her eyes got round as...well, pearls! She was speechless for a moment and Miho guessed that didn't happen very often. When the middle-aged woman recovered her speech, she said, "I will not bother him! He isn't well. As a matter of fact, there is no lesson tomorrow. You tire him out! Go home!"

And with that, she slammed the door and snapped off the light. Now it was Miho's turn to be speechless. *Is Sensei really sick? Maybe she just didn't want me inside. I tire him out?* Miho had walked there feeling hopeful. She walked back feeling dejected. She would just have to face Ojisan with what she had, what she knew, what she...understood.

She sat on the veranda and watched the waxing moon rise in the east. It beamed a lane of light across the inky sea. Miho, as always, wondered if a whale would appear.

Thinking of whales made her think of dolphins, and soon she was thinking of the strange lumps she had seen in her friend, in Curly.

She sighed. She knew what cancer was. A friend of her parents, and of Mr. Hernandez, had died from it. After the funeral, when the grownups sat around and talked about how sad it was, Miho and a black-eyed boy named Carlos had tiptoed into Mr. Hernandez's office and gotten on the Internet. Miho had seen tumors, how they grew and reached out and grabbed on more and more until they grabbed vital things. She worried about Curly. Did he know? What did dolphins do when they got sick?

Suddenly, she realized—she knew who to ask! She ran into her room and dug into her backpack. In the small photo album was a picture her father had taken of Mr. Hernandez squeezed into a wetsuit and about to tip over the rail of his boat.

It was a funny picture, because his eyes were bugging out. Mr. Hernandez had laughed when he saw it and drew a cartoon bubble over his own head. In the bubble it said, "CALL ME!" and there it was—his phone number. Miho couldn't believe she hadn't thought of this before! He would love to hear her story, and maybe he knew how to fix dolphin cancer! She could hardly dial the phone fast enough.

"Hola?" the familiar, gravelly voice said. Miho knew this was Spanish for "Hello?"

"Hola! This is Miho Rivolo!" She started laughing, happy to have reached him.

"Miho! I wondered when I would hear from you!" When she realized that this wonderful person from her old life, halfway around the world, had been waiting to hear from her, her laugh turned quickly into tears.

For a minute, she could do nothing but cry. But it felt good, like the last of the ink going down the drain. He had loved her parents. He loved her too. She understood this now and would never again let so much time go by before reaching out to him.

"Miho-Miha!" He used her "Japican" nickname. "What's wrong? Where are you? Can I come get you?" His concern made her smile, and she sniffed the hot snot back up her nose and wiped a hand under each eye.

"No. I'm fine. I'm fine. I'm in Japan with my uncle. Well, kinda not with my uncle right now. But, well... that's not why I called. Mr. Hernandez, do dolphins get cancer?"

There was a long pause on the other end. Finally he said, "Miho, it is 5 o'clock in the morning here. Why are you asking me about dolphins and cancer?"

Miho thought about how to explain her strange new life in Japan. Should she tell him about Nagoya? Wave wishes? Sensei and Shodo? Gaia? How could she ever explain Gaia? She didn't even quite understand Gaia herself!

"Well, I'm in Goza, it's on the Pacific and there's all these Pacific white-sided dolphins; you know, like the ones you study."

"Yes?"

"Well, there's this..." she thought about how to say this in a way a grownup might believe. "There's this researcher who can talk to the dolphins and can see the cancer in them too."

There was another long pause. "There is a researcher who can talk to wild dolphins? Or dolphins in a tank?"

"Oh, they're wild! There's a lot of them too. We were out and then there were like, hundreds of them... maybe thousands!"

"You were with this researcher?"

"Kinda, yeah! It was cool because they showed us where all the pearls were!"

"What?"

Miho knew she had said just a little too much and needed to get the conversation back on track. "Mr.

Hernandez? Do dolphins get cancer? What do you do when they do?"

A third long pause filled the space between Goza and Baja. "Well, to answer your question, yes, dolphins get cancer. Actually, they get a lot of cancer. Because they have so much fat and are at the top of the food chain, chemicals that go in the water end up in dolphins and whales. A lot of chemicals. Miho, why..."

Miho cut him off mid-sentence. "How do you make them better?"

"What?"

"How do you help them?"

"Miho-Miha, if they are wild dolphins, you can't help them. This is part of what I study, how many babies die before they are one year old, how many females can't have babies at all. I still don't understand..."

"You can't do anything?" Miho interrupted again.

The sigh Mr. Hernandez heaved swept all the way across the Pacific Ocean and Miho could hear the sadness in it. "Well, until people stop using certain chemicals, we can't. Miho, who is this researcher? Why do you say he can talk to dolphins?"

Miho was busy thinking about what he said and had to shake her head to answer his question. "Oh, uh, she is new...kinda young. I'm sure you haven't heard of her. And it is like this, new ummm…technique. Yeah, a new technique!" Miho was proud she remembered such a great, grownup science word.

"A new technique?"

"Yeah and," an idea leapt from her mind like water from a spring, "if you came here, she could show you, maybe even teach you!"

Could what Gaia had given her, be given to anyone else? The idea of Mr. Hernandez in Goza made her giddy. Her phone began to beep repeatedly and she realized that the battery was low.

"Hey, Mr. Hernandez, my cell phone is dying. Did you get my number with your caller ID?"

"Si. I have it. I will call you. I want to talk to this researcher. What was her name?"

"Uh…" her mind scrambled through all the names she knew, from all the places she'd been. "It's uh, Pearl. Yeah! I forgot her last name."

"Is she Japanese?"

"Sorta."

Miho was trying to think of more, when the phone let out a final beep, and went dead. She plugged it in. She was sorry she hadn't been able to see what Ojisan sent her and happy she hadn't had to make up anything else to tell Mr. Hernandez.

She lay on her futon and worried. Ojisan was coming back tomorrow. She wasn't sure if pearls would be enough to make him want to stay. Sensei was sick. Curly was even sicker, even if he didn't look it. Why had she told Sensei she wanted understanding? Understanding could actually be really confusing.

# 31
# Nice Speech

The first thing Miho did Friday morning was make sure the house was clean. She opened every shoji screen she could to let in the fresh morning air. And it was fresh. The wind was wild and brought the fresh and the cold from far out in the open ocean.

When she was done, she went to Sensei's. Even if he couldn't teach her, she could still learn. In her pocket was a piece of paper. On that paper was the hiragana for "Welcome Home." She wanted to draw it for Ojisan.

Tomiko met her at the door. She didn't even say, "Ohayo." Instead she said, "Why are you here? I told you my father is sick!" She was making shooing motions, as if Miho were some stray cat that could be pushed back out.

Miho kept her head high and didn't pause. "I am his student. I am here to practice." And with that, she walked straight past the woman, out the far door, and through the garden.

Miho stepped out of her shoes, stepped over the threshold and bowed. The irises on either side of the sword were crinkled and brown. She wanted to get to work on her Shodo. But she knew keeping fresh flowers in the tokonoma space was important to Sensei. She replaced the old flowers with bright, new ones from the garden, then stepped back to look at the calligraphy hanging over the sword. She understood it now.

"From the heart, comes the truth."

Miho prepared her ink and thought about that. She began to write out her welcome home message and thought about what true thing her heart said.

Her heart loved whales and dolphins as much as her parents ever did. Her heart wanted Ojisan to love her as much as her parents ever did. Her heart loved the ocean—so she tried to stay in Goza. Her heart loved Sensei—so she tried to understand. Her heart even loved Gaia, although she didn't understand her yet. Her heart loved.

By the time she finished her sixth copy of "Welcome Home," she had decided that that was what hearts were for—loving. It was what they did best, and love was the only thing that ever did any good.

Miho was surprised to find a bowl of miso at the doorstep and decided she must love Tomiko too, just a little bit.

When her Shodo was dry and her tools clean, she headed back to Ojisan's. She placed the calligraphy in the tokonoma, the nook in the entryway. She hadn't realized until then, a properly adorned tokonoma had been missing in this house.

She fetched a vase and ran across the road to pluck two small daylilies. With the living flowers next to her Shodo, coming into the house really felt like coming home. Now she just had to wait for Ojisan. She sat on

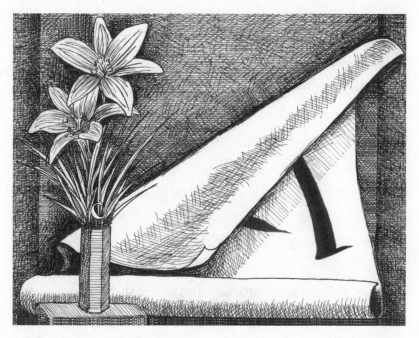

the veranda and watched the water. She also watched the clock on her phone and waited. She couldn't wait to see Ojisan's face when he came in and saw her Shodo!

As Miho walked to the ferry, she thought about how excited Ojisan would be. She could see the approaching ferry as she crested the hill. The ever-present cloud of clamorous vega and slaty-backed gulls circled the boat as it chugged through Ago-wan. Miho shaded her eyes, wondering if Ojisan would be standing at the rail, shading his, looking for her. She listened to the men yell back and forth between the deck and the pier as they secured the ferry. She hoped she would hear a yell of, "Miho-san!"

But she didn't. Not only didn't she hear her name called, she didn't see Ojisan. She looked around the people milling past her and searched the deck, the dock, and even the surrounding shoreline of Ago-wan. No Oji. She couldn't believe it, couldn't move, until the diesel churned to life and began to back the ferry out of its slip.

The setting sun made the top of the hill shine a golden red, and flickers of sun skipped around the hill and across Ago-wan, as if calling a goodbye to the ferry. Miho bit her lower lip and looked around, hoping no one saw her standing alone, looking lost. She turned and walked up the hill. As fast as she had gone earlier that day, she now felt lead-footed and slow.

In the house, the phone beeped. There were now three messages. The first one, the one she couldn't read the night before because her phone went dead, said, "Interesting video. Explain."

The second message was from that morning. It said, "Delayed. Can you take ferry and subway to Nagoya?" Miho felt a hot anger begin in her belly. *What kind of grownup is he? I can't go all that way all by myself!* Then she remembered that she had flown all the way across the ocean by herself. So her anger cooled a bit and she moved to the next message.

"Be there Saturday morning. You OK?" Miho snapped the phone shut and cocked her arm back to throw it across the room. She couldn't believe it! He should be there, in Goza! In his house, with his niece! He should be more like Mr. Hernandez and want to come rushing to be with her!

The thought of Mr. Hernandez stilled her arm. It would be stupid to break her phone. It was her link to the outside world. She flopped down at the low table and typed out a text message. -U should B in Goza. Promise B worth it!-Then she sent the message, to Baja, to the man who loved dolphins as much as she did.

She was feeling lower than whale poo. Even a hot shower didn't make her feel much better. She ate a little and then fetched her portable CD player from her backpack. She tucked into her bed with the one friend who was always, always, always there when she needed her—the matted, gray Shinju. She closed her eyes and let the great, stretching, singing poetry of the humpback whales send her to sleep.

Somebody was shaking her foot. Her nose caught a whiff of cigarette and for a weird moment, she thought she was somehow back in Nagoya. "Oh, Ho! Miho!" Ojisan's voice came through her sleepy fog, and then a giggle. She sat up.

"Ojisan?" The light from the main room made him nothing more than an uncle-shaped shadow in the doorway.

"Hai! I here!" He giggled again and went to the main room. Miho pulled herself from the futon and followed him, rubbing her eyes.

"I don't...but...you weren't at the ferry!" She yawned and then opened her eyes a little wider, hoping it would help her understand his answer.

"I at ferry." He waggled a finger at her. "I come early ferry to see what my hafu niece do to find all this pearl." He swayed a bit as he gestured to the bowls of pearls on the table. He leaned in close to her face. The hot, spicy smell of some kind of drink came off him like a wave and made Miho hold her breath. "So, how you find? You...steal? Hmmm?" He pulled his pack of cigarettes from his shirt pocket.

Miho snatched them out of his hand! He jerked upright, surprised. She squeezed the pack in her fist and felt most of them crush. She glared at him, angry that he had lied to her, angry that he just accused her of stealing, mostly angry that he had called her his, 'hafu niece.' He still thought of her as half, gaijin, not just his niece.

She waved her pack-clutching fist under his nose. "Don't you know these cause cancer?" she yelled, and then threw them to the floor. "Some people can't help it when they get cancer and you do this on purpose. You...You're the one stealing! You're stealing yourself from me and from yourself too!"

Her heart was pounding and sweat sprung from her upper lip. "And those pearls...I FOUND them because I AM AMA!" She screamed the last part, then turned on her heel and marched to the entryway. She snatched up her Shodo from the tokonoma.

"Did you see this?" She waved the paper under his nose and watched his red eyes try to follow it back and forth. "In America we say, 'Home is where the heart is.' Maybe you don't have a heart! Because in Nagoya, you don't have a home!"

She thrust the paper against his chest and brushed past him. She grabbed the lip of each bowl on the table and flipped them up. The pearls flew! They arched in every direction, the light blinking off their iridescent skin, and pattered down on the tatami like raindrops. Miho spun about to face her uncle, still clutching the bowls.

Ojisan's eyes were wide as he gazed around the room. He pulled the crumpled paper from his chest and read the words. He looked up at his niece, threw his head back, and began to laugh.

The sound jolted Miho. It was a deep, long laugh, like the one she had heard him share with his friend. He staggered over and slapped her on the back. "This good speech!" He laughed more and then knelt down and began to pick up the scattered pearls.

He kept chuckling and occasionally squeaked out, "You have no heart!" and "I am Ama!" as he picked up the pale, round spheres and dropped them on the table. "Oh yeah, nice speech! Although," he picked up the crushed pack of cigarettes. "I wish you no do this!" He put them in his pocket and continued to pick up the pearls.

Miho didn't say anything. Maybe she had already said everything. Even though she had thrown the pearls, she didn't help pick them up. Something felt different. Like there was some kind of…understanding.

When Ojisan had returned the last pearl to the bowl, he went out to the veranda and searched through his crunched pack until he found a cigarette that was bent, but not broken. He lit it and inhaled deeply.

Miho padded out and sat next to him. She said, in her most polite Japanese, "I am sorry I yelled so loud. I am very sorry I threw the pearls. I wouldn't do these things if I didn't care."

Ojisan didn't look at her, but reached over and rubbed the top of her head a few times. He continued to smoke and look out over the water. "Goza is nice, isn't it?"

"Hai." She didn't dare say more.

"Did you really find all those pearls yourself?"

"Hai."

"Hmmmm. You really think I steal from myself?" He held the cigarette out in front of him as if he were really seeing it for the first time.

"Well, it costs money. What do you get for your money?"

"Good point." He ground it out, then stood and

chuckled again. "Nice speech."

He didn't say goodnight. He didn't say he was sorry for his lying text message. He just went to his room. Miho was left staring at the bowls of pearls and feeling odd. He had laughed and that made her happy.

32
# Deal

Miho woke to the smell of food. Ojisan had risen before her and had the table full of good things when she came out. "Sit," he said and folded his legs, lowering himself to the table.

Miho, still clutching Shinju, sat. Ojisan was already lifting his chopsticks and dipping into the bowls. "You tell me why you think we need to be in Goza. I want good speech, like last night."

He chewed and raised his eyebrows in expectation. Miho pulled Shinju up under her chin and thought about it. "It's nice here. The ocean breeze makes it cooler than Nagoya. The house is bigger here and you don't smoke in it."

She glanced up, worried he might get mad. But he was chewing thoughtfully. She continued. "It's like you have friends here. I see you laugh with people. Sensei likes you. And, well, I like him. I'm learning a lot." She paused, not sure if she should keep talking.

Ojisan motioned with his chopsticks, so she continued. "Uh, the fish is always fresh and I can find pearls and stuff, uh…" She had no idea how to make a money argument. She didn't know what he did in Nagoya or what he could do in Goza.

"Ojisan, don't you like it better here?"

He set his bowl down and laid his chopsticks across the top. He leaned back on his elbows. "Hai. This always my home. But, it just…hurt to be here." He picked up his chopsticks and waved them at Miho. "You kinda fun here. Maybe for you, hurt more in Nagoya."

Miho couldn't believe her ears. It was as if a pinprick of light at the surface was widening. She swam toward it. "Ojisan, what do you do in Nagoya? I mean, can you work here too?"

Ojisan started to laugh and almost sprayed his mouthful of food out. He gulped it down and told her, "I make website, graphics, e-mails…you know what for?" She shook her head. He snickered, "Air spray." He mimicked spraying a can through the air. "Air spray!" His snicker turned into an out-loud laugh. "Air spray that smell like ocean!" He waved his hand to the opened wall letting the blessings of the sea into their home. "Everyone wants house to smell like this one!" He laughed so hard he fell over sideways.

Miho began to laugh too. When she thought of his small, stinky apartment and then imagined him at an office, making websites to sell...well, this! It was hilarious. They both ended up collapsed on the floor cushions until tears peeked out of their eyes.

When the hilarity ended, Miho asked again, "Why can't you do something like that here?"

He answered in Japanese: "I never think about that— until you came." He looked at her and shook his head. Then he looked out at the bright morning light. "There was no Internet when I left Goza. Maybe now I can have my computers here. I am uncertain though. I have been with this company long time. It would be disloyal."

"Why is it disloyal to do what makes you happy?" Miho asked.

Ojisan's jaw clenched and his eyes narrowed. "Why. I hate this question! This is what your mother said to me! It is not right. If everyone ask why, no one make a commitment! No one do the right thing."

Miho took a deep breath and felt much like she did when she went deep with the lags; she couldn't see where she was going, but there was another way to understand. "Please excuse me, Ojisan. But you say that Ama are no longer in Goza, why?"

He seemed startled. He cleared his throat. "They know how to make the oysters create pearls. No one has to go find them anymore. They are cultured on farms and always come out perfect. I will show you. I will take you to Toba."

"So, they do it a new way, because it is better?"

Ojisan looked at her, an odd look dancing across his face. "I need cigarettes. I'll be back," and he went out the door before she could say anything else.

He was the strangest grownup she had ever met. It was like he didn't understand himself. But he was thinking about Goza! Miho thanked her windy-wave wish, grabbed a few more bites, and cleared off the table. She hoped Mr. Tomikoro was saying nice things about her. Maybe he would say something that would help Ojisan. After all, he had been her Oji's teacher, too.

When Ojisan returned, he was quiet. He went from room to room, standing still and staring at the walls and sliding them back and forth a little. Miho didn't know what to do. She finally asked him if she could go to the beach—thinking, of course, she would head down to her cove and look for her friends.

Ojisan held up one of the bowls of pearls. "Do you know how much these are worth?" Miho shook her head. "Very few people risk diving for this kind of pearl anymore." He dragged his fingers through the bowl. "And you have so many."

"Do you think I found so many because no one is diving for wild pearls anymore?"

He frowned at her. "You ask too many questions! I thought American girls only want to go shopping and talk on the phone." He shook his head and began to rub the bridge of his nose. "OK. I will make you a deal. If you can find ten more pearls by the time we leave on Sunday, I will find a way for us to come back...for good." Miho grabbed his hand and shook it...deal!

"So American," he muttered.

# 33
# Futo

**M**iho couldn't believe it! Ten pearls would be easy, especially if the pod could help her out. She yelled out to Ojisan that she would be back before dinner and set off at a run to the cove. The summer sun perched high in its vault of blue, and by the time she reached the rocky ledge, she was wet with sweat.

There were no dolphins, no Gaia. She dove in anyway and began to slap the water and yell, "Ohayo!" She slapped and yelled and had just begun to feel silly when the now familiar high, warm voice of Gaia, came from behind her.

"That is a lot of noise for one little human to make." Gaia was floating on her back, rubbing her paws, but not looking at Miho.

"Gaia! Where is the pod? If I can find 10 pearls, I can stay in Goza! Isn't that cool?" Gaia didn't look at her.

"Then I can come!" She added, "Whenever you need me, whatever you need me for."

Gaia rolled and looked at her with dark, sad eyes. "I suggest you find them on your own, my dear."

"But Gaia, the lags are so much faster than me! I mean, if they're all here and they help me, they can find ten before dinner time! Ojisan will be so surprised." Miho's imagination was already off ahead, seeing Ojisan congratulating her and setting up his new office in one of the empty rooms.

"Sometimes faster is not better," Gaia said, and began to rub her black paws over her whiskered face.

"C'mon, Gaia! You're the one that's been saying, 'Hurry, hurry.' Why did you say that if faster isn't better?"

The otter rolled a few times and shook her whiskered face. "There are times to hurry, to understand, for example. There are times to go slow, to follow my breathing, just like you followed the breath of the dolphins."

Miho thought about that. *Follow her breathing? I don't get it.* Miho forgot about her Shodo, forgot about understanding. All she could think about was being able to live in Goza. She shook her head. "No, Gaia. I gotta get those ten pearls today."

Gaia floated over. The sunlight that bounced off the water reflected off her dark, otter eyes and pierced right into Miho's mind. Gaia's voice seemed to be carried right on those flecks of light. *Be patient and more pearls will come right to you. I breathe: in, out—life, death. You took the oysters; they will return. Everything has its own cycle. Everything will go around if you wait.*

Maybe it was because Gaia used the word 'death.' Miho suddenly felt that the pearls were owed to her. She had given her parents to the sea. She had been lost in this strange world of Japan, and it was her turn to get something. She wanted to stay in Goza!

"I'm not waiting! I'm gonna get ten pearls so I can stay. I'm staying for YOU, Gaia!" She reached out to the otter, but Gaia was now nothing but a ring of ripples on the water. Miho spun around, looking for the round, bobbing head. It appeared far off, a speck on the horizon.

Gaia's voice drifted back, sounding like far-off thunder. "Sometimes the old way is best, sometimes the new, sometimes the quick way, sometimes the slow. Do you have understanding? Until you do, you do not know the Way of Water."

Miho was left, rising and falling in the swells considering these words. But the desire she had nursed all week came back to the surface of her mind. Ojisan had said ten more pearls to stay in Goza—that was what she would do!

On the horizon, the curling of fins broke the surface. She went under and sent out her best Dolphinese greeting. She was overwhelmed with the flurry of echolocation scans and greetings. The pod was sharing news of the school of anchovies they had successfully bunched up and eaten. They were scanning her, checking her, inside and out and they were pinging her pictures of where they were going.

Of course, Miho didn't recognize their pictures of the shoreline. Even if she had been there, she would know it from the top down, what the hills, the buildings, and the beach looked like. The dolphins sent pictures of the ocean floor rising to become the land—a sort of reverse beach.

They dipped and swirled around her; some pinged out pictures of a pod of pilot whales, some flicked her with their pectoral fins and re-sent the picture of the reverse beach. She knew it was their way of saying, "C'mon, here is where we're going; go with us!"

Miho began to send out her own pictures—pictures of oysters with pearls. It became an acoustical debate. Miho insisted on her picture, what she wanted; about half the pod insisted on heading to the beach. Even their pictures of wave-riding, surfing waves in toward the shore, something she loved to do, couldn't sway her.

The pod split in two. Miho was pleased to see that Notch, Star, Shinju, Curly, Larry, and Moe were among the 15 or so lags that stayed to help her. She grasped the now-familiar notched dorsal fin and they went west, while the rest of the pod peeled away to the east.

Star and Shinju again flanked her, no matter who pulled her. She liked that; she felt part of their small family. She wondered if maybe Notch or one of the Three Stooges was Shinju's father. She couldn't begin to know how to ask such a thought in Dolphinese, so she didn't.

The top layer of water was very warm, so the lags went deeper to stay cool. While they were down in the murky dark, the sun only a memory above, Star sent her pictures of where they were going. It was a ledge, outside of a small bay. The bay had boats, but they wouldn't be getting that close. The oysters clung to the ledge and no humans swam that deep. Star sent Miho several different pictures, showing that there were perhaps as many as 20 or 30 pearls!

Miho was elated—Goza was in her grasp! She kicked her own feet in anticipation and the dolphins sensed her urgency. They began to cruise shallower and leap free of the surface to breathe. It was faster that way and Miho now knew how to breathe and keep up. Shinju sent her small ping forward and Miho could barely make out the shelf. They were getting close.

They slowed and began to go deep. As promised, just past the place where the ocean depths rose, turned and began to level out, the rocks were clustered with oysters! Miho let go of her ride, Moe, and started scanning the oysters for herself. She tugged free the first one containing a pearl within its fleshy belly and rose to the surface.

When Miho broke into the air she realized her dilemma; she had no way to open the tough oyster shell. She banged it between her two fists, but knew that like a sea otter, she would need two rocks.

She called to Notch. She showed him an oyster getting crushed between two rocks and pinged him the image of the rocky jetty that framed the bay. Notch became agitated. He pushed back her image at her. She re-sent it over and over, not understanding.

She couldn't carry home ten oysters! She needed to bust them open and stuff the much smaller pearls into her pockets. Couldn't he see that? Shinju rose beside them, an oyster perched between her small black lips.

Miho took it from Shinju, glad that someone was helping her.

She sent the image of the rocky end of the jetty to Shinju and the youngster didn't hesitate; she pushed her small dorsal into Miho's hands. Miho was hampered by holding the oysters, but able to hold onto Shinju anyway. They set off slowly across the surface of the choppy sea.

Notch kept pushing in front of them and slowing down. He was blasting sounds at Miho that made her wince. *What's his problem? I need rocks to open these things!* She dropped one oyster to grab his black-tipped rostrum and gave it a shove to one side. If she could stand up to Ojisan, she could stand up to Notch too!

Shinju continued to tow her toward the jetty. As they reached it, Curly, Larry, and Moe each arrived with an oyster. Miho stuck out her tongue at Notch, who was now swimming back and forth a few feet from the jetty. She used two rocks to pop open the oysters and soon had four large pearls snug in her pocket. She dove back in and began to swim back toward the oyster bed.

Shinju was there, offering her dorsal fin for a ride. Before Miho could grab on, Notch sent out a call and Miho found herself surrounded by white stripes and black lips. Star rushed up and pushed Shinju away from her. Miho didn't understand. She dove further under, where maybe she could hear better. The pod dove with her. A sort of argument ensued.

Notch sent her the very pictures she had put out earlier—pictures of whole oysters. Miho kept sending pictures of pearls freed from the oysters and instead, safe in her pocket. Star kept deflecting Shinju's ideas away, a sort of dolphin, "Don't interrupt!" It was then, as they squabbled near the jetty that their whole world split open.

The sea was torn apart with a sound so big and meaningless that it blanked everything. It was like having someone turn out the lights and slap you hard in the face at the same time. Her head filled with a buzzing sound that crowded out all but the most important thought, *Hold your breath!*

Miho now understood the phrase, "dazed and confused." She didn't know which way was up! She couldn't understand the frantic dolphin calls that filled the water around her. When she felt a fin thrust in her hand, she grabbed on. It was one of the Stooges—she wasn't sure which one. His swimming was erratic, first up, then down and rolling too much. He didn't seem to be aware of her need to get a breath. Miho started getting her wits about her and blew a short stream of bubbles. Her eyes followed them up to the ring of bright blue above. She needed to breathe!

The world exploded again! This time, Miho lost all thought and lost her air. When she bobbed to the surface she was coughing and gagging and spitting sea water. She heard an outboard motor fire up. An inflatable zodiac boat sped toward them and in the bow, a man was lighting a fuse! To her left and right, two more boats closed in. A dorsal fin was thrust into her hand. By reflex, she grabbed hold. She went under just as the third explosion hit the pod like a wall and pushed them forward. The pod went past the jetty and into the small bay.

Notch was sending fast, repeated pictures of swimming past the zodiacs, out to the open ocean, but the buzzing of the outboards was like a curtain. The pod's sonar couldn't see past it, so they didn't dare go there. Miho could see the bottom rising and knew they were getting close to shore. The boats were closing in! Above the water, she could hear the muffled sound of men yelling.

Cold fear began to grip her in a way she hadn't felt since the bull shark had rushed her so long ago and so far away. Where was the lifesaving ring? No one was yelling, "Pull Miho, pull hard!" Instead, as the water grew even shallower, she heard horrid cries—cries of pain.

Miho saw two long poles with gaffing hooks on the ends plunge into the water and, right in front of her, the hooks dug into Moe's flesh! Her friend was yanked from the water! Miho had to come up. She had to breathe. She had to know what was really happening.

The scene in the fierce light of day was beyond imagination! Directly in front of her, a boat had its deck rails down and there, on the wooden planking, was Moe. Blood streamed from his wounds. Two men pushed against his head, moving him back from the water. A third man wound a rope around his tail.

The water was frothing with dolphins, desperate to escape. She saw men wading into the water carrying ropes and hooks and knives. It was like the kind of Halloween movie her parents would never let her watch. And now, it was all happening in front of her, for real.

Miho ducked under, not wanting to see and hoping to remain unseen. Below the surface, the water was filled with wild calls and sonar zinged about. Calls of what to do and calls of pain intermingled, filling the water with as much confusion as the explosions had.

Notch sped past her, his tail thrashing furiously in

the shallow water. He was still sending the image of swimming out past the three zodiacs hemming the bay. Miho turned to follow him, but ran smack into little Shinju. Her small tail was beating the surface trying to get away from the men in the zodiacs, who were now hitting the surface with paddles. Miho saw a gaffing hook cut through the water toward little Shinju!

Miho threw her hip into Shinju's side, moving her out of the way of the cruel, grasping hook. She felt the hook grab the back of her shorts! As Miho tried to move away from the bite of it, she threw both her arms around Shinju's diminutive dolphin body.

The two of them were pulled from the water! Miho tightened her grip as she felt the full weight of the baby dolphin. Out of the water, Shinju was heavier than Miho! The two frightened mammals were slung onto the wooden deck! Even in the air, Miho could hear Shinju calling for her mother.

Miho looked around for Star. The water beneath them was a boil of tails and dorsal fins and frantic dolphins throwing their heads in the air in an attempt to turn and run. The zodiacs closed in tighter. Miho looked to her left in time to see Notch, cruelly snared at the end of two gaffing hooks, land beside her. One man began tying a rope to his tail and another approached his head. The man had a knife!

Miho jumped to her feet, but had to turn away from Notch. The man who had pulled her and Shinju out of the water stood, wide-eyed, yelling, "Hey! Where did you come from?"

Time seemed to slow for Miho. From the corner of her eye, she saw the man with the knife kneel down by Notch's head. In front of her, the man who had yelled lowered the bloodstained hook of his long pole and poked it at her!

Miho looked down. She meant to look at Shinju, but her eye was pulled to the cresting wave of scar on her hand. That scar was proof of her courage. *Kimo.* Trying hard not to see the horror all around her, she put that kimo into motion.

Her Hokusai hand flashed out and grabbed the shaft of the gaffing hook. With a quick twist, she had it out of the man's hand! She spun the pole in a way that made the end of the shaft connect with his cheek with a wet, "THOCK!" The man fell to the deck, holding his face. His howls mixed with the high, agonized squeals coming from the dolphins.

*Good!* Miho thought.

The deck was now red and slick. Blood was running into the bay, staining it pink. Miho had the gaffing hook in hand and turned side-to-side, wanting to know where to run, what to do. She heard an engine fire up and looked up just in time to see dear, sweet, Moe being pulled away by his tail.

He called out to her, but she could only stand there, frozen in horror as the asphalt began to darken in his wake; the rough road rubbing the very skin from him. Her stomach lurched and her vision began to narrow. It was if her mind wanted to shut down completely and not face this grim reality.

A hand grabbed her shoulder from behind. The rough grip snapped her back to herself. Miho whipped the gaffing hook around and under her right arm. She felt it connect with her assailant's rib cage. He too, hit the deck, but this time there was no howl of pain, just a "HOOOOF" sound.

Miho looked down at her feet, willing them to move. She was ankle deep in water and blood and there was little Shinju, kicking her small tail and trying to do… something, anything. Miho knew how she felt.

She let go of the gaffing hook, dropped to her knees, and placed her hands against Shinju's back. She braced her feet against the second fallen man and pushed with all her might! Shinju began to slide to the edge of the deck. Miho felt a hand close around her ankle!

Without knowing what she was going to do, she flipped onto her back and swung her free leg in a high, wide arc. Miho felt her instep connect with the third man's knee and saw the joint bend out sideways at a most unnatural angle. But then again, everything about that boat was unnatural!

Because she was on her back, she could see upward. There above her, swinging in a sling, was Star. She was pumping her flukes hard, trying to swim. Her calls fell on Miho like hideous rain. As hard as she could, Miho sent Star the picture of herself the silly, long, legged gaijin, pushing baby Shinju back into the water.

It was all she could do. She didn't know what might happen next. But that image was now a promise. Miho flipped over and gave one final, hard shove that pushed herself and Shinju over the edge!

The water below was still as much a horror as the deck above. Now many men were in the water, knives in hand. Miho could still hear Notch calling to the pod. His call stopped suddenly. Miho didn't want to or need to know why. It was all too much.

She stood up. She felt twice as tall and twice as angry as when she had yelled at Ojisan the night before. She placed her left hand on Shinju's back and balled her scarred hand into a fist. She plunged her fist into the horrendous pink water and began to swish it back and forth.

Instantly, the scene of the dolphins' demise was overtaken by waves. Like water sloshing in a bathtub, the water that pounded into and out of the bay set the zodiacs tumbling and the men on the boat deck scrambling for handholds. Miho grabbed Shinju with one arm and dove. She kicked hard and said in Dolphinese, "Swim fast!"

They passed under the zodiacs and finally Shinju began to pump her small flukes, helping their escape. Miho heard an outboard fire up. When they rose to breathe, she saw one of the inflatable, motorized boats swivel and begin to follow them! She wanted to run, or to swim—as the case may be. But she knew that her pathetic human feet and Shinju's small, inexperienced tail was no match for the motor.

She turned and faced the boat. *Face him, Miho! Turn and face him!* Her father's voice rang in her ears as she drew both her hands out wide and shouted, "NOOOOOOO!" She clapped her hands together. It was if her hands dragged half the ocean along with them!

Two great waves drew up behind her hands and curled toward the unspeakable scene in the bay. The zodiac in pursuit was swept up the sheer face of the wave. *Into the washing machine!* Miho actually smiled when she heard the satisfying sound of men crying out. The small boat was flipped and the lip of the great wave began to fold over.

The two waves coming together looked like watery jaws coming to eat the bay and swallow the horror. Miho didn't see the rest of what happened. She grabbed Shinju and raced away.

# 34
# Orphans

Miho kicked harder than she had ever kicked before. She had to turn herself and Shinju upward when she needed to breathe. Behind them, the roar of the giant waves had overtaken the cries and the yells. For a long minute, there was nothing but the roaring and the hissing of the water pounding, receding, and pounding back into the small bay.

For Miho, within the roaring and pounding came her father's voice.

*"Under heaven*
*nothing is more soft*
*and yielding than*
*water.*

*Yet for attacking the*
*solid and strong*
*nothing is better.*

*It has no equal."*

Miho didn't know if any of the other pod members had escaped. She hoped that her waves hadn't flung any of them onto the boats or the shore. She turned once to call out, "Follow us!" and sent a picture of herself and little Shinju. She listened for an answer. She kept her ears open for the sound of outboard motors, but the motors didn't come.

Miho kept swimming, trying not to hear Shinju's repeated cries for her mother. Miho just kept telling her, "swim," over and over. When Miho felt the buzz of sonar pass over her, she stopped swimming and turned. She called out, "Hello?" wishing desperately that she knew how to say, "We are here."

Shinju and Miho waited, and waited. They surfaced to breathe twice before the dolphin reached them. It was the one she thought of as Lightning, the one with the zigzag mark. Although now, she was marked by more than a light colored zigzag.

Lightning was swimming slow and trailing blood. A gash along her neck revealed her thick white blubber. The gash angled back and had partially separated her pectoral fin from her flank. It was there the blood streamed out, a dark testament to the reality of what should have been a bad dream. Miho's throat tightened with tears. *Why? Why would they do this?*

Lightning sent Miho pictures of sharks. Miho understood. Sharks would be coming, drawn to the blood. Beside her, little Shinju began to shiver. Miho remembered how she had shivered uncontrollably the day she had met her own shark. She knew that shock was beginning to overcome Shinju.

"Swim," she told this new, tiny pod. She didn't know what else to do. They moved pathetically slowly. Lightning had to keep correcting her course because, without the full use of her pectoral fin, she kept rolling and drifting left. Shinju was worn out, her little tail, little help. When they surfaced, Miho scanned the shoreline. When they dove, she did her best to scan the seafloor. She needed to find the right spot.

As the sun began to slide down the west side of the sky, a breeze brought a greater chop to the water. It was getting harder for all three of them to continue to surface and dive, surface and dive. And Miho knew the sharks were coming. It was what sharks did—remove the small, the weak, and the injured from the sea. Miho also knew big sharks didn't like shallow water.

The sun had slid behind the mountains by the time Miho found what she needed. A rim of living coral hemmed a sandy beach. The sharp rise of the reef broke the waves long before they reached shore. Because the waves lost their energy on the reef, the water close to the beach was calm and relatively protected from the hunters of the deep.

Miho led the way through the breaking waves and sharp coral. When she tried to stand, she found her legs shaking and barely able to hold her weight. She knelt down and wrapped her arms around Shinju. She didn't think that dolphins gave hugs, but people did, and it was all she could think to do to calm the distressed baby.

Lightning bobbed on the surface, her breathing sounding a little ragged. Now that Miho had found them a safe place, she had to slow or stop the bleeding. Miho pulled off her shirt and tore a long strip from the bottom. She put her shirt back on, wadded up the strip and went to Lightning.

Miho did her best to make a picture of what she was going to do. Lightning gave a short, Dolphinese, "Hai." Miho rolled the injured lag onto her side. The gash on her neck was deep, but the cut had not gone past the warm and protective blubber. When Miho looked lower, however, she felt her knees weaken and her belly turn to liquid. Lightning's fin was hanging loose and useless; a little puff of red stained the water with each heartbeat.

Miho concentrated, willed her belly to harden and

her mind to focus. She took the balled-up cotton strip of her shirt and began to push it into the gap between Lightning's fin and body. She pushed it in tight, trying not to notice the way Lightning's body tensed and kicked with pain.

When Miho was done, she sat back on the sandy bottom, the gentle remainder of waves swirling by her. She placed Lightning's dark rostrum on her bent knees and did her best to send a picture through the air, one of no blood, no sharks. Lightning was quiet, the only sound, her odd, raspy surface breathing.

Shinju pushed her small, black-tipped snout up against Miho's hip. Miho looked to the east at the darkened horizon. Was the rest of the pod wondering where they were? Was Ojisan wondering where she was? Should she leave the beach and try to find a phone to call Ojisan? What would happen to darling little Shinju? *She's an orphan—just like me!* Miho stopped thinking and simply cried.

# 35
# No Why!

It was the second longest night of Miho's life. The longest had been waiting for her parents to come home. She had sat on the dock with a wool blanket around her shoulders, ears straining for the familiar sound of the boat's engine. She wished she had that blanket now.

Miho began to shiver. When she was with the dolphins, she didn't get cold as fast as she normally would. But she had been in the water for over 12 hours now. She had neither blanket nor blubber to prevent the chilly Pacific from stealing her heat. Each time she tried to tell Shinju she was going up on the beach, the little white-side clasped the hem of Miho's shorts in her teeth and wouldn't let go.

Lightning didn't say anything, just pulled each breath in with a rattle and exhaled with a slow sigh.

Miho finally had no choice but to forcefully pull

herself away from the insistent baby lag and get out of the water. Up past the sandy beach there were trees. Miho snapped leafy branches down until she had enough to cover herself. It was as close to a blanket as she would get.

Miho wanted to sleep, but from the shallows came the repeated, plaintive cries of little Shinju. She had her snout in the air and called for her mother, called for Miho, called for the pod. Miho would yell back, "I'm here." She yelled it in English, in Japanese, and even in Spanish, hoping the frightened little girl would understand.

What little sleep Miho had was punctured by hideous images from the bay, images of her parents, and the sound of Ojisan yelling, "Where you been?" It was a very long night. It seemed like she had only been in the deepest, darkest place of sleep for a moment when the rising sun sliced across the water and stung her eyes.

The cries of sea birds pierced the hazy sky and the rim of coral was alive with breaking waves. Miho shaded her eyes and looked toward the beach. She could see Shinju's small dorsal fin, bobbing on the surface. She waited for Lightning to surface. The sun rose a bit higher, but Lightning didn't rise at all. She wasn't there.

Miho ran into the water and dove under. She began

to call, but the only call that came back was from Shinju. The wee dolphin bombarded her with images and clicks, "my stomach is empty, where is my mother, where is Lightning, my stomach is empty, where are we going?" A flurry of possible destinations flew past Miho like a slide show. Miho realized that this small child of a dolphin knew much more about the world of the ocean than she did, and yet she was looking to Miho for guidance.

Miho's own stomach was growling like an elephant seal. She didn't feel old enough or big enough to deal with this, but no other pod members were here. She was it. She rubbed her scar with her thumb; she only knew one place to go. She sent Shinju the image of the mermaid cove. She also sent her a picture of Gaia. Gaia would know what to do.

It was a long trip back. Shinju's little tail could give little bursts of power, but not the sustained speed of adult dolphins. Miho had to scan carefully and listen out ahead to avoid boats, jellyfish, nets, and sharks. Her mind was fixed on getting to the mermaid cove.

Miho knew that she and Shinju both needed food. She hoped Shinju was old enough to eat fish. When one of her scans showed a shoal of sardines, she sent Shinju the idea of eating them. It was a sad thing, a bumbling human and an inexperienced baby dolphin trying to ball up a school of sardines, but Shinju managed to grab three or four and stopped talking about her stomach.

Miho wished she could snatch a raw fish and flip it down her own throat. Her stomach was a knot of complaints by the time the ridgeline of Goza came into view. As much as her stomach ached, it was nothing compared to her legs and arms!

Miho's grumbling stomach sank when she found the bay empty—no Gaia, no white-sided dolphins. She wasn't sure why she thought they would be there, but she believed they would be. The tide was rising and the waves were booming against the rocks. Miho couldn't leave Shinju there! She would tire out completely trying to keep from being pounded against the rocks.

Miho clenched her teeth and tried to tell Shinju that they still had to swim around Goza and into the safety of Ago-wan. If dolphins could whine, that's what Shinju did. She was tired, she was scared, she was hungry, why were they here? Why? Why? Why?

Miho yelled, "No why!" then clamped her hand over her own mouth! Her flash of understanding for Ojisan was powerful. There are some things you just can't explain. They are what they are, and you have to do what you have to do. Miho grabbed Shinju's dorsal fin and began to tug her out of the mermaid cove.

In Ago-wan, Miho found a calm spot behind a tiny island, out of sight from all the shoreline activity and well away from the ferry route. She did her best to show Shinju that she should stay there. Miho tried to say that she would be back soon. But even with her best explanation, she had to swim away with the sad sound of Shinju's calls following her.

～

The police car in front of Ojisan's house made her stop and take a good look at herself. Her shirt was torn off at the bottom. Her shorts were stained red. Her skin was a sick pale color and wrinkled. Miho patted her head and knew that her long, dark hair must be matted and frightening.

She wanted to run somewhere to clean up. She didn't want to tell the terrible story of what had happened. However, she had no choice but to continue down the lane to the gate. She had no choice. When she pushed the gate open she heard Ojisan yelling. For once, he wasn't yelling at her, but *about* her!

He kept repeating in Japanese, "She told me she was going swimming. I don't know where! You should be looking—not asking stupid questions!" Hearing Ojisan express such concern for her was nothing compared to what met her eyes when she stepped over the threshold.

There was her grumpy, stinky uncle—red-faced, red-eyed, and clutching her raggedy stuffed dolphin in his hands. Miho couldn't help it; she yelled out, "Oji-san!" and ran to him. He turned and as his eyes opened wide, so did his arms.

Miho didn't know how many hugs this grumpy, stinky Japanese uncle had ever given, but it was one of the best hugs she ever got.

# 36
# The Whole Story

The police had a lot of questions. Miho played a game of using bad Japanese and a lot of fast, slang-laden English to tell a confusing story of being bumped by a boat and waking up on shore. She could clearly understand the police talking amongst themselves, talking about her being American and not knowing how to be in the water. She let them believe whatever they wanted to make them go away. Ojisan watched with a strange look on his face and said nothing.

When the police finally left, Ojisan brought her a steaming mug. "Shogayu," he said. "Drink it. It will make you feel better." The shogayu, hot ginger water, did indeed, begin to warm Miho from the inside out. Ojisan sat, not looking at her, pinching and squeezing the bridge of his nose with one hand. "Eat, take shower, then we talk." He was pulling his cigarettes from his shirt pocket even as he finished talking. It seemed to Miho hug-time was over, and the Oji she knew was back.

Miho filled her empty, aching stomach with a rice porridge called okayu. Belly full and insides finally warmed, she went to the shower to wash off the salt and blood and memory of her journey. Miho didn't really want to talk; she wanted to sleep. But Shinju, the living, breathing one, was waiting for her. She would have to talk to Ojisan if she were to be able to go back and help the little orphan.

Miho went to sit next to him on the veranda. There was a long silence, except Goza was never truly silent; the heartbeat of the waves was always there. *'Seeking the shores forever.'Who said that?* she thought, and felt the pang of not being able to ask her dad. That steady, salty heartbeat filled the space between Miho and her uncle as the sun slid downward in the Sunday sky.

"I…have been fired," Ojisan finally said, giving his head a quick nod, as if to affirm that statement. Miho stared at his profile. He continued to gaze out at the darkening sky, his face not showing how he felt about this new development.

Miho had learned by now not to ask why. She could guess anyway. It was too late for today's ferry and he probably had to call, yet again, with a story about his American niece and why he wouldn't be at work in the morning.

She steeled herself against the expected yelling, the tirade about the gaijin-ko who was making his life so difficult. But Ojisan didn't yell. He turned to smile at her and said the most unexpected thing: "I rather lose job than lose niece."

Miho bit her lower lip and searched for words, English, Japanese or Dolphinese. Finding none, she turned to look out at the water. A flock of terns made a last attempt at feeding before the light left for good; a crisp breeze whisked the day's heat away. Her uncle continued. "So, Miho-san, I very curious, where you been. If you tell me whole story, maybe I help you get rid of this."

He reached out his thumb and rubbed it between her eyebrows. Miho hadn't realized it, but she had her brows knit tightly together. When Ojisan rubbed the scrunched-up line away, the tensions of the last five months seemed to get smoothed away as well. She could think again, and words flooded her mind.

Miho threw caution to the wind and let the whole story pour out. She told Ojisan about first seeing the otter in Alaska. She told him about following the otter to the water her first night in Goza. She told him about the night of O-bon and about meeting the dolphins. She told him how dolphins talk to each other and how they have names and how they laugh and play, gossip and argue—just like people do. She told him how the dolphins had taught her to go deep and see in the dark. These were the friends that helped her find the pearls.

By the time Miho finished, it was dusk, lit by the glow of the setting sun and of Ojisan's cigarette. He exhaled and said through the plume of blue smoke, "This is most interesting story. But I still not know story of where you have been for two days. Hmmm?"

Miho sighed and pulled her knees up to her chest. She wished she had Shinju, the stuffed one, tucked under her chin. Instead, she laid her forehead on her knees and directed the rest of the story into her lap.

She told him about making the pod help her find the ten pearls. She told him about the explosions, the gaffing hooks, the trucks, the knives, and their escape. When she told about the two thunderous waves, she sat up and held out her hand.

Ojisan took it and examined the scar. He traced the scar with his finger and Miho wondered if he was imagining the great waves. When he let go, she told him about Shinju and Lightning and their long, risky journey north. She choked back tears as she described her long night and waking to find Lightning gone.

And then she told him that Shinju was in Ago-wan. Her remark caught him mid-inhale and he started coughing plumes of cigarette smoke. "You mean this little dolphin is in Ago-wan *right now?*"

"Yeah, I think she's really hungry. I gotta feed her, I'm all she has."

Now Ojisan had a line between his eyebrows just like Miho's. "Show me," he said, and rose to his feet. It felt like a challenge. Miho had the sense that if Ojisan saw Shinju, he might believe her whole story. Miho gathered up the hamachi, yellowtail tuna, from the refrigerator. She tried not to get nervous at the odd way Ojisan stared at her.

They walked over the hill and down to the docks. Miho felt very uncomfortable. She hadn't thought too much about how strange what she had been doing really was, until she got ready to do it in front of someone else. She hoped her Oji would understand. He didn't speak, just stood with his hands on his hips as if he were waiting for her to admit she lied about everything.

*Satoru satori,* Miho thought, bowed, and dove into Ago-wan. She felt so slow without her speedy dolphin friends pulling her. She kept swimming and calling underwater. When she surfaced for air, she could see the small, dark form of Ojisan standing with his hands still planted on his hips. Of course he thought she was spinning some wild tale. Maybe he had already called the psychiatric people to come get his crazy American niece and have her locked up with other crazy people!

Miho began to angle around the island and, finally, her calls reached Shinju. The little dolphin zipped through the gloom, buzzing her sonar, and calling Miho's name excitedly. Miho realized for the first time that there was a Dolphinese version of her name.

She also realized that her name was, indeed, Japanese. In English it meant, "Beauty in the crest of a wave." In Dolphinese, as far as she could tell, it meant "Bridge." It was an image of a link between the water and the land, complete with long arms and legs and a big smile.

Shinju peppered her with pictures and chirps and whistles. Miho knew that about every third one was a reference to her mother, Star. Miho knew exactly how it felt to wonder when, or if, your mother would come home. She also knew that knowing was better than wondering. She had to tell Shinju.

But in order to help her, Miho also had to prove to Ojisan what she said was true. She felt bad, but asked Shinju to jump. "Why?" was the Dolphinese response. If

Miho hadn't been underwater, she would have sighed.

There was simply no way to explain, so Miho repeated the call for jump over and over until Shinju shot to the surface. Miho came up in time to see Shinju pass the apex of her beautiful arch. The last bit of daylight winked off the drops of water that trailed out behind the little dolphin. In the distance, Miho could see Ojisan's hands drop to his sides.

Miho asked Shinju to pull them halfway back to the dock and then jump again. Shinju did it beautifully and only asked 'why' three or four times. Miho saw her Oji pull out a cigarette and noticed the way the glow of the tip shook in his hand.

*Enough with the dolphin show!* All Miho wanted to do was take care of her fellow orphan and let her know what had happened to her mother. Miho pulled out the fish. When the hamachi was gone, she shared the pictures of Star being lifted from the water. She wished she could tell the little one where her mother was going. She wanted to be able to tell her that she was sure her mother was thinking about her too. But she didn't know those answers and those kinds of thoughts were beyond pictures. It hurt Miho to not know how to say those kinds of reassuring things. *Like Ojisan,* her mind whispered before she could stop it.

Shinju fell silent. Miho didn't know what else to do but give her another human hug. She again told her of the plan for the next day. But she also knew that the little dolphin's heart was breaking. It took a long time to swim back to Ojisan. She couldn't stay under long while she was crying. She ended up doing a backstroke, so her tears could fall while she stroked through Ago-wan. She cried for Shinju. She cried for Lightning and Moe and the others. She cried for her parents. She cried for herself.

Ojisan helped her out and started to ask questions. "Sumimasen," Miho began, hoping what she was about to say wasn't too disrespectful. "I am very tired, and you ask too many questions. We should talk tomorrow."

To her great relief, he simply said, "Hai." She leaned on his arm as they walked back over the hill. She needed his help just to keep her legs moving. Her heart ached and the line was once again firmly set between her eyebrows. She had to find the pod for Shinju. She had to.

# 37
# Oikomi

In the morning, a fierce, crisp wind blew in through the opened shoji screens. The day seemed electric with potential. Miho tore through her breakfast and went out to find Ojisan pacing the veranda, talking very fast on his cell phone and smoking his cigarette even faster.

He finally snapped the phone shut and made a movement like he might throw the phone against the fence! Miho knew the feeling. But he rolled his shoulders, cracked his neck, and slipped the phone in his pocket. "Ohayo, Miho-san."

"Ohayo," she replied, cautiously.

"I must go soon." He spoke in Japanese, but Miho understood every word. "I have to go back to Nagoya. There is a lot to do if we are going to be here." Miho's heart skipped a beat. *Omigosh...we're staying!* He sighed and Miho could sense a long, grownup to-do list forming in his head.

"Sumimasen, but, I can't go to Nagoya!" Miho said. "Shinju needs me to take her out to find her pod. We have to at least find Gaia! I can't leave. I..."

Ojisan held up his hand and stopped her mid-sentence. "Hai. Hai, I know this." He laughed, tipped his head back, and smiled at the sky. "Your story is too crazy not to be true! Ever since O-bon, things are different. I don't belong in Nagoya. I have been so busy being angry, I forgot something very important: I am Ama too."

The news rocked Miho back on her heels. It was like her dream. Her uncle would be just as much Ama as his sister or his mother. But were men Ama? Miho thought it meant 'woman of the sea.' She wanted to know more, but Ojisan was talking. She wanted to hear everything he had to say before she bent his thoughts in a new direction.

"When I found out about Yoko, my sister," his voice tightened up when he said 'sister.' "I tried not to care," he continued. "But then I learned about a niece. My niece. And you were coming here. Every day I had to think about why I was still in Nagoya, about why I did the job I did. At first, I did it for Yoko, but she left me long ago."

He smiled down at Miho. "Now I sound like an American, eh? Why? Why? Maybe the dead really do come back at O-bon. It was like my mother, my father, my sister, maybe even your Ameko-father..." he sighed. "They shook me awake, like I was waking up from a long dream and not sure why I had been sleeping so long. And maybe Gaia is doing something to me too. Last night..." He looked around like he was afraid someone else might hear him. "...I thought I heard something. You told that little dolphin about her mother, didn't you?"

Miho was speechless. She nodded. It was amazing— she had never heard her Oji say so many words in a row before! His cell phone rang and startled them both. He answered it and swept into the house before she could ask any of her thousands of questions.

By the time Miho came in, he had a duffle bag over his shoulder. "I must go back to Nagoya, and you have things you must do, too. I understand." He placed a hand on her shoulder and Miho felt very grown-up.

She nodded and said, "I'll call you before I leave and I'll call you when I get back. Don't worry Ojisan. I don't think Gaia will let anything happen to me. But I gotta...I must, take care of Shinju," she looked at the floor and felt a flush climb her neck. "Just like you are taking care of me."

"Hai. Hai. You call. Text. Let me know you are okay." He walked toward the front door and then turned back. "Oh, this is for you." He handed her a rolled-up newspaper, "Page 7."

After Ojisan left, Miho sat on the sunny veranda with her Japanese/English dictionary next to her hip and the newspaper folded back. It was a report from a town called Futo. It seemed rogue waves had disrupted the beginning of the annual dolphin drive! *They should call it murder!* Miho thought fiercely. The dolphin hunt was called Oikomi in Japanese.

Miho struggled with the translation. But it was worth it to read how the fishermen were scared. The older ones suggested that a Shinto god or two might be displeased in some way. Miho's frown gave way to a small giggle. *If only they knew it was Gaia, the whole earth that is displeased with hurting the minds in the water! Well, Gaia and me; Gaia through me?*

The men in Futo bragged that they managed to get one live dolphin that would be sold to do shows in a marine park. *Star! That's why she was lifted up like that!* The article said that the live dolphin was worth ten times more than the dead ones. What Miho read next had her on her feet and searching the house for a map.

The fisherman in a town called Taiji were going forward with their dolphin drive. *Murder,* Miho corrected the phrase.

*Oh no, they're not! They are not! No! No more Oikomi! Not when I'm here!* Miho knew what it felt like to have your parents disappear. She couldn't stand the thought of more lost little "pearls," like the one waiting for her in Ago-wan. She knew she could stop it.

She stormed from room to room searching for a map that could tell her where Taiji was. Her cell phone rang. Her phone; her phone had a GPS! She could find Taiji and stop this horrid Oikomi. It was Ojisan. "I forgot to tell you, go visit Sensei; he is not well and asked for you."

Miho thanked Ojisan for calling. Her anger waned and she sat, limp-limbed, wondering what she should do. Any dolphins swimming near Taiji would be in danger. She wanted to go see Sensei; he was the first person in Japan to treat her as a friend. But Shinju needed her. The first thing she had to do was find the remaining lags. She hoped Sensei would understand. She would explain it next time she saw him. He had Tomiko; Shinju was alone.

Miho ran over the hill to Ago-wan and, when she was sure no one was watching, she dove in. She made the journey through the dappled blue out to the small island, calling Shinju the whole time.

She felt the buzz of sonar long before she saw the little dolphin. Shinju rushed up to her from below, and they did a sort of twirling dance in the gloom of Ago-wan. Miho sent her pictures of the mermaid cove and then began to swim toward the tip of Goza.

Shinju understood and gave Miho her little dorsal fin. The travel was much slower than it had been with the full pod, but faster now that they were both rested. When they finally reached the mermaid cove, Gaia was waiting.

Shinju was so excited she leapt over the whiskered otter several times. Miho wanted to know that everything would be okay. But the air around Gaia felt charged. The day was still electric with possibilities.

"Ohayo, Gaia-san."

"Ohayo, my dear. Why are you and this small one all alone?"

Miho didn't know what to say. She hadn't anticipated this question. She couldn't tell Gaia what had happened. Miho's stomach knotted when she thought about how she had wanted her pearls so much that she had led her friends into a deadly trap.

"Well?" Gaia prodded. The way she said it filled the

air with the tang of a coming storm.

"Gaia I...I didn't listen to you. I didn't understand what you were trying to tell me."

The otter sighed and looked sad. "So very few listen anymore. This is why I come to you, all of you: because I think you can truly listen. You, more than the other three, must understand. Water is everywhere: in the air and the soil as well as in the deep bowls of the seas."

Miho only had a moment to wonder what others Gaia was referring to before the otter twitched her broad, black nose and continued. "I am taking this small one with me. You shall go home."

Miho was stunned. Her mind had been so focused on how she could find the pod that she hadn't considered another option. "But Gaia, I want to take her home. I want to help."

"And if I let you take her home," Gaia began, her voice sounding like a cold night. "Would you tell the story of what happened? Would you help the others understand?"

"Of course I would! I..." Miho fought to find the right words. "I hate not knowing things! I get scared when I don't know what's going on. They need to know, so, yeah! I'll tell them. I'll show them what people can do to them!"

"What if they don't listen? You didn't listen when your friend tried to tell you. How do you convince those who will not listen?"

Miho's heart felt like a cold stone. It was true. Notch had tried to warn her. He had known about the danger, but she had only her selfish wants in mind. "Gaia, I will try to tell them what happened when I didn't listen, when I was thinking only about myself."

"Ahh. We may make a Gaia Girl out of you yet."

*Gaia Girl?* The phrase rang like a bell in Miho, but she didn't have time to think about it. The little dolphin and Gaia were still circling her and Gaia was still talking—giving her directions.

"You go back to your human teacher today. I will care for this little one until tomorrow. I expect you here in the morning. I expect more humility, understanding, and a sense of duty. You cannot think of only yourself if you are going to do what is best for all."

Miho returned home, ate a bit of lunch, and went to see her Sensei. The store was open and as Miho walked in, Tomiko came rushing out from the back room. Miho clenched her jaw and prepared herself for any rude or unkind thing the grouchy woman might fire at her.

Tomiko, surprisingly, gave Miho a quick bow and motioned for her to come around the counter. Miho followed, wondering about this unexpected courtesy.

Through a doorway behind the counter was an office, the desk covered in papers, a computer screen glowing a dull blue in the dim light. Through a second doorway, however, was a room that reminded Miho of Ojisan's.

Portions of the wall had been wheeled back to let the Pacific-cooled breeze flow through. Across from the doorway hung beautiful Shodo and a vase of white daisies. Miho wondered if Sensei had made the Shodo. When she looked into the room beyond, there was her teacher, in a plain brown robe, seated at the low table near the open shoji.

"Konnichiwa, Miho-san," Sensei said, and motioned for her to sit. She took a seat in front of a steaming cup of matcha, green tea, and a platter of wagashi, sweets that were shaped to look like daisies.

Sensei lifted his cup of tea and Miho noticed the tremor in his grip. He took a long, noisy sip, and turned to her. His eyes twinkled in a way that was like the happier version of Gaia's fierce glint. "I think this Ama has been adrift at sea; I have not seen you in so long," Sensei said.

Miho wasn't sure how to respond. Was that his way of saying he missed her? Did he really know what she had been up to? He was as full of riddles as Gaia!

"Sensei, I have been seeking...understanding." And without planning to, she made the motions, as if she were holding her brush and making the kanji.

Sensei sipped his tea, his eyes peering over the lip of the cup. He set the cup down and said in such a conversational way that Miho almost missed it, "I have asked Masuaki-san to return. I believe the school in Goza can have new life. I believe that you, little Ama, will be a good student, the first of many who will seek understanding through the way of the brush." He paused, leaned in close to Miho and whispered, "Ishin denshin."

"Sensei! What is...why are you..." but her teacher held up his hand, cutting off her questions. The sweetness of the wagashi began to turn sour in her throat. Sensei started to push himself up from the floor. Miho rushed to take his elbow and help him rise. Tomiko was there in a flash, doing the same thing. Their eyes met across the weave of his robe and Tomiko's look held the same worry Miho felt.

The moment passed and Tomiko said with her customary bit of a growl, "Go home. Go home to your own family." Miho was left in the doorway between the house and the store wondering what *ishin denshin* was, wondering what makes a family, and trying not to wonder too much about what Gaia had in store for the following day.

# 38
# Gaia Girl

As she walked back from Sensei's, the wind doubled in strength, and a chill in the breeze spoke of some event that was streaking their way. The waves sounded as if they were pounding to come in and be understood by the strange, long-limbed creatures that insisted on venturing out into the blue.

She looked up *'ishin denshin'* right away. It was like a heart-to-heart communication. Miho wasn't sure what Sensei meant by saying that. But between Gaia and Sensei, she was used to being a little confused and waiting to understand.

A "beep" from her phone alerted her to an incoming message. It was Ojisan!

-You OK?-

-KONBANWA, OJISAN. I M OKAY-

-GOOD-

-SAW SENSEI-

Miho's thumbs hovered over the tiny keys as she waited for Ojisan's response.

-IS HE WELL?-

-NO-

There was another long pause, which Miho chose to fill with one of her father's poems.

*"The bleat, the bark, bellow and roar.*
*Are waves that beat on Heaven's shore."*

She repeated this four times before Ojisan typed back.

-BE HELPFUL-

Miho didn't know how to respond, so she didn't. She stared at the blue screen and wondered if Ojisan had his own poems to fill such moments as this.

-IS SHINJU HOME?-

Miho was surprised he asked. Her heart felt warm with the knowledge that he cared, at least a little bit, about the small, orphaned dolphin out in the big blue.

-GAIA TOOK HER BACK I SEE HER SOON I HOPE-

Another long pause filled the air between Goza and Nagoya. Miho repeated the poem.

*"The bleat, the bark, bellow and roar.*
*Are waves that beat on Heaven's shore."*

She seemed to remember her father raising his sandy eyebrows and giving a knowing look. "Blake," he would say. This particular poem was swirling through her mind because the waves were bleating and barking and roaring against Goza.

-GOING 2 SEA 2MORROW. UNSURE HOW LONG-

-SHOULD I WORRY?-

-NO. GAIA LEADER-

-CRAZY AMERICAN TALKING-

-AMA TALKING-

Another long pause.

-BE SAFE!-

Miho smiled and knew she was free. Ironically, just as her Oji was letting her be what she needed to be, Gaia began talking about duty—not duty as daughter or as Japanese, but as a Gaia Girl. Miho smiled the first smile she had all day. *Gaia Girl.* It sounded good and made her feel brave. She was ready for whatever lesson Gaia was going to teach her. She finally knew where home was. She knew who her family was. She understood.

Miho fell asleep listening to the bleat and bellow

and roar of the sea. It was a sweet lullaby, the booming of the waves like a mother's heartbeat, the hiss of the foam and spray like a mother's shushing.

In the night, the lightning and thunder and tremendous pounding rain finally showed up. Miho wasn't afraid of the storm, but she sat up in her futon, afraid she wouldn't know the sunrise when it was wrapped within such a fury. She sat awake, determined to do her duty, to do exactly what Gaia said.

When the storm finally carried its bluster inland and a hint of gray could be seen within the black, Miho rose and dressed. She paused only to send a quick message to both Ojisan and Mr. Hernandez.

-WISH ME LUCK-

-AND UNDERSTANDING- She added, deciding it was more important than luck.

As she walked to the mermaid cove, her heart pounded harder than the waves at the shore. She tried not to be nervous about what was to come next. She would have to take each moment as it appeared. *Breathe-enso-breathe-enso.* She was trying to remember Sensei's lessons without worrying about Sensei himself.

A red sun ripped across the frothing cove, making the swells an almost unnatural rosy color. Gaia was waiting, bobbing high and low on the storm-whipped high tide. Miho stared down for a moment. How could it be that this magical creature had so much power to steer her life?

"Jump in, my dear; the water is fine!" Gaia called up. Her voice seemed to flicker on the rays of the rising sun.

Miho hoped she had rested enough to tackle whatever task lay ahead. She took a deep breath and reached into her memory to grab her father's voice. She raised her arms to the angry, red morning sky and yelled,

> *"She will start from her slumber*
> *When gusts shake the door*
> *She will hear the wind howling*
> *Will hear the waves roar.*
> *We shall see, while above us*
> *The waves roar and whirl,*
> *A ceiling of amber.*
> *A pavement of pearl.*
> *Singing, 'Here came a mortal,*
> *But faithless was she…"*

Miho stopped there. She knew there were a few more lines, something about kings of the sea. But, darn it, she wasn't faithless, she was here! She decided to redo the ending of that grand poem.

> *"Singing 'Here came a mortal,*
> *powerful was she*
> *A true Gaia Girl*
> *That dove into the sea!"*

Miho felt powerful! She did something she had never done before. She spread her arms wide, like wings, and leapt from the cliff's edge—no climbing down today—then plunged into the crazed, red, morning surf below! When she came up, Gaia was clapping her black paws together and laughing in a way that sounded like the chatter of happy dolphins.

"Wonderful! That was simply wonderful! It never ceases to amaze me how some humans are so deaf and others take what I say and turn it into the most glorious human song! Come, my love, the skin of the sea is whipped, but below, it is a beautiful day."

Gaia reached up and placed her paw on the back of Miho's head. At that moment, all the air left Miho, as if she had never needed lungs or air or sunlight, and down they went. Miho equalized her ears and reminded herself to relax. She took a quick peek toward the surface and saw that the blue sky of the day was now the size of a basketball, a softball, a golf ball, a pinprick, and...gone.

Gaia was right; at the depth the light of the new day failed, the sea was calm. Down in the blackness, there were only endless flowing currents pushing the water to the east. Gaia steered them into this current and with one small kick of her little otter feet, they shot off at a speed twice as fast as her dolphin friends!

Miho felt the excited chatter long before Gaia lifted her toward the light and towards her friends. As Gaia brought them up, the lags surrounded them. The images and squeals and clicks and buzzing began bashing Miho from all sides. They all wanted to know what had happened. Miho had no words.

A small snout nudged her ribs. Shinju! The young dolphin sent Miho a fast picture of the bay where the pod had been waylaid. Miho could feel her own heart, and Shinju's, break with the memory. *Ishin denshin.* Shinju began to share with the rest of the pod. She was telling the story.

For a long while, one in which Miho never needed to come up for air, members of the pod came to her with images and sound combinations that Miho knew were Dolphinese for, "Is this true?" and "How?" and "Why?" Miho did her best to share what she knew. All the while her heart beat out, "I'm sorry. I'm so sorry! I'm sorry! I will help you. All of you, I promise."

Shinju came to Miho and sent her pictures of the bay where they spent the night, of Ago-wan, of the yellowtail tuna Miho had brought from Ojisan's, the mermaid cove, and meeting Gaia. She then sent Miho a pulse that felt like it cooled the heat of Miho's shame. "Thank you," was what the small dolphin seemed to be saying.

"Come now," Gaia said, and began to place her paw on the back of Miho's head again. Miho didn't want to leave. She wanted to stay and help her friends, make it up to them. But this seemed to be her life—wanting to go back, but Gaia pulling her forward.

# 39
# Leviathan

Gaia and Miho journeyed along the very pulses of the ocean. Miho waited and wondered where Gaia would take her next. Their pace began to slow and they began to rise into the warmer water, the bluer water, the water kissed by sunlight and alive with the life that loved it.

When they broke the surface, it was a beautiful day. Whatever storm had stomped across the ocean and pounded into Goza was only a memory. All around Miho, nothing could be seen but deep blue swells rising and falling against a lighter blue sky. Far off, toward the impossibly distant horizon, clouds were being born. Miho could see the haze and each perfect puff growing as the day grew warmer.

Miho turned around a few times and saw that she was alone! Gaia's otter face was nowhere to be found. Miho had a brief moment of panic. But Gaia brought her here and she was certainly here for a reason. Miho floated on her back, eyes up to the fierce blue of the sky. Something was coming. Miho could feel a deep pulse and a building pressure below her. The fear left her completely and she laughed out loud when the whale blew.

"PPHHHHHHHOOOOO—AAAAAAAHHHH!" The blowhole atop the great grey mountain beside her sent a blast of steamy, mammalian breath up into the air. Miho rolled onto her side. Her nose was inches from an eye that was almost as large as her face! Miho could see her own smile reflected in the deep, dark iris of the

whale's eye. They looked at each other as if they were both trying to set the memory in place, every detail.

"Hello, my dear." The voice sounded like every wave-wish Miho had ever missed making. Gaia's whiskered sea otter snout appeared up over the rim of the wide, whale face.

"Gaia! Why did you leave me here? Why..." She wanted to know why the whale was with them. She wanted to know why she should feel fear, but didn't. She wanted to know...why.

"Well, I had to go fetch our friend here! And, there you go with that question again. Why ask why? Just be and feel the way of water. Haven't you been listening to Sensei?"

"You know Sensei? How? Does he know you?" Miho couldn't believe that Gaia had mentioned her teacher.

"You don't think you are the only one that talks to the earth, do you? A lot of people talk, but few listen and learn. I am the Sensei of every teacher, through all of history. Everything you smart, smart humans know, began with someone learning from me. Wakarimashtaka?"

Miho smiled. Yes, she understood, "Hai."

Gaia tilted her twitching nose down toward Miho. Miho felt the laugh passing from Gaia to the whale and, from the whale through the water, to her. She couldn't help it—she began to laugh too.

"Climb aboard, my dear! We have work to do, and you need to travel very far, very fast. Let us sail for a while and we will talk. I think maybe you are beginning to understand. It is time to go further and deeper."

Miho knew this was a humpback whale. She had seen its bumpy face and now, as it rolled up on its side, an impossibly long pectoral fin rose. Drops of water shimmering in the sunlight dripped off the long fin that was rising higher into the air. Miho grabbed on and was pulled onto the mottled grey skin of the leviathan.

A breeze that carried the smell of land, far off beyond the horizon, began to freshen and whip across the waves. The humpback whale raised its long pectoral fin into the sky and caught the breeze.

Miho leaned back against the fin and felt the push of air move the humpback's entire bulk through the sea. It was astounding—they were sailing! Miho remembered her mother talking about seeing humpback whales do this. But hearing about it and being a passenger on a whale-sailboat were two very different things!

Gaia began to pace back and forth in front of Miho and Miho knew it was time to settle back and listen. "To truly know the way of water, you must master waves."

Miho blurted out, "But I already know waves pretty good. I've been on boats in the deep ocean and been around rocks and tide pools, and I can even ride the waves!"

"That is but one kind of wave. All the world is waves. Even the hard earth on which you walk and live and feel so steady is moving in waves. The sun that is warming this ocean reaches us on waves, and the sound of my voice is coming to you as a wave."

Miho thought about that, all the world being made of waves. It was a hard thing to think about when there was something she wanted to know so badly, she just had to ask. "Gaia, I like whale-sailing, but I thought you said we had to go a long ways."

"First you must listen, deeper than you ever have before. Not only deeper inside, but deeper outside." Gaia resumed her little roundabout walk and Miho again leaned back against the whale's fin. "I know you understand a bit of the way of the great whales. You know they are often alone and making such a deep sound most people cannot hear them."

Gaia paused in her pacing to send her dark gaze deep into Miho. "Most people cannot hear, but you do, yes?"

"I've heard them, Gaia, those pings. My mother

would slow down the tapes and you could hear the tones. Sometimes I thought I could hear them in the boat, too."

"You have heard them more than you know. They have been calling you. It is the whales who helped me find you."

"Will I be able to talk to whales?" Miho asked, her voice a thin whisper that could barely be heard above the sighing wind.

Gaia laughed. "It may be hard for you to talk to them. You simply are not large enough to make the sounds their ears can hear. However, the language of the heart is not lost with whales."

*Ishin Denshin! Heart-to-heart communication! Is this why Sensei wanted her to know this?* Miho held her breath.

"The song of the whales is yours to use," Gaia continued. "The waves of sound they send through the seas will be like the waves you ride to shore. They will get you where you need to be." Gaia stopped pacing and set her front paws up on Miho's folded legs. Her broad, black nose flared and twitched, and every whisker on her bushy face had a little quiver to it. Miho sensed that Gaia was scanning her in an almost dolphin-like way.

"Are you ready?"

Miho had as many questions for Gaia as the pod of

lags had thrown at her: *Why? How?* But there was only one thing to say.

"Hai."

Gaia slid off the humpback and Miho followed her in. The humpback rolled and exhaled a wondrous plume of breath into the sky. It tilted its large whale head downward and rolled its massive weight up and through the balmy air. The tail lifted, glistening and dripping golden droplets of water down on Miho and Gaia.

*Whale wishes,* Miho thought, looking up at the glimmer of sun passing through the droplets. She watched the tail slip effortlessly into the depths and turned to Gaia.

"Is she leaving?"

"No dear, she is preparing to send you, finding layers of warm and cold water and setting the course. Whales have their own talking lines, you know. I hope you don't mind, but you will need to let our large friend here take you into her mouth."

"Her mouth? You mean, like, swallow me?" Miho's own mouth opened in shock and disbelief. Let a whale swallow her? That was crazy!

Gaia said, "She will let you sit on her tongue as she heads to the great shelf of earth. She will take you down to transmission level. You will feel the call coming. Listen deeply. See the wave and grab on. It will be the best wave ride you have ever had."

The whale surfaced again and the BOOM of the blow made Miho jump. Her heart began to beat double-time! The tingling in her arms and legs felt a bit like the fear that had gripped her when she punched the shark.

The whale parted its lips, and the dark space beyond the brushy, hanging baleen looked as large and dark as a garage. Miho parted the baleen, like stiff curtains, and swam on in. She turned to look back at Gaia.

Gaia, in her very sea otter-like fashion, floated belly up on the sea with her feet poking out above the waves. Miho couldn't stand the suspense any longer. She yelled out through the closing baleen curtains. "Where am I going?" She didn't remember if she yelled it in English, Japanese, or maybe even Dolphinese, but she remembered Gaia's answer.

It came on a laugh that sounded like every fun beach Miho had ever played on, "NEW YORK!"

# 40

# Ping

N *ew York?* Miho thought she must have misunderstood. But the whale's mouth was closing; there was just time to catch Gaia's last call, "See you on the other side!" It sounded like the last flicker of sunlight before the whale closed its mouth and all went dark.

Miho now crouched in utter blackness. She felt a push in the water and behind her the giant, thick, fleshy whale tongue lifted and pressed forward. Miho was pushed right up against the baleen! She knew how whales used their tongues and baleen, so she wasn't surprised to feel the water around her draining out through the long bristles.

When the tongue retreated, she was able to ride it down and stand hunched over upon it. She gripped a few strands of baleen and held her mind back from wondering what was coming next.

Behind her, great blasts of air began to pump. She could hear the snap of the blowhole opening and closing. The long, deep inhales and vibrating hollow exhales continued three, four, five times.

*She's gonna dive deep*, Miho thought. She had watched enough whales to know when they were priming their lungs for a long dive. Miho was just starting to wonder if she too, should take a deep breath, when the whale, tongue and all, tilted and began to roll.

Miho's feet lifted right up off the tongue! It was as if she were in an airplane going into a steep dive! She clutched the baleen and squeezed her eyes shut. She opened them again when she realized—whether her eyes were open or not—she saw only the same deep black.

She sensed the pressure outside getting stronger; inside the whale there was only a slight change. After a time, the whale leveled off. Miho loosened her grip on the baleen and felt a tremendous pressure building up behind her. She sent all her attention to her ears and waited.

The whale's ping issued forth! It looked like wild bands of blue around her! She focused her eyes (her ears?) on one waving blue band. Miho grabbed it and held her breath as the whale's mouth opened. Out into the black realm Miho flew!

She clung to the blue strand with both hands and was pulled violently forward. The cold blackness that rushed by had hints of sounds and creatures, but before Miho's mind could even begin to wonder, she was miles ahead. She heard the oncoming, rhythmic chugging of a big ocean liner, but it passed overhead and was out behind her before her mind could finish thinking, *big ship*.

She flew on and on, not hearing the sound, but being borne upon it. She hooked her elbow over the racing blue line and let go with one hand. She relaxed and lengthened her body, streamlining herself as she did when she rode with the pod of white-sided dolphins.

The cold, cold water was rushing past her so fast she didn't have time to *be* cold. She flew like this for many minutes; sometimes her blue line—her wave of whale ping—would angle up and bump against the warmer layer of water. Sometimes it angled down and bounced off the colder, denser water below. The bumps and bounces didn't hurt, but they did make her tighten her grip. She couldn't imagine what would happen if she bounced off, way down here in the darkest, coldest place of the world!

She sensed a change ahead. She wasn't sure how she

knew. It was like falling asleep in the back of the car and somehow knowing you are close to home. She felt the blue line she was clinging to bend sharply. Miho was rising along a seamount—an underwater mountain. It rose up until it was only a few hundred feet from the surface. Someday, this seamount would lift its face from the sea and become a new island.

But for now, it was still far below. Miho was dragged up its steep side. She wished she could stop at the crest and explore the thousands of creatures that flourished where the warm and the cold of the sea met. But she only had a moment to regard the wondrous whirl of living things around her before she pushed right up against, and then through, baleen.

Miho rolled onto another hot, wet tongue! Thousands of gallons of water rolled in with her and for a moment she was trapped in a spinning, swirling whirlpool. But as before, the enormous tongue began to lift and press forward. Miho, understanding what was happening, grasped tightly to the baleen and waited for the water to get pushed out.

She dropped back onto the tongue. She sensed the immensity of the creature and a feeling like, "Welcome." She had no idea if this great being would understand her or not, but, in her heart and mind, she bowed in respect and said, "Ohayo, most honorable whale."

With her greeting, Miho felt the snout tip up and the quick rise to the surface pressed her down into the fleshy tongue. She felt the huge body bend and roll and all around her the great "PPPPPOOOOOOOSSHHHH-WHAAAAAAAAAAHHHH" signaled the whale's arrival on the surface. The lips parted and Miho was first pushed back by the incoming water, but then swept out into the warm, turquoise sea. Gaia was waiting for her.

# 41
# Crushing Cold

Miho's heart was beating triple time! She wasn't completely sure what had just happened. She looked around and found that she was still in open water, no land in sight. She was still next to a great humpback whale, one whose laughing eye was inches from her own and Gaia was there too, laughing. "You did it! I knew you could!" Her round, sea otter face was alive with joy.

"Gaia, what happened? And how can you be here? You were there! I think it was a long ways back. It felt like a long way." Miho paused to catch her breath. "What happened?"

"Grab on and I will explain," Gaia said, and paddled over close to the whale. As the first whale had, the great, grey creature rolled on its side and lifted its long pectoral fin from the ocean. Miho grabbed on and was hoisted onto the broad belly of the humpback. This whale too, caught the breeze with its fin. Miho leaned back and told her heart to slow down. Gaia began to walk and talk in her weird otter way.

"You, my dear, just rode a wave halfway across the big sea, I believe you call it Pa-ci-fic. Yes?"

"Hai, Yes. It's called the Pacific, but that was no wave! What was that? Where are we? How are you here too?" Miho couldn't help it. The questions were piled up so thick that some spilled out. She needed to know.

"I am here because I am the whole of the earth. I am everywhere because I am everything. But enough about me. You, my friend, just rode a whale's call. A sound is a wave as much as a wave on a beach is a wave. You surfed this one marvelously!"

"I..." Miho wanted to ask another question; but now the questions faded, all dried up on her tongue. She was sitting on yet another whale, out in the middle of the Pacific Ocean, maybe a thousand miles from Goza, talking to an otter. There probably were not enough answers to explain all this. Miho decided a practical question was best. "Where am I going next? And, am I going on a whale's ping?"

"Smart girl! Yes. Your next stop is quite cold. I don't want you to be frightened by that. You will be fine."

"Will you be there?"

"No. I must go on ahead. There is something I must attend to in New York. I will see you there. This is your first mission. Do not worry; you have friends to help you get there."

"But Gaia! How..." Miho's question didn't have a chance to come out because the humpback whale rolled and dumped them both into the water. When Miho came up for air, Gaia was again...gone.

Miho gritted her back teeth together. This was all very confusing, and she had no idea what was really happening. It was like...well, it was like Shodo. No one could really tell you how to do it. You just had to do it. She waited for the whale to dive, presumably to find the 'talking lines,' as Gaia called them. She treaded water and watched as a large albatross flapped in its big, lazy way across the horizon.

She wondered how far away New York was and how many whales it would take to get there. She had never been to New York, but knew that not a heck of a lot of it bordered the ocean. She wondered if she would end up at the Statue of Liberty or maybe out on Long Island somewhere. She tried not to think about the thousand and one reasons Gaia might want her in New York.

When the great humpback resurfaced and parted its lips, Miho didn't hesitate; she swam in past the baleen and turned to face forward. The bright day closed down as the whale closed its mouth. She clung to the hard bristles as the water around her rushed out and then felt her stomach flip as the steep dive began.

Miho sat on the hot cushion of the whale's tongue and thought about where her next stop might be. Gaia said it would be cold. She thought about the map of the world in her Social Studies book.

If she were going to New York, she would have to get around South America to reach other side of North America! She must be heading south, into Antarctic waters. Miho hadn't been there, but her parents had. Many whales—blues and seis, right whales and bowheads, fin whales and even the smaller minkes—went there to feed on huge swarms of krill. She pressed her body closer to the warm tongue and tried not to think about what her mother had called, "crushing cold."

She felt the humpback whale level off and began to sense the same buildup as before. She took a deep breath and waited for the ping. The big sound began to swirl around her. She saw the waving blue lines and grabbed on. As soon as she did, the whale parted its lips and she shot off into the blue!

She gripped the sound wave close to her heart

and squeezed her eyes shut. Not that it made much difference at this depth. Gaia was right: the world of water was mostly black. No wonder listening was so important! Again, the ride was so fast that she could barely scan what was around her.

She began to send a constant scan to the ocean floor. It was amazing to "see" all the hills and valleys, just like on land. Some of the chasms she flew over would put the Grand Canyon to shame. The mountains too, were mind-boggling in their scale.

Miho got hints of the life thriving in this hidden world. As she raced through the sea at the speed of sound, she got glimpses of clusters of living things. Sometimes they were bunched around what seemed to be plumes of smoke. Miho hoped someday Gaia would take her that deep.

Once, she passed over the shape of a fallen whale— mostly bones, but still teeming with life. Miho stopped scanning and thought back to when Gaia said that every day some things live and some things die. The day that whale died, a thousand other things found a source of life.

Miho gripped her blue ping wave tighter and let herself think about her mother and father. They were dead. But, because they were, she had gone to Japan, to Goza. She had met Gaia. Maybe because of all this, more beings would live.

She imagined that if she could use what Gaia had given her to tell everyone the real world of dolphins, no one would want to hurt them. She imagined if Ojisan could make people want to buy air freshener, maybe he would know how to tell them about the huge eyes and heart and love that whales possess.

Miho tightened her grip as she felt the ping hit a seamount and begin to rise up. She opened her eyes— the black was becoming a lesser black. She smiled, as best she could in the crazy speed of the ping, thinking of her Shodo ink washing down the drain. The lesser black turned to gray and the gray turned to a thinner gray and then she hit a whale!

This whale didn't open its mouth to let Miho roll onto its soft tongue. She banged up against the whiskered face so hard it felt like the time she had fallen from the crow's nest on Mr. Hernandez's research boat. Miho had been horsing around and lost her footing. Landing on the deck had driven all the air from her body and made her see stars. All the grownups agreed it was a miracle that none of her bones had been broken.

Miho lost her breath this time too. But after her massive exhale, she inhaled a thousand knives! The intensely cold water hit her lungs and seemed to steal all sense from her. The whale, mercifully, opened its mouth and let her roll in with the frigid seawater.

Miho gagged and gasped as the whale tongue pushed the water out through the baleen. This wasn't the same kind of mouth as the humpbacks. This mouth was much longer and narrower. Miho thought it could be a fin whale...maybe even a rare blue whale!

Part of her wished she could be outside to see. The more sensible part was grateful to be in the hot, mammalian mouth instead of out there in the icy waters. She continued to cough, ejecting the last of the salt water from her lungs. She felt the whale begin to rise.

She lay flat on its tongue, knowing the whale would have to breathe before sending her onward. *Northward?* She patted the tongue a few times, wondering if this massive creature could feel this gesture. She rolled onto her back and called up toward the hairy, baleen-fringed roof of the mouth, "Domo arigato. Thank you."

Miho waited. And waited. She began to feel sleepy. It had been a very long and crazy day. She had just begun to nod off when her whole body lifted off the cozy, warm tongue. The huge whale began its deep descent. Miho was quickly alert and prepared herself for yet another 'ping ride.'

This time, as she shot off into the black, the shock of the cold almost made her let go of the sound wave. She squeezed the wave tighter and squeezed her eyes closed against the tremendous speed. This time, she didn't try to scan; she simply rode.

Minutes passed as she streaked northward. Miho could feel the water become noticeably warmer. How many more whales would it take to get her to New York? And then what? Was she supposed to swim to shore and ask for Gaia? She clenched her jaw, still frustrated with the lingering questions of this mission.

The ping wave bounced a bit against the layers of warm and cold, but Miho now expected that and didn't worry too much about the bumps and jolts. The wave hit the rise of yet another seamount, and she began to anticipate hitting yet another whale snout.

But as the ping-wave crested the seamount, she encountered something other than a whale.

# 42
# Gaia Chica

As the sound wave crested the ridge of the seamount, it began to lose its structure! The water was in turmoil and there was no greeting whale. Instead, the water was full of debris: bits of coral, bits of fish, bits of the seamount's very earth! It all spun and churned and filled the water with a great confusion.

The ping-wave that Miho had been clinging to disintegrated into whorls of muck-filled water. Her ears filled up with dreadful clanging, dragging sounds! She tried to send out a scanning sonar, but couldn't overcome the hideous scraping that filled the sea with both the sounds and sights of utter destruction.

Miho was adrift, spinning free at a depth that would be unsafe to free dive to. She let loose a few bubbles of air to know which way was up. Looking skyward, she saw a pinprick of light blue. There waited her life-giving air. Her panicked heartbeat thrummed the question, *Can I get there?* She began to kick. *I may have enough, I could have enough air...but...Oh! The, what are they called? The bends!*

Anyone who ever donned a mask, snorkel, or scuba tank had to know about the bends. When one rose too fast, the life-giving air bubbles in the bloodstream would expand—just as a bubble blown underwater did. But the air bubbles that traveled veins and arteries could get too big, too fast. The bends could twist you into knots of agony—the bends could kill you!

Miho didn't have a choice. She had no scuba tank and therefore couldn't pause in her ascent. If she had a scuba tank, she could stop and wait for her body to adjust to the releasing of pressure from the deep. But she had to breathe—just like a dolphin, just like a whale.

Miho kicked hard for the surface. Gaia had gifted her the ability to scan with sonar, talk to dolphins and ride the ping-waves. She hoped against hope that another gift from Gaia would now allow her to surface without being twisted into a thousand painful knots.

The circle of light above her grew and the water around her began to dance with spinning strands of sunlight. She released the last of her air and burst to the surface. Miho turned her face to the hazy sky above, treading water, and waiting for the twisting pains of the dreaded bends. But the bends didn't come. Miho laughed a laugh that came from the deepest place in her body—the place the bends would have pretzeled and crushed had Gaia not given her yet another power to take into the water!

Still smiling, she looked around. Chugging away from her was some kind of fishing vessel, surrounded by a cloud of screeching gulls. Miho hoped they couldn't see her. Then hoped they could. Then hoped they couldn't.

She twirled her arms and legs in the green-gray sea.

The surface was choppy and the sun pounded down. Miho was glad she was in the water, because the heat of the day was intense. Not knowing what else to do, she kicked back and lay prone, ears underwater and eyes to the sky.

Did Gaia know that the last ping-wave would be disrupted by whatever created that man-made mayhem? Did Gaia know that she was adrift in what was surely the open water of the Atlantic Ocean?

"At-lan-tic," Miho whispered, imagining how Gaia might say it. The Atlantic, after all, was part of Gaia and that word, Atlantic, was just the human way of describing the place. "At-lan-tic," Miho whispered again.

She closed her eyes against the bright sun. She could hear her own blood squooshing through her ears with a rhythmic, "shooosh, shooosh, shooosh." She focused on that sound, her circulation, the fluid movement that was her life force.

The oceans and the rivers and the rain were like Gaia's blood. Miho listened to the rhythm of her own blood in her ears and imagined that each "shooosh" she heard was her brush making one stroke of the kanji for satoru satori—understanding.

She floated, the sound of her heartbeat making Shodo in the sea. Maybe she slept. Maybe not. Her body felt light. "Shooosh, shooosh" went the sound of her blood. Perhaps she slept. Perhaps not.

"Hola, Gaia Chica!" A girl's voice and bird-like twitter of laughter startled Miho. She sat up and started to tread water. Except, she was no longer in the water!

Miho's arms and legs twirled like egg-beaters in a cold gray-white thickness that she didn't understand. It was like the thickest fog she ever saw. But it wasn't fog! "Where am I?" Miho called into the bleakness. "Gaia? No... You're not Gaia! Who are you?"

Miho hoped her voice didn't show the fear beginning to grip her belly. A dolphin would know, but that voice didn't come from a dolphin. That voice had said, "Hola," just like Mr. Hernandez!

As she waited for an answer, a deep boom echoed around her. It was almost like a whale's call, except a wild, white light chased the sound through the gray.

"Relaje, Gaia Chica," a girl's voice said. The high-pitched chirping voice surrounded Miho.

"Wakarimasen," Miho called into the gloom. And then she realized her linguistic mistake. Miho scrambled through her mind for the long-unused Spanish words she knew. She dug deep into her memory. She flipped through all the warm, happy days in Baja.

"Yo no entiendo," Miho said, hoping her Spanish for

"I don't understand," was as decent as her Japanese.

The girl's voice swirled around her in tight, practiced English, "Gaia tell me, tell you—this my mission, take *you* to *your* mission!"

"Your mission is to take me to my mission?" Miho hoped her voice was able to penetrate the cold, thin grayness. She hoped her voice wasn't shaking.

"Si," the voice answered. Miho knew this was Spanish for 'yes.' "Sea valiente-Be brave, Gaia-chica."

Miho's quick mind had already made the translation of "Be brave, Gaia Girl." She thought, *I've lost my parents, been sent to Japan, been lost in the ocean, seen my friends skewered and hauled from the sea! I have kimo!* Miho was grateful for the reminder.

The chirping, happy voice said, in English, "Rain falls down." Whoever, or whatever, had held Miho up, let go! Miho began to fall! As the gray around her began to thin, she realized she was falling from the sky! Her arms wanted to pinwheel, to grab onto something, but she couldn't feel her arms!

Streaking toward the green earth below was as exhilarating as zipping through the ocean, but it was more terrifying! Miho was completely powerless; gravity had all the control. She wanted to yell. But what could she yell? She wanted to close her eyes, but

330 | Lee Welles

a morbid curiosity wanted to see where she would land and what it would look like when she did.

Because she was curious, she found the guts, *kimo*, to look around a moment. All around, fat raindrops fell with her. A flash streaked around her. The flash lit each and every drop with a hot white light. It was like a wave-wish magnified a thousand times!

*I'm raining—I'm water and I'm raining down!* When the next flash of lightning coursed around her, she wished, *Please, let me land in one piece!*

Miho looked down. A thin, brown squiggle could be seen, winding its way through puffs of green trees and squares of light and dark green fields. Miho knew from all her years of looking at maps that the squiggle must be a creek or river.

She wished desperately for the comfort of a whale-ping to hold onto! But there was no whale-ping to hold, to trust, just the memory of a high, bird-like voice telling her to, "Be brave." The squiggly line of the creek grew bigger and bigger. The creek was rushing up to meet her! Miho squeezed her eyes shut.

# 43
# Be Brave

SPLASH! The sound of her landing was so loud that it seemed to fill every pore of her being! The fresh water was a startling slap after so many days spent in the sea. When Miho surfaced, she realized she was moving at great speed.

She barely had time to look around at the mist-coated tall hills. This rich, green place was swollen with rain and alive in a way that almost sang. The leaves that dangled out over the creek winked at her from their rain droplets. Miho imagined that each droplet whispered, "Be brave. Be brave."

Miho didn't feel very brave; she felt out of control! The creek was bloated and rushing like the subway during O-bon. She did what she could to keep her head above water as she was swept downstream. The roaring creek was more frightening than any wave she had ever ridden.

Miho tried to swim against the flow. It was as tiring and pointless as swimming against a riptide. *All rivers flow to the sea.* Her father's voice bubbled up in the muddy, frothing water. Miho held the thought and kept repeating, *To the sea. To the sea. To the sea. I can get back home. I am Ama!*

"You may be a woman of the sea, but you are forgetting the way of water, my dear." The voice had a deep laughing quality, much like the bumping, roaring brown creek Miho was caught in. Her mouth popped open in surprise. She almost took in a mouthful of water. *Gaia's here!* Gaia was riding the same muddy creek as Miho. However, Gaia had changed a bit—thinner and sleeker, her nose a bit more pointed with fewer whiskers.

"Gaia! This is awful! I can't…hardly…ugh…keep my head above water! Why…" Miho's question was cut short as an unexpected eddy pulled her under and filled her open mouth with nasty, muddy water.

Gaia laughed and it sounded like the very raindrops that still pattered around them. "Silly girl! Who said you had to stay above water? I thought you would know by now you can stay under as long as your dolphin friends. You can not only stay under, Miss Ama, but you know how to look with your ears and not your eyes, yes?"

Miho didn't want to open her mouth to that horrid brown water again, so she simply nodded.

"Well then, let's go under and do some good! Your mission, my dear, is to find the knife and then find the girl. That is all. I will care for the dog. Just find the knife and then find the girl. Help her if she needs it. Wakarimashtaka?"

"Hai." What else could Miho say? A load of questions would only prolong her time on the bouncing, unpredictable surface of the storm-bloated stream. She took a deep breath and dove.

Once under, the roaring of the creek became a constant sort of background noise. Miho scanned out in front of her. As the waves of sound came back, she perceived the rise and fall, the twists and turns, that made the contours of this stream. The storm had made the stream into an obstacle course. Miho could "see" branches, soda cans, plastic bags and bottles, trout and crawdads doing their best to keep their places and…

Miho intensified her scanning. Up ahead, there seemed to be a whole bush bobbing and turning in the water. Caught within were two creatures! Miho's scan revealed two wildly beating hearts. There was a four-legged creature, a large…dog? Yes! A very big dog and a…a girl? It was a girl about her own size! The girl and the dog and the bush were caught in the tumble of the mindless, whirling stream.

Miho had found the girl, but what knife was Gaia talking about? Miho wondered if her Hokusai hand had any power in this freshwater place. Could she reverse such a furious flow of water with a wave of her hand?

She was just dismissing this idea because she still had some doubts that she had indeed created the rogue waves. Suddenly, the two creatures separated. The dog and the bush were pulled into the center of the raging creek. The girl began to pull toward the shore. A thin object sliced down through the middle of Miho's sonar-scan. The knife!

Miho kicked hard and let the raging stream double her efforts. She scanned the turning, gravel bottom more intensely. It was harder than looking for pearls! The noise of the turning rocks confused her scan and it was hard to ignore the image of the large dog trying to fight to the surface as it was swept downstream.

But Gaia had told her what her mission was—find the knife, then find the girl. She ended up having to turn and kick against the current to stay where she first saw the knife enter the water.

Finally, the form became apparent. Miho reached out her hand to grab it. When the bone-like handle was

safely in her grasp, she turned her scan toward the girl. Miho could see the girl's heart beating wildly, but there was a slow, leaden quality to the way she swam.

Miho kicked as strongly as she could to reach the struggling girl. She finally set the knife between her teeth and carefully bit down to hold it. She needed both hands. She looped three fingers of one hand through the belt loops of the girl's pants. Her other hand kept pulling toward the bank.

When she felt the exhausted girl pull herself onto the shore, Miho let go and let the stream take her away. She was tired too! Remembering her lessons of traveling with the lags, she relaxed her body, let the creek do the work, and simply rolled to grab air when needed.

Soon, she felt the tight, fast energy of the creek begin to slack into a larger, wider body of water. She surfaced to see that she was in a river. The river, like the creek, was fat with rainwater and lined with trees. Miho swam to the muddy bank, grabbed some willow roots and pulled herself out.

Gaia had said, 'find the knife and then find the girl.' Miho figured 'the girl' was the one she had just helped to shore. She knew she shouldn't go further downstream. Should she walk back upstream or stay here? Miho brushed her hair from her forehead and kept her eyes on the delta where the creek met the river.

A girl with brown braids, tangled with debris from the stream, came stumbling around the bend. She was calling, "Maizey! Maizey!" Miho assumed Maizey was the dog and hoped that Gaia had seen to her safety. The skinny girl with the mussed-up braids staggered along. It was obvious that fighting the raging stream had exhausted her. She cried, "Maizey," once more, then turned and grabbed her belly.

Miho heard a retching sound and figured the poor girl had tossed her cookies onto the muddy river bank. She knew exactly how this girl was feeling. She felt the same when she saw Star being lifted from the sea. She felt the same sick feeling knowing the Three Stooges were gone. She also knew what a bit of hope could do.

Miho saw the exhausted girl fall to her knees in the mud. A breeze began to stir and it was as if the rumbling of the angry river merged with the anguish of the kneeling girl. A sort of song tickled Miho's ears.

"Ohayo! Hello!" Miho called out and began to walk toward the girl, mud squelching up between her toes. But the girl didn't look up. It was as if her grief and exhaustion kept her face turned toward the muddy ground. The girl didn't look up until Miho's feet were right under her nose.

Miho wondered what to say and in what language to say it. She decided words didn't always say what someone needed to hear. *Ishin Denshin*—Miho simply smiled and held out the knife. The poor girl's eyes bulged with astonishment. Miho had to hold back a laugh.

Gaia's voice tumbled along on the breeze. What she said seemed like an answer to a question Miho hadn't heard. "We did come to help," Gaia said. "We helped you reach the shore."

Miho turned to see Gaia's new, sleek river otter face poking above the roiling water. The brown-haired girl yelled, "You helped? You helped this happen?"

"No dear," Gaia said, "You did this. We just helped you out."

Miho knew the sad, wet, scratched-up girl kneeling in the mud before her was feeling the same confusion she did in the wake of Gaia's riddles. So Miho decided to pass along the advice given to her by the voice in the clouds. "Be brave," Miho said in a small voice, barely loud enough to be heard above the river. Then she set the knife before the angry, tired girl. Miho turned to dive back into the river.

Miho scanned and kicked or pulled to change course

and avoid the debris that was swept along with her in that wide, unknown river. She scanned and saw that Gaia was with her. She wanted to speak to Gaia, but wanted to stay underwater, away from the bouncing, wild surface. She did her best in Dolphinese. She sent a picture of the kneeling girl along with the sound of questioning. "Who was that?" Miho asked.

Gaia's voice blended in with every burble and clatter and chatter of the river. "She is like you. But she is of the flesh and the bones. You are of the blood." Another Gaia riddle! Miho resisted the questions. She knew that there was no way to ask such abstract things in her newfound underwater language of image and sound.

She sent Gaia a picture of the mermaid chair, of Goza, coupled again with the dolphin way of implying a question. Gaia's voice came rolling through the foam and debris. "You will get back the way you came. All water flows to the sea. This is my blood, the seas, my heart. That is why I need you, dear one; my heart is being broken."

Miho's mind flashed to the destruction that had disrupted her last whale ping. She surfaced for a breath and Gaia was there, her large brown otter eyes filled with a longing that Miho knew. It was the longing for understanding, for love, for help. It was the longing she had carried in her own heart every moment of every day since she last saw her own mother and father.

Miho spoke aloud, risking another mouthful of the vile, muddy water. "Gaia, I'll do everything I can to help you." Thinking of Sensei, she asked, "What do you need most?"

"Understanding," Gaia said. Miho's mind flashed to the kanji form. "The minds of the land do not understand the minds in the water. They are blind to the very deepest places of my heart—the dark and cold, but very alive places. They forget their fates are combined with mine. You are the bridge of understanding, Miho-san."

Miho's mind held this last statement as tightly as she held the dorsal fins of the lags. *Understanding—satoru satori.*

"Come, my Ama friend. I will speed your return." Again, Gaia placed her small otter paw on the back of Miho's head and ducked her under. The river around them became a passing, creamy blur.

Time blurred. Miho didn't think and never needed to come up for air. The water became saltier and colder and when Miho came back to herself she was once again alone in the open water of…of Gaia's heart.

# 44
# Three Names

Miho leaned back in the gray swells and listened to the rhythm of her own heart. The whooshing in her ears was as comforting as the constant sounds of waves and tides and seabirds that had always wrapped around her life.

She wasn't afraid. She wasn't brave. She was simply certain that Gaia knew how she would get home. Into the quick rhythm of her own heartbeat came a low repeat, a low thrum that she knew.

The thrum became a push—a push of displaced water, followed by a heat, a presence and finally a great POOOOOOOSSHH-AAHHHHH! The great breath of a great being of the sea. Miho laughed and looked into yet another huge, deep, thoughtful eye.

Miho wished she knew the whale's name so that she could greet it with the proper, honorific Japanese. As this thought crossed her mind, an image chased it.

The picture was of a hot, blazing sunset—the kind that set the horizon on fire. Against the backdrop of this sunset, a whale leapt. The breaching whale crashed to the surface of the sea with a boom and a splash that made the sunset shimmer in delight. It was as if the ocean applauded at such a performance!

The name rippled through Miho's mind on the heels of the image, *"Sunset Dancer."* She closed her eyes. *My mother was right—they do all have names! And I'll learn them all.*

She wiped the hint of tear that teetered in the corner of her left eye and said aloud in her best, most polite Japanese, "It is an honor to meet you, Sunset Dancer-san. Please send me south to your friends."

The whale parted its lips and Miho gladly allowed herself to be swept in along with thousands of gallons of water. She knew this gift now, this Gaia power. Her heart warmed with a new thought, *This is how I will get to Taiji!*

She held the baleen and waited for the thick flesh of the whale's tongue to push the water out and for the deep dive to begin. Riding the whale ping was not as scary, now that she knew what was happening and why and how it would end. *Understanding. Nothing is as scary when you understand what is happening.*

As before, another whale scooped her from the biting chill of the southern waters. It must have been a right whale, for its mouth was tall enough for her to stand in! She inquired and learned this whale's name too—*Ice Runner*. Maybe it was "Racer." She couldn't actually hear the great whales speaking. It was more like having a thought that was not her own swish through her mind. She barely had learned this whale's name when it dove, leveled, and sent her on her way to the warm and balmy blue of the mid-Pacific.

Miho had no idea how long each ping took to send her through the hundreds, maybe even thousands of miles of open water. But she sensed the sky above graying, darkening, and lightening up once more. As she streaked along, she tried to combine what little she could glimpse of the sky with what she knew about time differences around the world.

She finally gave up. It was like a super-hard word problem in a math book. Miho knew that in this case, understanding didn't help her much. It was what it was. She would know when she was in her room in Goza and could look at the time/date stamp on her cell phone.

In the endless clear water of the Pacific tropics she met a humpback whose name could only be thought of as *Laughter*. And why not? She once met a lady named

Joy. Why couldn't a whale be named Laughter?

By the time Miho did see the familiar shoreline of Goza, she was full to bursting with love and laughter. Her mother would have loved this! Miho could learn the names of whales and knew how to travel between them as they shared the news of the wider seas.

She called a few times to see if the lags were anywhere nearby. Nothing but the pops of snapping shrimp and the endless rumble of waves came to her ears. *It must be time to get home*, Miho thought, then laughed. *Home. I guess Goza is home.* Miho was looking forward to seeing her Oji and Sensei and even grumpy old Tomiko. She was also starving. For all she knew, it had been two days since she had last eaten.

She climbed the hill on leaden legs. The light of the full moon was just beginning to skip across the crest of the hill, as if it were already bored with Ago-wan and sought the wilder water of the sea. Miho was relieved to see that the lights were on at Ojisan's house. *Our house.*

The smell of Ojisan's cigarette signaled his presence. Sure enough, after she passed the front gate, there he was.

She wanted to rush to him for a hug and gush out the story of her wide-ranging travels. Instead, she gathered what was left of her energy, bowed politely, and said, "I am pleased to see you, Ojisan. How have you been?"

A strange expression twisted his face; he opened and closed his mouth several times. Miho could tell that he was testing out several things to say to her before he said anything at all. Finally he gave his head a couple shakes, as if to clear out the competing words and simply said, "Konbanwa, Miho-san. I am...relieved to see that you are well."

Miho had her own competing words. Part of her wanted to say, "Wow! Ojisan, you're not yelling!" Part of her wanted to tell him the wonders of traveling by whale-ping. However, Miho, being more Japanese every day, continued the polite conversation. "Shinju is with her pod, her family."

Ojisan smiled, pleased. It was a real smile, and it was startling how much he looked like her mother. "You must be tired from your journey," her polite and understanding Oji said. "Take a shower and I will prepare a meal."

Miho's more American half couldn't stand it any longer. She took a giant, bounding step and wrapped her arms around his waist. "Thank you. Domo," she whispered. He ruffled her salt-laden hair and said, "Come."

# 45
# Yabai!

Miho told Ojisan the whole story. She watched him go from astounded to skeptical and back again. One minute he would look wide-eyed, like a little kid; the next he would guffaw and roll his eyes. But he kept saying, "And then what happened?"

She was relieved to hear that Sensei was a bit better. Sensei had even beaten Ojisan at a game of Go! Miho laughed as Ojisan described Tomiko hovering and hinting that Sensei should be in bed, not playing games. As the evening deepened and Goza quieted, the spaces in the conversation lengthened. Miho didn't mind. It was a comfortable silence.

When Ojisan began patting his pocket, looking for cigarettes, Miho didn't hesitate. She reached out and grabbed his searching hand. "Don't," she said in English. "Don't steal yourself from me."

"It not so easy," he replied, also in English.

"Was learning Aikido easy? Was it easy to move to Nagoya? You're smart; you know how to do hard things."

"Good point." He wiped his hand on his pant leg, as if to brush away the urge to let his fingers climb into his pocket for cigarettes. "So what is next? What does this Gaia want you to do?"

Miho was about to say she didn't know, but found she did know! "I am going to Taiji. They have planned a...Oikomi." She hated the bouncy sound of the word that meant so much sadness and destruction to the minds in the water.

"Yabai!" Ojisan almost shouted. Miho's mind whispered, *Risky? Yes. Yabai means risky.* She watched the lines of Ojisan's face deepen as his old, familiar scowl came back. "This is no game, Miho-san. People have gone to Taiji many times to stop Oikomi. People get hurt, go to jail."

Miho thought about this. "They won't see me. I won't get close. And I'll make sure that no cetaceans get close."

"Cetaceans?" Ojisan didn't get the English word she said.

"Hai—whales, dolphins, porpoises." Ojisan still looked concerned. "Yaranakucha," She added, amazed that, just as she understood Ojisan's 'Yabai,' she somehow knew how to say, "I gotta do it!"

Ojisan didn't look convinced. As a matter of fact, he began to look anguished, trying to think of what to say to her. Miho reached out her hand to clasp his, this time gently, and said, "I am Ama."

"Hai."

～

The next morning Ojisan and Miho went to see Sensei. Tomiko was busy with customers and barely gave them a second look as she waved them out the back door toward the garden. But Sensei wasn't in the garden. Miho saw the pair of shoes outside the classroom door and knew where he was. She nudged Ojisan in the ribs.

They both entered and bowed. She let Ojisan make the greetings and looked closely at her teacher. He was pale and, if possible, even smaller than before. But his eyes brightened at the sight of them, and he rose to make his return greetings.

Miho left the two men murmuring together in the front of the room and wandered back to the shelf that held the brushes, stones and ink. A few times, she heard her name in the conversation. She got the idea that Ojisan was seeking Sensei's advice. Would he tell her teacher all she had told him? What if Sensei didn't believe her, called her a liar? What if he said it was too dangerous for her to go to Taiji?

She used a brush to write the courage kanji, kimo, over and over in the dust on the windowsill. She needed courage, not so much for Taiji, but to be patient as these men discussed her future. She knew what her uncle had thought of her mother running off to talk to whales and dolphins, and she worried.

The windowsill was laced with kimo when Ojisan barked, "Miho!" It startled her and as she spun around; she dropped the brush on the floor. She retrieved it and hurried to the front of the room, heart pounding like drums at O-bon. She stared at the floor and clenched her jaw. What would she say if Ojisan commanded that she couldn't go? But he didn't command anything. He asked her a question.

"Sensei and I would like to know why you feel you must go to Taiji." Miho looked up at the two sets of dark eyes and had to bite her lower lip to keep from laughing. They were asking her 'why!' An impish part of her wanted to snap, "No why!"

When she was sure the urge to laugh or make fun had passed, she said, "Satoru satori. Those men in Taiji don't understand what they are doing...that Oikomi!

They don't know those are mothers and children and friends." She had to swallow hard as the memory of Notch and Star and the Stooges flashed through her mind. "Those men in Taiji don't understand the one they take away may know something the rest of them need. They don't understand; until they do, I will stop it another way."

Sensei stroked his chin. Ojisan looked over her head and stared out at the garden. Miho waited and the silence of the moment stretched out until it made her twitchy. "Ojisan, if you don't want me to go, you must find another way to help them understand. You. Because I'm just a little kid, not even Japanese—just gaijin-ko."

Ojisan looked surprised and Sensei laughed aloud! His laugh turned into a long cough; Miho and Ojisan helped him out of the classroom and back into the store. After he sat down in his chair and Tomiko brought him a glass of water, Sensei told Miho to go home while he talked to her Oji alone.

Never in her life had Miho wanted to ask 'why' so badly.

# 46
# Hokusai Surprise

When Ojisan returned, he wouldn't look Miho in the eye. He brought a laptop from his room, hooked his cell phone to it, and spent the afternoon pointing, clicking, and occasionally cursing. His credit cards were strewn across the counter, and she heard him give their Goza address more than once.

Miho kept herself busy programming the global positioning feature in her phone and trying to figure out how long it would take to get to Taiji. She wished she knew for sure if she would travel with a pod (which might take too long) or by whale ping (how would the next whale know where to catch her?) or if Ojisan could charter a boat! Maybe Gaia had something else in store for her. Did Gaia even know about Miho's Taiji plans?

Miho finally asked if she could go to the beach. "Are you going to disappear for two days?" Ojisan gave her a very parental look.

"No. I just want to walk a little, think, maybe find some shells."

"Hrrmmff. One hour." He returned to his pointing and clicking.

It was as fine a beach day as one could hope for. It was hot, but not too hot. An onshore breeze kept things cool, but it wasn't too windy. The waves were well-formed, but not too big. The sand was dappled with families escaping city heat, and Miho had to wend her way around them to get to the water. She tried not to notice mothers unpacking food and fathers swinging their kids through the waves. She tried not to notice the dark ache that began to thrum in her chest.

She put her toes in the water and stared out at the sparkling, blue Pacific. The whoosh and hiss of the incoming surf was almost hypnotic and the sounds of family laughter seemed to fade away. All Miho heard was the water. *"You will do well, Miho-san,"* said a familiar otter-voice! Miho spun around, looking for Gaia, shocked that she would come to this busy beach where anyone could see her! *"Why do you still insist on using your eyes? I am in the air and the sand and especially in the waves that you hear so clearly. You don't need to see me."*

"How am I hearing you?" Miho said out loud. A little

boy digging a hole in the sand stopped and looked at her.

"*The ocean is my heart.*"

"Ishin Denshin," Miho whispered.

The waves rose higher, broke, and swept to shore with a happy hiss. Gaia's voice exclaimed, "*Hai, very good! Now speak to me from your heart.*"

Miho reluctantly focused on the dark ache in the center of her chest. That ache was for her parents. She loved them. She missed them. But she had work to do. From her heart she saw the dolphins and the terrible day in Futo. She pictured the map and zoomed her mental image in on Taiji and then…she wasn't exactly sure yet what she was going to do.

"*You will know, my dear.*"

"*Gaia, will you be there?*"

"*I am everywhere because I am everything.*"

Miho struggled. Just because she knew how to make the kanji for understanding, satoru satori, didn't mean she could always understand Gaia's riddles.

"*Will you help me?*" Miho asked from her heart.

"*You are helping me.*"

The little boy who had been digging the hole in the sand was now tugging on Miho's shirt. She looked down at him and for a moment his eyes went wide. *He sees my green eyes, my gaijin eyes.* Miho smiled, hoping that the stranger-ness of her wouldn't scare him.

"Who is Gaia?" the little boy asked.

Miho's knees felt shaky. How did he know?

She remembered that Gaia had said, "*You heard me every time you went to sleep listening to the waves come to shore. You heard me when you turned your ear toward the horizon and heard the breath of whales. You heard me when you sat on your boat and listened to the sea birds cry and call. I am Gaia. I am the whole of the earth. And the earth is the sea, the river, and the rain.*" Miho squatted down so she could better look the little boy in the eyes and gestured to the sea. "Just listen," she told him.

Miho walked away feeling different—a little older, maybe even a little wiser. She had to smile thinking that small boy probably felt like she had given him a riddle. Knowledge flowed like water. *Mujo.* She had just handed a drop of knowledge to that boy.

The people in Taiji needed knowledge and understanding if they were ever to stop slaughtering the minds in the water. It occurred to Miho that she could stop the Oikomi, but until the people in Taiji had knowledge and understanding of what they were destroying, nothing would really change.

And even that might not be enough. As she climbed

the hill to her house, she considered the destruction she had seen while traveling to New York. If the bottom of the sea were destroyed, how would the dolphins ever live? Where would their food come from? And, for that matter, where would the people of Japan (*and America, don't forget you're American too*) get their fish?

All this understanding made Miho feel as if she were carrying a hundred pounds on her back. When she came through the front gate, she instantly forgot about everything when she saw Ojisan with a cigarette!

"Ojisan! You…"

Ojisan held up his hand, cutting her off. "Hai. Hai. Miho, I will quit this." He rubbed the cigarette out with the heel of his shoe and stared over her head at the endless blue below. "I will quit when you come back from Taiji."

Miho threw up her hands and yelled, "Yeeaaaaah!" which means the same thing in every language.

Ojisan told her she couldn't leave for two days. Before she could ask why, he showed her an article about the Taiji dolphin drive. The local police were securing the land access to the inlet so no photos or videos could be taken.

Over those two days, Miho watched his worry lines

deepen. She also watched an impressive number of trucks stop in front of their house. Boxes of all kinds were showing up. Ojisan lugged most into a spare room, but one small box had her name on the shipping label.

Miho had just come back from a short lesson with Sensei when she saw the package on the counter. Ojisan chewed his new stop-smoking gum noisily while she opened the box. Inside, was a sort of plastic bag with a strap attached to one end. It said, "AquaTalk" on it.

Miho knew what this was. Her mother had one. *Used to have one*, her heart whispered in a chill voice before she could shush it. It was a waterproof case for a cell phone! She held it up and grinned at Ojisan. "Would you like me to call in reports?"

"Zettai!" Again, Miho knew this meant, "absolutely!" although she had never heard this word before. Her heart warmed, appreciating the Gaia gift of understanding.

"Although," Ojisan continued, "we will set it up to be fast and easy. I just want to know you are okay."

He spent the next 45 minutes fiddling around with her phone until it was programmed to send a special ring to his phone: *1 when she was okay and *9 if she were in trouble. They tested it out a few times and then Ojisan reminded her to plug it in to charge it fully.

He also reminded her about the importance of getting sleep.

When Miho unrolled her futon, a wonderful surprise tumbled out. It was her Hokusai print! Miho didn't know if she were more surprised to see it, or shocked that Ojisan had gone to the trouble to roll it into her futon and set up such a cool surprise.

Miho tacked it to the wall and stared at it as she waited for sleep. Unfortunately, Miho couldn't sleep. She rubbed her scar, stared at her print, and began to doubt that she could do anything to stop the Oikomi in Taiji. Maybe she was fooling herself because she felt so bad about Notch and Star and especially little Shinju. Miho knew how hard it was not to have your real parents. She hoped the real Shinju was okay.

"I gotta know for sure," she whispered to the stuffed Shinju, who was nestled in the crook of her elbow. "Do you want to come?" Miho imagined her ragged, one-eyed dolphin exclaimed, "Zettai!"

Miho tiptoed through the house. She thought about waking Ojisan to tell him where she was going and what she was doing. But if she failed, she didn't want anyone else to see. Except Shinju! Stuffed Shinju was very good at keeping secrets.

# 47
# The Test

Miho went to the mermaid cove. However, she didn't climb down to the mermaid chair. She sat high up on the rocks and turned her ear to the sea. She wanted to make sure none of her white-sided friends were nearby. When she was sure that no one would get hurt, she set Shinju to one side and got to her feet.

She rose, balled her Hokusai-hand into a fist, and raised it into the air. She squeezed her eyes tight and saw the big wave coming, crashing, foaming. Nothing happened. She tried again...and again. When her temples began to throb with the effort, she sat back down.

"I must be crazy," she said to Shinju, who had her one good eye turned toward the sea. "I swear I did it before. I was swimming with the real Shinju and..."

Then it hit her. She was standing on the rock; before,

she had been in the water. Miho climbed down the rock enough to put her feet into one of the small tide-pools. She wondered if the water in the tide-pool, the memory of the high tide of that day, would be enough. Again, she clenched her scarred hand.

This time, the water in the cove dropped as if someone were sucking it out with a straw. It continued to drop. Miho felt a whisper of fear at what she was doing. She released her fist and stared across the water. *Here it comes!*

Her elation was replaced with panic as she realized the approaching wave was much higher than the highest tide! It would dash upon the rock. It would dash *her* upon the rock! It would drag her down and continue to throw her against the rock until all its energy was spent.

She turned and began to climb as quickly as she could. But the wave was faster. The wall of water fell upon her with a sound like the end of the world! It flattened Miho, but then something curious happened.

Miho felt all of her skin that was touching the rock— her hands, her feet, her forearms, her knees, and even her right cheek—begin to tingle. She knew the wave was churning over her and dragging back across her, but the pull of it was small. She took a deep breath and waited until the second wave came. It rose only to her knees.

The ocean resumed its regularly scheduled lapping. Miho got up on shaky legs. When she examined her arms she saw they were patterned with small circles. She had seen such a pattern before. When she was six, her family had pulled into a slip in Moss Harbor somewhere in California. She was shocked when they winched the research vessel up and it was covered with what looked like dollops of cement.

"Barnacles," her father had said. Miho had watched, fascinated, as her father used a rented pressure-washer to knock the little organisms off. Her mother and father then spent three whole days using paint scrapers to remove the remaining husks. Miho hadn't known there were creatures so tough they could hang on to the bottom of a boat! From then on, she noticed that in many places, you could tell how high the tide got by seeing where the barnacles clung.

She rubbed her skin, feeling the last of the bumps recede. She knew this was another power—another Gaia power. Being able to stick like a barnacle was the only thing that kept her from being swept off the rocks by the big waves. "Wow! I guess *that* will come in handy! Right, Shinju?"

She looked up, but her small stuffed friend was gone! Miho turned and squinted out at the dark sea. There was Shinju: floating up and over small swells, heading out to the open ocean. The moonlight winked once off her single eye, and then Miho lost sight of her.

She wanted to cry. An ache greater than the wave she had just created rose in her chest. She was about to give it permission to fall over her when she remembered that there were real dolphins who needed her. She curled her Hokusai-hand into a fist and put it up to her mouth. She now knew for sure. She knew the way of water and would use this understanding to help her friends.

Back in her room, she lay in her futon, stared at the print, and tried to convince herself she was too old to talk to stuffed animals. It was only after she decided Shinju had swum off to be with her parents, that she could finally fall asleep.

The next morning Ojisan began driving her nuts. Why was Gaia an otter? How did she make waves? How would the whale know where to take her? Just what was she going to do when she got there? Miho found it tiring because these were all questions she was asking herself over and over. She finally suggested he go visit Sensei. Ojisan suggested she should go too and say goodbye.

"Ojisan, you wouldn't believe how fast a whale's ping travels. I'll be back in a day. I'm not saying goodbye to anyone."

Her Oji started to answer, but then he realized that she was sending him to Sensei so she didn't have to say goodbye to him either. "Is your phone charged?" he asked, indicating he knew she was ready to leave for Taiji.

"Hai."

He ruffled her hair as he went past and then called over his shoulder. "I'll tell Tomikoro-Sensei that you will come tomorrow evening for Shodo."

Miho smiled. She liked this idea. It was as if the appointment with her teacher was strong enough to ensure her return. She braided her hair tightly back, got a big drink of water, made sure her phone was sealed tightly in its case, and then went to the mermaid cove to begin her mission.

# 48
# Mama

At first Miho was disappointed that Gaia was not waiting there, toes up and whiskers twitching. But she remembered that she didn't need to see; she needed to listen. She clambered down the rock and sat in the mermaid chair.

It was like the first day she had come to the cove. The rising tide sent the smooth, small swells occasionally sliding across her lap, like a liquid blanket. Miho sat on the smooth seat and listened to the endless heartbeat of the incoming waves.

*Gaia?* She thought. *I'm here. I need the pod; I need to travel.* The water continued to rise until Miho was bobbing up and out of the mermaid chair with each wave. She finally gave up trying to hang on and allowed herself to float out into the cove.

She slapped the surface of the water, then dove under to call and to listen. She was just starting to really worry about getting to Taiji when the wonderful high whistle/ click of dolphin greetings reached her ears. They were coming!

The real Shinju was the first to meet her. It was almost overwhelming to be with the pod again. They all talked at once and took turns buzzing past her. "Let's go!" Miho said. She suggested they head east.

It was an exhilarating ride. They met up with another, much larger group of lags and being one in a group of a few hundred was amazing. Occasionally they all let out what was like a group cheer. It was only after the group had fallen into a nice rhythm of breathing and leaping and chatting that Miho dared to say anything. She asked to find a whale. "Why? Whale! What kind? Why?" images of all manner of whales zipped through the water around her. The group slowed and Miho did her best to explain. She had to show again the awful day in Futo to do it, but if her mission were to get going, she would need the pod's help.

A group of ten young, strong lags peeled off and sped south. Most of the group agreed that it was the most likely place to find a whale. The pod slowly followed the same path as the group of ten. Miho began to worry. What if she couldn't find a whale to send her to Taiji? Would she have to read a horrid story in the newspaper about how they captured dolphins for amusement parks and killed the rest?

But soon enough, the ten returned with a happy vision of a sei whale to the southeast. The pod gained speed and soon they were leaping free of the water. Miho was going to be extra careful on her mission; she wanted to be around to take this kind of wild ride again!

The sei whale was waiting for them. Miho's breath caught at the enormity of the great being. It was 50 feet long and the water around it seemed to hum with its great living energy. Its grooved throat was pale, almost white compared to the dark gray of its back. Miho used her heart to send a greeting and said out loud. "Yoroshiku," which meant "pleased to meet you."

She felt the return greeting like a hot shiver through her entire body and the whale's name followed. *Big Boy* was the best translation her mind could conjure up. She looked into the dark well of the whale's eye and wondered if this whale could possibly know what she needed to do. Before, Gaia had started the chain of whale pings and Miho had trusted that Gaia knew the way.

As if in response, Big Boy opened his big mouth! His throat grooves expanded as thousands of gallons of sea water rushed in. Miho was swept in as well and could see the lags milling around the whale. She ducked under the water and called to them, "I'll be back!"

As the whale closed its mouth and the brightness of the day vanished, Miho hoped with all her might she would see her friends the following day. As before, the whale began to press the water from its mouth, straining it through the baleen. As before, the steep dive took them to the 'talking lines' that whales used. As before, Miho could feel the buildup before the ping resounded and she was yanked out into the blackest of black places.

Going this fast, she could almost forget she was in the water. Miho had just gotten her arm securely hooked over the wave of sound when she felt the ascent begin. *Already? Well, duh! You're not going to New York, just Taiji.* Miho barely had time to wonder how close she might be when she rammed into the waiting whale.

She tumbled onto the soft tongue, relieved to be, in some small way, safe. The whale squeezed out the chill water and began to rise. Miho wondered about its name and the answer came in the image of a dark and angry storm at sea. In the midst of the storm the whale rolled one eye to watch the heavens. *StormWatcher.* "Yoroshiku, Storm Watcher-san," Miho called into the wet cavern of the whale's mouth.

Miho was allowed to swim out once they were on the surface. The sea was choppy and gray. Miho had to work hard with her arms to keep from taking in mouthfuls of water. She could see the shoreline in the distance and studied it up and down.

Storm Watcher began to blow repeatedly, priming for a long, deep dive. "Aren't you staying?" Miho asked, in English, not sure what language whales preferred, but feeling certain that it would understand the intention in her heart. *Ishin denshin.*

As she looked into the dark, thoughtful eye, she got the sense of another whale and a much smaller, lighter colored one. Storm Watcher was an auntie and needed to return to her duties, traveling with the mother and calf.

Miho was scared. What if she wasn't in the right place; what would she do? Would Gaia come? How long could she bob here like driftwood? She was a strong swimmer and knew she could make it to shore, but ocean currents can be tricky and she could be miles away when she did.

The leviathan's eye was still fixed on her. If she could speak, the whale would say, "Don't worry, Gaia Girl." Miho nodded, mostly to herself. The whale gathered her energy, ploughed her massive head downward, and Miho felt privileged to watch every inch of the magnificent creature slide past her into the gray waters.

The tail rose high and water rained down on Miho as if blessing her. Miho waited for the whorls of water, the whale's footprint, to diminish before turning her attention back to the shape of the shoreline. Yes, this was where she needed to be. She could see high cliffs and the sharp inlet of Taiji to her north and judge that the current was gently pulling her that way.

Miho dove and began to swim underwater, away from the chop. She felt ridiculously slow after riding with the lags and being rocketed on the whale ping. She scanned in front of her and didn't see much except a swarm of jellyfish out to her right, a scattering of flounder far below her and the usual human detritus: plastic bottles, plastic bags, plastic bottle caps, plastic packaging of all shapes and sizes.

Miho knew that these were just the kind of cancer-causing things that Mr. Hernandez had spoken of. The chemicals in the plastic leach into the sea, into the fish, and eventually into the dolphins as well. She cursed the plastic and kept swimming.

She saw men preparing boats. Oddly, other men were setting up huge expanses of blue tarp between the cliffs.

*So no one can see, take pictures and tell the world. Pictures!* She thought of her phone and sent what she hoped was the first of many "*1...I'm okay" messages.

Miho dove again to scan, hoping no dolphins or porpoises were coming. Then again, if they didn't come, how would she save them? That was a puzzle that kept Miho's mind busy as she treaded water.

Miho had to dive and swim against the current in order to maintain her position. She knew this would get tiring in due time. When she came up, she listened hard to the intertwining sounds of the sea, the birds, and the wind and tried to ask Gaia for help.

Miho used her phone to keep time and dove every ten minutes to scan for cetaceans at risk. After an hour and two more swims against the current, she decided to test her powers, just a little bit.

She drew her right hand back, gathered her intention and gave a slow, but steady push through the gray water. She waited. Even the largest of waves sometimes were hidden until they came up against the rising sea floor and in to land.

Sure enough, about 45 seconds after she pushed, the boats milling around Taiji began to rise and fall sharply. She could see men, looking like scurrying ants, trying to secure equipment. She heard engines rev as the antmen pushed their boats out away from the rocks. She smiled.

~~~

The day wore on. The sun traveled unseen, its daily trek hidden by thick clouds. Miho worked continuously against the choppy swell and the ever-running current. Her stomach growled and her eyes were tired of watching. A bump against her foot snapped her to attention. In the sea, a predator bumps things like a human checks a menu. What is this? Can I eat it? Then again, it could be a piece of driftwood.

She held her breath and dove to scan. What her ears saw confused her. It was like a rock with wings. The odd rock turned and came toward her! Only when she intensified her scan did she know what she was seeing: a sea turtle, and a large one at that.

Miho was delighted when it came straight toward her. Now she could see it with her eyes. Before she could tell what kind it was, it did something amazing. The sea turtle took a sharp dive under Miho and then rose directly beneath her!

Miho found herself draped across the turtle's upper shell. *Carapace*, she reminded herself of the word for the upper shell. She slid partway back into the water so she could see the turtle's face. Its eyes reminded her of

Sensei: old and patient and a little amused. Miho studied the shape of the head and decided that this must be a loggerhead turtle. She didn't know if the loggerhead was sent by Gaia, but she was grateful for the break.

The turtle floated patiently and occasionally flapped its long front flippers to push them back against the current. Miho periodically slid off and dove to scan. The day stretched out. She tried asking the sea turtle its name. All she saw in her mind's eye was the thousands of eggs this turtle had laid over her long lifetime. Miho thought about the thousands of wee little turtles that had gone flippety, floppety, down the beach and into

the sea, either to become food or more loggerhead turtles.

"Well," Miho declared, "I'll have to call you Mama!" Mama didn't seem too impressed with her new name.

The day wore on and Miho began to feel dull. Her eyes were very tired and she began to wonder if this had all been for nothing. Just as she was about to send Ojisan another *1, a series of sharp clanking noises grabbed her attention.

It was the sound of the fishermen banging pipes that were held in the water. The dolphin hunt had started—the Taiji men were scaring the dolphins to drive them into the bay! Miho climbed higher up on the loggerhead and shaded her eyes.

The men had gone further out into the sea and made a wide arc with their boats. How had she missed this? As they clanged the pipes, they started to tighten the arc toward the inlet. Miho felt frantic. Her hope had been that she could talk to any dolphins and tell them to run. But it was too late now. She could see dorsal fins breaking the surface!

# 49
## Taiji

Miho needed to get closer. She dropped her legs in the water and had only given two kicks toward the shore when Mama dragged them five feet under and began to fly! She flapped her long flippers and Miho clung to the ridge of shell behind her neck. The banging of the pipes filled the water, filled Miho's mind, and made sonar useless.

Miho let go when she felt she was close enough. *Close enough to what?* She popped to the surface like a cork and hoped that her small head would remain unseen in the choppy water.

She needn't have worried. All the men had their attention focused to the inside circle, drawing tighter around the... *what are those?* As if in answer, one made an awkward leap half out of the water. Shining out from the fat, black body was a large patch of white that marked its side and ran under its belly. *It's a panda porpoise!*

Well, that was what Miho had always called them. The mostly black Dall's porpoise has a very distinct white "belly saddle." Its dorsal fin and tail fluke were also black with white gracing the trailing edge. Dall's porpoises were short and stocky but boy, did they love to bow ride! Miho had seen them often in her travels. She used to call out, "The pandas are back!" each time they zipped along the pressure wave that pushed out ahead of the bow of the boat. This was the first time Miho wished she wasn't seeing them.

Five boats. She looked down at her hand—five fingers! She curled her scarred, but powerful hand into a claw shape and pushed it out in front of her. Behind her push was a feeling that was a strange combination of her shame from Futo and her love: love of her parents, Ojisan, Sensei, Shinju, all the whales and dolphins she had ever known, and the ones she had yet to meet.

Miho knew the wave had gone out. What she didn't expect was the form it would take. The water rose up in five tall reaching fingers. It was like seeing Hokusai's "Great Wave" come to life! Each boat was pounded, doused by the falling wave! The power of the crashing water flattened men to the decks and swept some into the sea!

She pulled her hand back again, ready to push those

men down into the water, never to come back. But her heart spoke...*They are fathers.* Miho knew those men had children at home. She couldn't imagine being the reason another kid had to say their father was "lost at sea."

Instead she dove and called with all her might, "Swim! Here! Swim!" The Dall's porpoises were as fast as she remembered and were arriving almost before she finished calling. Their speech was a bit different than that of the lags, but Miho could see all the pictures and knew they were discussing the strange waves and what had happened.

Miho began to send pictures from Futo. Slowly, the chatter of the Dall's stopped as they all listened to her story. She did her best to relay the message that they should tell to other dolphins, but the group of forty was already heading south, anxious to get away from the shore, the men, and the story of Futo.

A few paused to give their version of thank you, but soon, Miho was alone with the loggerhead. The wise old face stared at her as if waiting for direction. Miho looked to the mayhem she had created.

Two boats were overturned. Small craft buzzed out from the shore and men were being pulled from the water. There was a lot of yelling going on and it made

Miho happy. But she didn't want this to be too easy for them. Perhaps the power of waves wasn't needed. She drew her Hokusai hand up to rub her eyes and saw that below it, tiny droplets followed.

She opened her palm and drew her hand up again. Like a delicate formation of cotton candy, a fog began to form around Miho. She laughed out loud, not caring if anyone heard. She began to wipe her hand across just the tips of the choppy waves and sent a wall of fog toward Taiji. Soon, all was hidden. They didn't need those blue tarps after all.

Miho sent Ojisan three *1's in a row and hoped he understood that meant, "Mission Accomplished!" She was so happy she kissed Mama on her hard, round head. If turtles could look surprised, this one did.

Miho grabbed her carapace and sent them both down. She was pleased to find the skin on her arms prickled, barnacle-like and she was able to stick fast to Mama's shell. Miho relaxed her grip and enjoyed the smooth ride the sea turtle gave.

She would go back to Goza and build an army. Not an army of kids with Hokusai hands. The shark had given her that scar and Gaia had come to make it something more. No, her army would be people who loved the dolphins so much that they would convince all of Japan that Oikomi should stop. No one would buy the poisoned meat. No one would want to see dolphins that had been caught in such a horrific way. It would no longer be entertaining...it would be heartbreaking.

Instead, they would seek understanding in the open water. Miho would help. She would make sure that dolphins would come. Miho would be like a...*bridge*, her mind whispered. She smiled, realizing how perfect her Dolphinese name was.

# 50
# Wakarimashtaka?

As Miho made her trip home—from turtle to whale to her friends, the lags—she marveled and lamented. It was astounding that she could do such things as ride a whale ping, but her mind was also troubled by all the challenges that the sea faced. Oikomi was really only one thing. The plastics and the cancers were another. And then there was that boat destroying the entire bottom of the sea. *Bottom trawling.* Miho had searched the Internet for an answer to her lost whale ping. She had watched bottom trawling on Ojisan's laptop.

It was almost worse than Oikomi. It was as if someone wanted to go squirrel hunting and took a bulldozer into the woods. Where would all the creatures live? What would they eat? The coral reef is like the woods. All the creatures in the sea need the reefs.

By the time the shore of Goza was visible, the fat but

waning moon was near its peak for the night. Miho was tired past her bones. Before she left the lags, she gave Shinju the image of a moon rising three times. In three nights she would come back to play with her. Shinju gave a short leap of approval. The lags peeled away and Miho wished them well.

When she got home, an odd ticking, tapping noise met her ears. A door in the back of the main room was rolled open and there was her uncle, hunched over a keyboard and typing so fast it sounded almost like sonar clicks.

The room seemed full of computers! Three large monitors sat in a line along a folding table. The audio equipment that lined a shelf along one wall caught Miho by surprise. This room looked a bit like her mother's office.

Ojisan was so engrossed in what he was doing that he hadn't heard her come in. She couldn't resist; she hit a *1 on her phone. His phone let out the special ring they had given it. Her Oji snatched it off the table. He stared at the screen and then muttered, "She's still okay! But where is she? Is she really okay?"

"Yatta!" Miho cheered. It meant "I did it!" The Japanese victory word had hardly left her mouth before Ojisan was out of his chair and striding toward her, a smile—her mother's smile—stretching his face. *I bet my parents would be happy with me too!*

"You shower; I have a surprise."

After she had washed the day's events away, was sipping matcha and leaning in the doorway of this newly outfitted room, Ojisan said, "Do you know where you are?"

"Should I get my GPS?" Miho asked, not caring if her sarcasm sounded, 'too American.'

He wagged his finger at her, getting the joke. "This is the home office of Kiromoto Center for Cetacean Studies!" His eyes crinkled in a delight that she didn't even know her Oji could feel.

Miho closed her eyes so the words could make more sense to her and she could be sure she understood his Japanese correctly. "Ojisan, you don't know anything about whales and dolphins."

"My sister did. This is for her. You talk to them; I will do all the marketing—those scientists never do any good marketing!"

Miho had visited her share of "Centers" and "Institutes" and they always had grownups with letters behind their names working in them. Like her mother, Yoko Rivolo, Ph.D. Miho wished she could feel excited by this room, but neither she nor Ojisan would ever be listened to in the world of science.

"Ojisan, I'm a just a kid and you are…" She tried to think of something nice that would explain this. "You are not a scientist like my mom was."

Oddly, he kept grinning. "Our Sensei reminded me that I am Ama too, and I'm smart!" He tapped his forehead twice. "I'm smart and I listen very closely to everything my strange gaijin niece tells me. Tomorrow, you'll see." He actually giggled before he turned around to sit back at the computer station.

"Now, make dinner!" The command that was tossed over his shoulder came from the Oji that she knew. The gruffness made her smile. She started up the rice cooker and wondered what tomorrow would bring.

That night her mother came. In Miho's dream, she climbed down to the mermaid chair to find her beautiful mother there, bathed in the waving bands of light bouncing off the water. "I'm glad you found it," her mother said. "I loved this place."

Part of Miho knew she was dreaming, so she didn't dare rush into her mother's arms for fear that such a physical thing would yank her wide awake. The water in the cove became alive with arching backs that were streaked with white suspenders.

Her mother laughed and looked up at Miho with

a grin she missed, but now knew she could find on Ojisan's face as well. "They are wonderful friends to have, Miho! But you need people friends too, friends your own age."

Miho still didn't speak or move, for fear of waking up. Her mother poked her bare toes at the black-lipped snouts of the lags. "They are beautiful, but like the sea, they are only the surface.

You have been to the bottom, you have seen how all water and all life revolves back through the sea. Tell me, Miho-san, how can we have dolphins or whales, if we don't have the all the life that thrives in the deep? Wakarimashtaka—do you understand?"

Miho looked out toward the horizon and saw there, the trawler, the boat engulfed by screeching gulls that she had seen while on her whale journey to New York. It was if her vision narrowed and zoomed in on that ugly ship. The nets that were being pulled onto deck had every conceivable form of ocean life caught and writhing within. The men on that ship were busy tossing most of it back over the rail. They plucked a few choice, market-worthy fish from the ill-gotten bounty and shoveled and tossed what had once been a riotous, living reef—including the ruined remains of what had once been a beautiful bull shark—back into the water.

What used to be glorious and vibrant and full of life was broken and gone forever. Miho's heart ached at the sight. She knew how vital the reef was and the sight of most of it being tossed away like garbage made her feel woozy and dizzy.

Miho's dream attention snapped back to the mermaid cove. But now, instead of her mother, a fat, furry sea otter sat in the chair. Gaia lifted her wide, whiskered face to Miho and said, "Miho-san, remember, the sea is my heart. Keep that in *your* heart as you meet the other three."

When Miho awoke, she sat on the edge of her futon, trying to put the words from the dream together with everything she knew. She could smell wonderful smells coming from the kitchen and could hear the clanging and banging of her uncle going from kitchen to table and back again. *I should be glad he didn't yank me from this dream to "Make breakfast!"*

When breakfast was over, Ojisan showed her the other surprise. It was a letter for Mr. Hernandez. Ojisan wanted him to come and help establish the Kiromoto Institute for Cetacean Studies. Miho thought that was an awesome idea! There were so many lags here and she could help him understand in a way he never could before.

Miho giggled a little at Ojisan's English writing. "Let

me write this again," she suggested. "I can write some in Spanish too; that's his real language."

"You can speak Spanish?" Ojisan looked surprised.

"Si, pocito. That means, Hai, a little bit." She felt warm to her toes at the look of admiration that crossed her Oji's face.

"I go work now," Ojisan said in English. She was amazed at the difference she felt hearing this now, as opposed to the first time she heard that statement in Nagoya. It now meant something very different. Ojisan was going to be the general in her army.

Miho went to the beach and again, tried not to look at all the happy families enjoying the day. The waves were wonderful. An onshore breeze shaped them perfectly for body surfing. The ocean had been such a source of stress and worry; it felt good to just play.

Miho was a master body surfer—especially now. She could anticipate the wave's movement and adjust her body so that the maximum amount of energy was turned into a smooth ride to the beach.

Miho noticed a girl and her little brother playing in the surf. They kept edging closer to where Miho came to shore. After one wave ride, Miho rose, smiled, and said hello to them. The girl said hello; the boy stared.

"How do you do that so well?" the girl asked.

"Mujo-kan," was Miho's reply. She used her toe to sketch the kanji in the sand at their feet. "You must feel the energy of the water and put yourself into the shape of the wave. Come on, I'll show you!"

The remainder of the morning, the three of them rode waves and dug holes and built fortresses in the sand. The summer sun pushed down on them, but the sea breeze came and lifted the heat off the sand and over Goza. Miho was happy.

She met their mother, who was very nice and gave Miho some juice. The girl, Sakata, asked if she and her brother, Koji, could meet Sensei and learn Shodo too. Miho loved that idea! The classroom would feel more like a classroom if there were other kids in it.

Sensei liked the idea too. In the classroom that afternoon, he told her that Mr. Masuaki would be coming to start the school back up. "But you will still be my Sensei, right?" Miho asked.

"I will always be your Sensei. Even when I am gone, you will be able to look at my work and keep learning." Miho chewed her bottom lip. She didn't like to think of Sensei being gone. He laughed, "Not for a while yet, Miho-san. Now, keep working."

She turned back to the long roll of paper in front of

her, consulted Sensei's example, and bent back down with her brush. She lost herself in the ebb and flow of the brushstrokes and soon, her work was done. Sensei was pleased.

She cleaned her tools and then helped Sensei back into the store, worrying because he needed both his walking stick and her arm to hold. She told Tomiko what Ojisan was planning. "Good!" Tomiko said, almost smiling, "that will mean more customers for the store."

Miho left her work to dry in the classroom and decided to go to the mermaid cove. She held her breath as she climbed over the rocks at the top. A little part of her wished that her mother would be there. But her mother wasn't there. It was Gaia, whiskers twitching and dark eyes sparkling, who stood in the chair waving her front right paw. "Konnichiwa, Miho-san!" Gaia called in her high, dancing voice.

"Konnichiwa, Gaia-san."

The slick otter slipped into the water and Miho took her place in the chair made from rock and relentless waves. Gaia rolled a few times and then stopped toes up. "An army, eh?"

"Not like a bombs and guns kind of army. A...a...an army of understanding! So they can love the minds in the water too!" Miho hoped that was what her mother was trying to tell her in the dream. She also hoped her army would have some ideas about how to set up her next mission. Miho had her sights set on the bottom trawlers.

"I knew I chose wisely." Gaia's pleased voice seemed to magnify every spark that leapt off every wave. "You have done well. Rest and enjoy the water as you did today. Soon enough you will meet the others; they will be the heart of your army!"

Just as Miho was about to ask who these others were, the brown eyes and twitching whiskers were gone. Miho smiled, now knowing that was just Gaia's way, to slip from the otter form that was easy to talk to, and once again become the soil and the sand, the wind and the water.

After dinner, she presented her scroll to Ojisan. He smiled and read it out loud, "Kiromoto Center for Integrated Cetacean and Oceanic Research." He looked at Miho with enough question to make him tilt his head a bit.

Ojisan asked, "Why 'Integrated Oceanic Research'?"

"It's all connected, Ojisan." Miho said. She felt kinda old and wise, as if her mother or maybe Sensei or maybe even Gaia were helping her find the right words. "How can we help the dolphins if the world they live in is ruined? We can't help them without looking to the deepest, darkest places. Wakarimashtaka?"

"Hai."

# AUTHOR'S THOUGHTS

Writing the second book in the Gaia Girls Book Series has once again launched me into the fun, yet scary, task of developing a good mix of real vs. fantasy. I want the reader to know what is real and what I made up to serve the story.

There is a lot about Japan that is real: O-bon, Shodo, Japanese words and phrases, and sadly, Oikomi—the dolphin hunts. In reality, the hunts happen from October-April. I placed them in the summer months to better fit the overarching Gaia Girls story. (Read Gaia Girls Enter the Earth to understand!)

The sad reality is that approximately 23,000 small whales and dolphins die each year during Oikomi. The people who engage in these hunts argue that Oikomi is their cultural heritage and should continue. There are many reasons why I disagree. There are many human cultural practices that are no longer appropriate—slavery is a great example. Early on in America, the culture told a story in which only men could own land or be educated, hold office, or vote. I think that story has been found to be fiction! Never be afraid to question what history says is fact.

Secondly, even if you believe that dolphins have no more mental capacity than your typical beef cow, understand that the resulting "food" from Oikomi is poison. Some dolphin meat has tested 400 percent higher in toxins, such as mercury and PCBs, than what is considered safe for human consumption! It is amazing to me that Japan allows this to be fed to their citizens. The people of Japan will ultimately be the ones to eliminate the demand for dolphin meat and I believe they are moving in that direction. Thankfully, the demand for dolphin meat is on the decline.

Sadly, the demand for live dolphins is increasing. Hotels and tourist destinations want "swim with dolphins" pools. Amusement parks of all kinds want dolphin attractions. I come from a bit of a zoo background and believe in the educational element of zoos, parks, and aquariums. However, I also believe that whales, dolphins, and porpoises are sentient beings like you and me. To pull them out of their natural, social state of living and force them into an amusement park setting is, in my mind, as cruel as slavery. I do believe that captive-born cetaceans can have a rich and fulfilling life when brought into excellent aquarium operations. They may even live longer in aquariums than they do in the wild because they have no predators and they receive excellent veterinary care. My suggestion is to be discerning about the parks you visit!

But if you really want to help the dolphins, you will have to care for their home. You can help the dolphins by signing the Seven C's Pledge that is included in this book. Visit Seas the Day http://seastheday.theoceanproject. org/ to learn more. The Ocean Project will love to have you on their team!

Bottom trawling is also real and one of the greatest threats to our oceans. Dave Allison at Oceana is the one who described bottom trawling to me as "hunting squirrels by taking a bulldozer into the woods!" The Oceans need our attention and yet, most of the ocean is unseen. We know more about the moon than the bottom of the ocean!

It is easy to assume all is well in the depths. However, the creatures of the ocean are threatened by wasteful drift nets and long lines. Worldwide, commercial fishing kills 800 marine mammals a day! What kinds of fish we choose to buy, and who we buy it from, will have a tremendous effect on the future of the ocean. Oceana is making strides worldwide to get governments to support the seas. You can help! www.oceana.org

Lastly, Goza is a real town in Japan and Ago-wan is the real bay you have to cross to get to it. I have used the name and the geography; that is where the similarity ends. The trains don't go "clickety-clack;" they are fast and smooth. The Japanese language, both written and spoken, is much richer and more interesting than I was able to convey within the story. I have no idea if there is a fish market or, if there is, what it looks like. Goza's beautiful beach is a popular summer vacation destination and I hope someday to enjoy the reality that was the backdrop for this fantasy!

Lee Welles lives in the Finger Lakes Region of New York State. She writes a weekly newspaper column, does corporate consulting and above all, loves learning.

Gaia Girls Way of Water is the second book in the seven book series. Look for Lee's next installment in the Gaia Girls Book Series—Gaia Girls Air Apparent.

Lee would love to hear from you. To let her know what you thought of the book, or to get information about her school and event appearances, contact her at gaiagirls@leewelles.com.

# ACKNOWLEDGEMENT OF POETRY

Nature inspires poetry. It is one of the many ways we humans try to capture the magnificence of our world. Some people can do this so well, their poetry is still read hundreds of years later.

I, however, can't write poetry for beans! I'm indebted to the masters of this craft and the beauty their words lent this tale. I hope you explore these wonderful works in their entirety.

Page 14 *"Once more upon the waters!..."*
   Lord Byron, Childe Harold's Pilgrimage

Page 53 *"The sea! the sea! the open sea!..."*
   Bryan W. Procter, The Sea

Page 163 *"The sea is never still..."*
   Carl Sandburg, Young Sea

Page 264 *"Under heaven / nothing is as soft..."*
   Lao Tzu, Tao Te Ching

Page 295 *"The bleat, the bark, bellow and roar..."*
   William Blake, Auguries of Innocence

Page 298 *"She will start from her slumber..."*
   Matthew Arnold, The Forsaken Merman

# ECO AUDIT

The Chelsea Green Publishing Company is committed to preserving ancient forests and natural resources. We elected to print this title on 100% postconsumer recycled paper, processed chlorine-free. As a result, for this printing, we have saved:

**40  Trees (40' tall and 6-8" diameter)**
**14,748  Gallons of Wastewater**
**28 million  BTU's Total Energy**
**1,894  Pounds of Solid Waste**
**3,553  Pounds of Greenhouse Gases**

Chelsea Green Publishing made this paper choice because we and our printer, Thomson-Shore, Inc., are members of the Green Press Initiative, a nonprofit program dedicated to supporting authors, publishers, and suppliers in their efforts to reduce their use of fiber obtained from endangered forests. For more information, visit: www.greenpressinitiative.org.

Environmental impact estimates were made using the Environmental Defense Paper Calculator. For more information visit: www.papercalculator.org.

# GLOSSARY / PHRASE GUIDE

Japanese syllables are pronounced fairly evenly. Most often, syllables are divided at the vowel. Pronounce each syllable without stress. Most consonant sounds are the same in English and Japanese. For the sake of simplicity, the author opted not to indicate long and short vowels, or the vexing "silent u" in the text of the novel. For read aloud pleasure, simply sound them out! For more information on pronunciation of these words, visit *www.japanese.about.com*.

**Ama** – Woman of the Sea

**Aikido** – Martial art that uses throws, joint locks, and the attacker's own energy against him/herself.

**Awabi** - Abalone

**Baka-da!** – "What you did was stupid!"

**Bento** – Single portion take-out food

**Chichi** –Father, referring to your own father (another person's father, is Oto-san)

**Domo Arigato** – "Thank you very much."

**Domo Sumimasen** –" I'm sorry to have bothered you, but thank you." Literally, "Thank you; I'm sorry."

**Ei**- Eternity

**Enso** – Circle, symbolizes the absolute, eternity, and the universe

**Futon** – Type of Japanese mattress, designed to sit on the tatami-covered floor

**Gaijin** – Stranger, foreigner, not Japanese

**Genkin** – Money

**Genki** - "I'm fine." (informal, used mostly with family)

**Gozaimasu** – Adds formality and politeness to phrases (Example: Ohayo gozaimasu – formal Good morning)

**Gochisosama** – "It was a feast." A compliment to the cook.

**Hafu** – Half Japanese. Considered a slur

**Haha** – Mother, referring to your own mother (another person's mother is Okasan)

**Hai** – Yes

**Haishi** - Chopsticks

**Hiragana** – 46 symbols used to represent the syllables of the Japanese language (ko, ha, wa etc.) Hiragana is most often combined with kanji and/or katakana

**Iruka** - Dolphin

**Itadakimas** – Blessing before a meal. Literally means "I receive"

**Kanji** – Ideographs (symbols) that represent ideas, concepts, or things. There are over 1,006 that are taught in primary school and 1,945 that are considered essential for everyday use!

**Katakana** – Symbols used to represent words borrowed from other languages, especially English. Foreign names are written in katakana.

**Kendo (Ken-do)** – Martial art using a sword. Literally means, "The Way of the Sword"

**Kimo** – Courage, guts

**Ko** - Child

**Konbanwa** – "Good evening."

**Konnichiwa** – "Good day."

**Nani** – "What?" or "What did you say?"

**Matcha** – Green Tea

**Machigata** – "Wrong."

**Majime** – Serious

**Mizu** – Water

**Motto** – "Keep it up!" or "Keep going!"

**Nemurimas** – Sleep

**O-bon** – 3-day celebration honoring the dead

**Ohayo** – "Good morning."

**Ohayo Gozaimasu** – Polite good morning

**Oikomi** – Annual hunt in which dolphins, porpoises, and/ or small whales are driven into bays and either killed or captured for sale.

**Oji (Ojisan)** Uncle

**Oka (Okasan)** Polite term for mother; used to speak of someone else's mother.

**Okayu** – Rice porridge

**Oke** – A round, floating wooden tub used by Ama to rest on and put catch into

**Okudasai** – "I would like..."

**Satoru Satori** – Understanding, enlightenment

**Sayonara** – Goodbye

**Sensei** – Teacher

**Shizuka** – Quiet

**Shinju** – Pearl

**Sho-do (shodo)** – Brush calligraphy. Literally means, "The Way of the Brush"

**Shogayu** – Hot, ginger water

**Sobo** – Grandmother, referring to your own grandmother

(another person's grandmother is, Oba-san)

**Sumimasen** – Excuse me

**Tatami** – Straw mats used to cover floors. Rooms are often measured by how many tatami mats will cover the floor.

**Tegane** – A tool used by Ama to pry abalone and other edible creatures from the sea bed.

**Uso bakkari** – "That's a lie!"

**Wagashi** – A sticky sweet treat

**Watashi no namae**- "My name is…"

**Watashi wa wakarimasen** – "I do not understand."

**Wakarimasen**- "I don't understand"

**Wakarimashtaka** – "Understand? Do you understand?

**Wan** - Bay

**Yabai** –"Risky!"

**Yukata** – Light cotton kimono

**Yaranakucha** – "I gotta do it!"

**Yatta** – "I did it!"

**Yoroshiku** – "Pleased to meet you."

**Zettai** – "Absolutely!"

# GROUP DISCUSSION QUESTIONS

1. Contrast the characters of Miho and Ojisan.

2. Describe the evolution of Ojisan's attitude toward nature's importance.

3. Describe how Miho deals with the shock of her new surroundings and culture.

4. How does the culture of the Japanese people lead to their treatment of outsiders?

5. Contrast the two settings of Nagoya and Goza.

6. Describe how the animals of the water communicated successfully with each other.

7. What is the central conflict in the book? How does Miho attempt to resolve it?

8. How does Miho find herself within the pages of *Book I: Gaia Girls Enter the Earth*?

9. Describe how Gaia acts more like a teacher to Miho than one who directs.

10. What is the importance of the character of Mr. Tomikoro to the novel?

11. Using the teachings of Shodo as a guide, how does Miho

gain an "understanding" about life?

12. Explain how respect is an important part of the Japanese culture, including respect for the deceased.

13. Water is often used as a symbol for life and rebirth. Explain how this technique is used within the novel.

14. After losing her parents, Miho rarely feels safe in her surroundings. In what circumstances does she feel some measure of safety?

15. Explain how Miho uses a mix of new technology and traditional techniques to reach her goals.

16. Why is it important that the story is told from Miho's point of view?

17. Ojisan continuously compares Miho to her mother. Why do you think Ojisan is upset that the two are very similar?

18. Three Gaia Girls are highlighted in this story. Which Gaia Girls appear in *Gaia Girls Way of Water*?

19. After reading *Way of Water*, what is one real-world ocean issue you took away from the story?

20. What do you feel would be the next step for Miho in her quest to help Gaia?

# HIDDEN PICTURES & SECRET CODES

Miho learns the *Way of Water* and she uses her new Gaia powers to truly see the hidden beauty of Gaia's underwater world. That is why we have hidden things for you to find! If you look carefully at the cover illustration, you will find hidden items within the waves. How many did you find?

Within the beautiful illustrations of *Gaia Girls Way of Water*, there are hidden codes! The twenty-six letters of the alphabet are hidden in the book's illustrations. The number under the space is the page number for the illustration. Use the hidden letters to solve this sample puzzle.

Take the ___ ___ ___ ___ ___      ___ ' ___
       90  15  335  15  54     235  90

___ ___ ___ ___ ___ ___; start your quest to help Gaia.
383 169 15 162 114 15

At *www.gaiagirls.com* you can solve other puzzles and games that require using your copy of *Gaia Girls Way of Water* and your best puzzle solving skills. You can also play Gaia Girls arcade games. Chelsea Green Publishing believes the Gaia Girls Book Series is Fiction with a Mission!

Go to *www.gaiagirls.com* to learn more about your mission.

# Protecting Our Ocean Begins with You!

## I promise to:

 **Commit** to making a real difference

 **Conserve** in my home

 **Consume** consciously

 **Communicate** my interests and concerns

 **Challenge** myself daily

 **Connect** in my community

 **Celebrate** our Ocean!

When you take the Seven C's Pledge, you help protect our ocean by promising to make each of the Seven C's a part of your daily life. Find out how! Visit **www.TheOceanProject.org**

---

## Mail in this pledge to receive your **free** Seven C's bookmark!

*Fill out the other side of this form* ➤

*Fill out the other side of this form* ➤

# Find out how you can learn and do more!

## Learn more!
www.TheOceanProject.org

## Do more!
www.SeastheDay.org

The Ocean Project continually strives to achieve its vision of a healthier and more abundant ocean supported by a society that acts responsibly to protect our blue planet for future generations. The Ocean Project partner network includes over 800 of the world's leading zoos, aquariums, museums, and other organizations interested in conserving our blue planet. We help our Partners inspire and promote behavior and lifestyle changes for sustainability, and promote positive policy changes for the ocean. Visit our website at **www.TheOceanProject.org** to learn more and connect with an Ocean Project Partner in your community!

**The Ocean Project**

**Cut off the bottom form and mail to:**
The Ocean Project, PO Box 2506
Providence, Rhode Island 02906

✂

# I'm making my pledge!
Please send my free Seven C's bookmark. Here's my info:

Name _____

Address _____

City _____ State _____ Zip _____

*If you would like to receive the Seas the Day ocean action update, an informative and inspirational monthly e-mail, please also include:*

Email _____

# Gaia ᘓ Games

The Gaia Games on pages 406 - 425 include illustration code games, crossword puzzles, scrambles, and wordfinds. Interactive games will be available on the Gaia Girls website www.gaiagirls.com.

Visit www.gaiagirls.com/quest to test your Gaia knowledge. Use this special code **PCDCP388** to log on, take quizzes, and earn prizes!

Teachers and librarians: you can receive master copies of these puzzles and more by e-mailing info@gaiagirls.com

Gaia is counting on you. Do your best!

# Character Names Wordfind

```
L O O S T A Z T Y S E A P R E S U M E D
D E J A D J E O O U P U V R D E H Z P R
D L H I Q I D Z B R V G G V K C H O Z D
B T F P S I N L G K C M N J F C N H N J
H M X O E A A Z I Z V N I Y O Q Q H Y S
B L J S L P N H B I M U N O T C H T M H
R I N G J L R R G O A A T Y L R U C C R
X E F A Y M E A E Z M D H Z J W I X R D
S N Q A N R H T F E V D G S T X P F T R
G V O O X I R S B M F D I I C L O V Q Z
N N A W A K M A O N S U L W H M A M A P
Q W U U G A R O L G Z J D T Y N P W O E
S R Y S Y U H C L M I H O N W W W K V V
C H K H I S S Z Z Z W R L N B D B R R I
Z A Q O M A S F F R Y P A T T B Z X N J
U Q I A W M E H Y D U X L T Y Y L R K D
K P Q A N R F L I N R H T A H Q O O C Y
I H D M G M G D W N R O K I M O T V H B
H M X Q U U A R V L J V Y D D B O Q A T
T P W D A M H Y R N H U S I Z A P V I S
```

| | | |
|---|---|---|
| BIGBOY | MOE | SENSEI |
| CURLY | MR. HERNANDEZ | SHINJU |
| GAIA | MR. MASUAKI | STAR |
| LARRY | NOTCH | TOMIKO |
| LIGHTNING | OJISAN | MAMA |
| | MIHO | |

*In the wordfind are the sad words Miho carried in a sealed envelope.*

__ __ __ __   __ __   __ __ __

__ __ __ __ __ __ __ __   __ __ __

# Character Names Crossword

## Across

3. a stooge
4. main character
5. a stooge
7. Miho's teacher
9. living organism of the Earth
10. stinky uncle
11. the leader of the pod
13. large sei whale

## Down

1. dolphin scientist
2. Sensei's mean daughter
6. young female dolphin
7. Shinju's mother
8. baby dolphin or stuffed dolphin
12. a stooge

# Fact and Fiction

Each illustration contains one hidden letter. Use the page number below the lines to find the corresponding illustrations in your book. Search the illustrations for their hidden code. Find out what is fact and what is fiction in *Gaia Girls Way of Water*.

1. ___ ___ ___ ___ is a real place in Japan.
   114   202   84   222
Lee Welles used this place in name only.

2. There are over ___ ___ ___ ___ ___
                 90   326   174   39   308
Japanese words in *Gaia Girls Way of Water*. In Japan they do use three different types of written communication.

3. Unfortunately, ___ ___ ___ ___ ___ ___
                202  326  154  202  78  326
is real. It is a tradition in Japan that continues today. What can you do to help? Visit www.seastheday.org and www.oceana.org to find out what we can do today.

4. ___ ___ ___ ___ ___ ___ ___ ___ ___ ___ ___ ___
  15  235  129  202  169  202  235  222  39  326  202  54
is the scientific word for how dolphins "see" and navigate using sound. It's fiction that Miho can talk to the dolphins because scientists have not yet solved the mystery behind dolphin communication.

5. Some ___ ___ ___ ___ ___ ___
      148   129   222   169   15   90

really do use pings to communicate, but it's fiction that Miho can ride them.

6. Some whales do use their fins to ____ ____ ____ ____.
                                                   90    222   326   169

7. Bottom ____ ____ ____ ____ ____ ____ ____ ____
            39  195  222  148  169  326  54  114
is a real type of fishing that destroys the entire ecosystem.

8. The ____ ____ ____ Gaia Girl makes an
      222   326   195
appearance in this book. Do you know where? What country do you think she is from? Read book 3 next!

9. In *Gaia Girls Way of Water,* Miho has to find the knife, and save the girl. Meanwhile, Gaia sets off to find

____ ____ ____ ____ ____ ____.
78    222   326   84   15   308

10. At Taiji the ____ ____ ____ ____ ' ____
           162  222  169  169  90
porpoises were in danger. A porpoise is slightly different than a dolphin. Look it up!

12. Miho learns ____ ____ ____ ____ ____
         90  129  202  162  202
from her Sensei (teacher). This means "The Way of the Brush."

# Japanese Language Crossword

## Across

3. I did it!

4. dolphin

6. Bay

9. Risky

10. Mother, referring to your own mother

11. Pearl

13. Teacher

16. Keep it up or keep going

19. Circle, symbolizes the absolute, eternity & the universe

21. Good evening

22. Woman of the Sea

23. Uncle

24. A round, floating wooden tub used by Ama to rest on and put catch into

25. Water

## Down

1. Goodbye

2. Absolutely

5. Ideographs (symbols) that that represent ideas, concepts or things

7. sleep

8. Understand? Do you understand?

12. Eternity

13. Understanding, enlightenment

14. Courage, guts

15. Type of Japanese mattress, designed to sit on the tatami-covered floor

17. A tool used by Ama to pry abalone and other edible creatures from the sea bed

18. Yes

20. 3-day celebration honoring the dead

Hint: Use the glossary

# Japanese Language

```
I X B O K T C B C I L N T O S N R H G Y
E R D Z E H W C J J O P W O A A O V X Y
D M O G Z R A N F M I Z U A M K B T A O
A K A T H S A M I R A K A W I U L B U D
R N C B A K T K A W Q A A Y R R A I P F
E O D O H S Q K N B E V K U U I F G O B
J C H G W T U A G Y D X C Y M N F O L N
M O T T O X B R Z D V Z U V E S W Y X T
P M N H U N S O O R Q Q Q Q N H Z N V X
S V M L O E N Y S T N J X I L I Q L Z B
G K Z K R A R A V N A A M U X N O A F A
O G U W S G G T A S E S W G X J H H N E
D B W F Z E J T N M C N P H V U O A N A
W X O X H D N A Z Z I N S A J J P H P E
M G A N B R K S L V X N R I I X B G C Z
S A Y O N A R A E I A T T E Z Y N Q L R
B A M D I Q R T A I G C U L P I O Q O E
H E E B U P N F R A D U V Z I J Y K C N
M Y A Y T U S N J E D W V Q M Y L I D E
M N Z K M O Y P A V Q J E K O O C M Z M
```

| | | |
|---|---|---|
| AMA | KONBANWA | WAN |
| ENSO | MIZU | YABAI |
| FUTON | MOTTO | YATTA |
| HAHA | NEMURIMAS | ZETTAI |
| HAI | SATORU SATORI | O-BON |
| IRUKA | SAYONARA | OJI |
| KANJI | WAKARIMASHTAKA | OKE |
| KIMO | SHINJU | TEGANE |
| SENSEI | | SHINJU |

— — — — —

"The Way of the Brush"

# Japanese Language Scramble

NEOTB ⚪__ __ __ __ (food)

IE __ __ (eternity)

KEIGNN __ __ __ ⚪ __ __ (money)

AKNATKAA __ __ __ __ __ __ ⚪ (symbols)

SUKAHZI ⚪ __ __ __ __ __ __ (quiet)

HIHCCI __ __ __ __ __ ⚪ (father)

CATHAM __ ⚪ __ __ __ __ (tea)

MAIJEM __ __ __ __ __ __ (serious)

MOKOII ⚪ __ ⚪ __ __ __ (dolphin hunt)

MAATIT __ __ __ __ __ __ (mat)

KYHRIUSOO __ __ ⚪ __ __ __ __ __ ⚪ (a greeting)

*Use the Japanese glossary in your book to help you solve the scrambles.*

*Then use the circled letters to complete the Japanese words below..*

__ __ __   __ __ __ __ __ __

is something Ojisan says to Miho. It means he thought she was
not being truthful about the pearls she found.

# Dolphin Species Wordfind

```
T L Z I L D V S Z K J V T W W O D O V Z S T X N B
C J Z K B E P A N E N A J O H E H K J F T O F O C
W T U G I T W J D O X Q U A D I D P H R R Y Z Y K
V I Z D G T I G Y I S U X I T P T Q H F I Z R G J
P N T Z O O O D L Q G R S P E A L E S U P W O D K
M U P L C P S O W J S E E J Z N B H B T E Z M T F
D Z K K F S L F Y F T A V M I T R N M E D P D C P
U Z T Z B A E N I I S A M Y M O J J J H A P L B A
S Q M I C O Q D H R O U G H T O O T H E D K M Y N
K I S C U W E W U Q T N W M N Q C Q X X L E E M T
Y X U U X Q C X O E Z H E I S Z E O C X L L S D R
P U R E S I U W D G F X Y S M A S O C O T O H R O
Z O P O F S E D I S I V A E H I O C N S S Q D P P
R N J I N G T W P L F L R D I I N H T S A X R G I
G H C T T F S H B C G Y Z A H L E N I O O G G J C
E A F V F E R A Q R U Y N E T A L R M V C L K C A
P K Q S B S Z A U C Z Q C A D P T R I B O Z D S L
M R U T S D I O S U B T B E O D T C Y V P K H R R
R G M E N W H Q C I O R D V W C O N O F A Y L B M
I R R A W A D D Y R E N E V W I B T Y M E M L E G
S W O T L D L E S H N R U N W G T A X D M A G E O
G Y H W O R H M A M T Z S E N E M Y L C C O D Q F
C S K O K C P U E L U Z R D J I I X F K Y O N O J
C N S D N I A F O M D L M K V H P G J I B P R S C
Z A Z I J E B Y O U Y M L O N F B S R I I C L P C
```

| | | |
|---|---|---|
| BLACK | HEAVISIDES | RISSOS |
| BOTTLENOSE | HECTORS | ROUGHTOOTHED |
| CLYMENE | HOURGLASS | SPINNER |
| COMMERSONS | IRRAWADDY | SPOTTED |
| COMMON | MELONHEADED | STRIPED |
| DUSKY | PANTROPICAL | WHITEBEAKED |
| FRASIERS | | PEALES |

Miho became friends with

__ __ __ __ __ - __ __ __ __ __ dolphins.

# Dolphin Facts

Thank you to Animal Diversity Web and Fact Monster™ for lending their resources in creating our ocean life questions. Visit both at of their great websites. *www.factmonster.com* and *www.animaldiversity.org*

1. ___ ___ ___ ___ ___ ___ ___ ___ .
  235   15   39   222  235  15  222  54
is the scientific term for the group marine mammals that includes dolphins and whales.

2. Pacific white-sided dolphins hunt in pods containing between 10-20 dolphins. Each eats about

___ ___ ___ ___ ___ ___ lbs of food a day.
 39  148   15   54   39   308

3. The strong horizontal tail of a dolphin is called a

___ ___ ___ ___ ___ .
371  169  119  154  15

4. The ___ ___ ___ ___ ___ ___ ___ dolphin
     90  383  326  54   54   15  195
is named after the acrobatic move they perform.

5. The ___ ___ ___ ___ ___ ___
    235  202  78   78  202  54
dolphin is frequently seen in warm waters and they are the biggest of the beaked dolphins.

# Whale Species Wordfind

```
J N W J N T R W W P E U V A A B V A V M B T L Q T
S U V H W C V U D F A D W F O G D B A Z X A F Q H
S V Z U U A K S N J S A Y T D G I V G J H Q B H N
Y H M N F X U Q H N J X T R O D O Y D W T I H Z Q
A S I T H G B F N B J L Z K B A H S R F O D C X P
J W F G R I M Q M I E F F P Q E M A E D L K F B U
K R H N K R U A B N X Z P I P H N A T I I I G B P
G O E A I L G C O I A P B Q N W B E Y Z P Q O N G
J I B G L Q J S V A J M V D W O T I D M F B U F O
I X H B O E E B V X K U A Q L B Y K G R E Y D I J
N T Z L N A R D I Z V R W E A Z Q G E T W L G N V
F X S T A Q S A Z O V K J G M P K J Q S M A D C F
U G N E M E R A D E J I K E B A B H W U O J W A M
C L J H I L N Z D D C Q F V D I G Y O Y Y K S J H
T U T L T R E V Y I U S P H M X B U Q W Y A I P N
C B W R B U A D A H C P P H U S J D A J W T F B M
E J M S L H X N F G L E L N E V H I W M G W F B H
V H D B J Y F L A D S R A C C E S F V I P Q J M E
F D Y S Y X Z S Q C A M E Z U Y N N M C O H Y S Y
K Y H A K R W W C Y C J J I A X D U J U B Q E M Y
M M K T N J Z Q G D S L H A P H F T A N G Q N T Q
W D G J A S T O U S C N A E R J Z U M B W O A E P
I E K N I M B L V T V H C P J Q O D F X O W F O S
J V K G S I R K R O Y F R S N P L Q Z P O D B V R
B E L U G A P R I K C A B P M U H G V I O O K N O
```

|         |          |        |
|---------|----------|--------|
| BELUGA  | FIN      | PILOT  |
| BLUE    | GREY     | RIGHT  |
| BOTTLENOSE | HUMPBACK | SEI    |
| BOWHEAD | MINKE    | SPERM  |
| BRYDE   | NARWHAL  | WHALE  |

Because Beluga whales chirp and squeak they are nicknamed sea

\_\_\_\_ \_\_\_\_ \_\_\_\_ \_\_\_\_ \_\_\_\_ \_\_\_\_ \_\_\_\_ \_\_\_\_.

# Whale Scramble

UBLE     __ __ __ __

EIS     __ __ __

HPBUAKCM     __ __ __ __ __ __ (__) __

NFI     __ __ __

MEPRS     __ __ __ (__) __

REYG     __ __ __ __

DAWBEHO     __ (__) __ __ __ __ __

GITRH     __ __ __ (__) __

NEKMI     __ __ __ __ __

DERBY'S     __ __ __ __ __ ' __

TEONETLOSB   __ __ (__) __ __ __ __ __ __ __

ULEBGA     __ (__) __ __ __ __

HLNAWRA     __ __ __ __ __ __ __

LIOTP     (__) __ __ __ __

__ __ __ __ __ __ __ the oceans by taking the pledge.

Hint: Use the wordfind

# Whale Facts

Thank you to Animal Diversity Web and Fact Monster™ for lending their resources in creating our ocean life questions. Visit both at of their great websites. *www.factmonster.com* and *www.animaldiversity.org*

1. The ___ ___ ___ ___ ___ ___ ___ has a
     54  222  195  148 129 222 169
tusk. This tusk is a tooth that grows up to 9 feet long.

2. The ___ ___ ___ ___ ___ whale is the
   90  383  15  195  78
largest toothed whale and it can be dangerous to small boats.

3. The ___ ___ ___ ___ ___ sperm whale is
   383  308  114  78  308
the smallest whale weighing as little as 300 pounds.

4. ___ ___ ___ ___ ___ ___ whales are whales
 5  222  169  15  15  54
that are toothless. Krill, their primary food, are filtered out of the ocean water.

5. ___ ___ ___ ___ might be the best
 114  195  222  308
known whales because they love to be near the shore. Also, they can be covered with barnacles that give them a spotted appearance.

6. Some whales sing ___ ___ ___ ___ ___.
      90  202  54  114  90

# Shark Species Wordfind

```
G X H T S I G Z I S S J P O L Y F M U W S Y E G F
R I O A S P V P E N J B O W M Z J E F B E Y L B E
G K P O M Q C M I K I A N G Y N B G L J D V Y J E
I N M E E M P E X R D L Y M N P O A X N B A H M R
F R O J C X E L X I U P B V N H E M R G I U T M P
K O R G G U P R J H D P P O J O L O K Y J N U U I
X E N E E L P H H E W P N K G A A U S O J J O Y T
Q I J P Y B Y B N E D P J X N C H T E B R A N U K
J H V S N L B I O L A C S H K W W H Q U K Q H G C
T R E R K V P O L O M D K X J G Z Z A X G M S H A
A W V M W S D U W R A B M F J T D U C L T E N I L
R Z Q Y H Y B M K D A K N L Q C B W G Y N C E C B
R T H W G Q Z A J S E V C U X X B U Q Z J H E J L
U T V T R P W E K J D T N I M D B U J Y I V X P W
G R E A T W H I T E Y M T J A H J G E R Z H O M Z
G B C A R J N M D B M W F O F B B U C S P C R T J
S G D W M G T M R G K X L R P C E O U J M R V Q A
J A Y B U D S R J M T M F H N S C E L G K A V M R
O J W N T U L I Q I L P F D Y X F M A K O K L P P
X C K A H E P O Y A H S I F G O D S S C U T L O B
G A R E T M X V T R Z B D O E W P T E M J B T N G
O A S Y T U R O Z G W F G V E I B I H Q Q H N W M
R A K W V B J A J N W F Y U N E N V E X N P Z N U
L P O E A U I A L D R A M B Y M H A E U B F L S F
D T R S S Y Q Q R R A M G K V E Y C M J H Q G Y B
```

| | | |
|---|---|---|
| BASKING | GREAT WHITE | WHALE |
| BLACKTIP REEF | HAMMERHEAD | SAW |
| DOGFISH | MEGAMOUTH | MAKO |
| GOBLIN | SPOTTED WOBBEGONG | SPINED PYGMY |

A \_\_\_\_ \_\_\_\_ \_\_\_\_ \_\_\_\_ shark gave Miho a
scare in Baja, Mexico.

# Shark Crossword

## Across

2. long blade-like snouts
3. has dark colored fin
4. jaws can protrude during eating
5. known for its head shape
6. has poisonous dorsal fin spines
7. 7 to 8 inches long
10. has no teeth
11. has 50 rows of very small, hooked teeth

## Down

1. famous movie shark
2. lives along coastline of Australia
8. biggest fish
9. incredibly fast swimmers; game fish

*Hint: Answers are in the Shark Species Wordfind*

Hint: Use the wordfind

# Shark Facts

Chelsea Green Publishing would like to thank Animal Diversity Web and Fact Monster™ for lending their resources in creating our ocean life questions. Visit both at of their great websites. *www.factmonster.com and www.animaldiversity.org*

1. The ____ ____ ____ ____ shark is the only shark
     5   119  169  169
that can live for a long time in fresh water.

2. Sharks ____ ____ ____ ____ ____ their
      235   326  195  235  169  15
prey before attacking.

3. ____ ____ ____ ____ ____ ____ sharks have never
  114  202  5  169  326  54
been studied in the wild. What we do know about them is gathered from sharks that have been caught.

4. A dwarf ____ ____ ____ ____ ____ ____ ____ ____ is
       162  202  114  90  129  222  195  154
the smallest shark in the ocean. They live and hunt in packs just like their canine name suggests.

5. A ____ ____ ____ ____ ____ ____ ____ ____
   39  129  195  15  90  129  15  195
shark uses its very large tail to stun its prey. It also likes to sweep food to its mouth with its most distinctive tail.

6. The____ ____ ____ ____ ____shark looks like a ray.
   222  54  114  15  169

# Turtle Wordfind

```
G K W B C C B O H O Z V I J P B L T O F N M V E J
O U C Y F B K A V R O L N O I F C J H L K O S N N
Q P R A Q O W S E U F J L E A T H E R B A C K I G
F M W B B K L P F R T R J E L M V O K L L D P K G
Y R V Z S P V I W T Z W X O J V G G Z T Y Y J H M
W X W B N R M B V W N K C A B T A L F C S L L S E
L G I V O M Z U P E I W Y P D N C D W M U K C A U
N L L Y K Z P Z H W R F K Q F M Y F C C K C C K U
L T C A G V N T E U X I F G L L K R I J A U Q C Y
A U Q F U C D L B R M O D P L Y Y U Y R N R C A G
U Z Z N Q U S C X D N I L L E Y X U L H B A X L U
K U I I O N J X B K Z P M L E R V V C G X B Y B L
S Z N U E K R F S Z D M D A C Y D T T O B G L V J
J M W E X W S G X V I I K V K A G P E L B J O R M
L Y R L H X C G M X R Q A G J Z Z Z J G A E Z A A L
O G X K V P Z X O S Y Q D G V A A Z W T K X W T Y
G B J N B Y M E P H P Q S A V Y C D T N G D Q J Q
G P T B Q M T M G T H D X K V E B S V O V S H D N
E R L A G T E T P J A G L S I G R R A Z I N I T F
R J J I Z K Y F J H V J M I Z L B Q I W S C T E Y
H F L K T O C P Z R U W K X W L K V F B X T Q P F
E I O Z O T C K Q X B P G Y O L Q Z T B S H O T O
A I C L J I D L K F O E N K I N H W K C L V E X U
D Q R Y G W J Z F X K N B J J U U S F E D F F T W
G Q Y E U B Y N V O S T S P U D B Q Z A G O N P J
```

|          |               |              |
|----------|---------------|--------------|
| BLACK    | HAWKSBILL     | LEATHERBACK  |
| FLATBACK | HUMPBACK      | LOGGERHEAD   |
| GREEN    | KEMPS RIDLEY  | OLIVE RIDLEY |

A __ __ __ __ __ __ __ __ whale was the whale that Miho's mom and dad were studying when she was born.

# Turtle Crossword

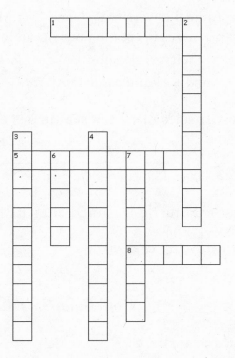

**Across**

1. named for Latin word "depressa"
5. has large head and powerful jaws
8. has a very dark carapace

*Hint: Answers are in the Turtle Wordfind*

**Down**

2. smallest of the eight species of sea turtles
3. named after a famous botanist
4. largest sea turtle, attaining weights of 650 to 1,200 pounds
6. named for the color of its fat
7. slender, streamlined appearance

# Turtle Facts

Thank you to Animal Diversity Web and Fact Monster™ for lending their resources in creating our ocean life questions. Visit both at of their great websites. *www.factmonster.com and www.animaldiversity.org*

1. The largest species of all the sea turtles alive today.

___ ___ ___ ___ ___ ___ ___ ___ ___ ___ ___
169  15  222  39  129  15  195  5  222  235  154

2. The loggerhead turtle is named after its large head.

It is also know for its very strong ___ ___ ___ ___.
                          303  222  148  90

3. ___ ___ ___ ___ from *Gaia Girls Way of Water*
   78  222  78  222
was a loggerhead turtle.

4. The ___ ___ ___ ___ ___ turtle
     114  195  15  15  54
feeds on the shoreline's abundant vegetation. So this turtles name is consistent with its diet.

5. Turtles can live a long time even in captivity, but one turtle in the wild was estimated to have lived over 150 years. The turtle species is old and has

been on the alive on this planet for ___ ___ ___
                               39  148  202
hundred million years. Turtles must be very wise.

# Turtle Scramble

BAKCL  __ __ __ __ __

LATBAFCK  __ __ __ __ __ __ __ __

GEENR  __ __ __ __ __

LABWIKHSL  __ __ O __ __ __ __ __ __

MBPAHKUC  __ __ O __ __ __ __

MEKP'S RYILED __ __ __ __ ' O __ O __ __ __ __

HECLATERKAB __ __ __ __ __ __ __ __ __ __

GERLDAGHOE __ __ __ __ __ __ __ __ O __

LEOVI LIDREY O __ __ __ __    __ __ __ __ __ __

In Chinese mythology the turtle represents

__ __ __ __ __ __ .

# COMING SOON!

## Gaia 🌿 Girls

### Air Apparent

## BOOK 3

### THE ADVENTURE TAKES FLIGHT!

Chelsea Green Publishing
www.chelseagreen.com

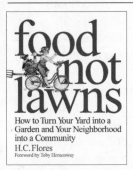
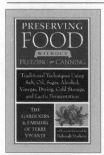

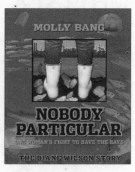
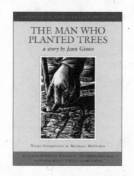